Once a Rake, Suddenly a Suitor

CHRISTI CALDWELL

Once a Rake, Suddenly a Suitor

Copyright © 2023 by Christi Caldwell

For more information about the author:
www.christicaldwellauthor.com
christicaldwellauthor@gmail.com
Twitter: *@ChristiCaldwell*
Or on Facebook at: Christi Caldwell Author

For first glimpse at covers, excerpts, and free bonus material,
be sure to sign up for my monthly newsletter!

Cover Design and Interior Format

OTHER TITLES BY
CHRISTI CALDWELL

ALL THE DUKE'S SINS
Along Came a Lady
Desperately Seeking a Duchess

ALL THE DUKE'S SIN'S PREQUEL SERIES
It Had to Be the Duke
One for My Baron

SCANDALOUS AFFAIRS
A Groom of Her Own
Taming of the Beast
My Fair Marchioness
It Happened One Winter
Loved and Found

HEART OF A DUKE
In Need of a Duke—Prequel Novella
For Love of the Duke
More than a Duke
The Love of a Rogue
Loved by a Duke
To Love a Lord
The Heart of a Scoundrel
To Wed His Christmas Lady
To Trust a Rogue
The Lure of a Rake
To Woo a Widow
To Redeem a Rake
One Winter with a Baron
To Enchant a Wicked Duke

Beguiled by a Baron
To Tempt a Scoundrel
To Hold a Lady's Secret
To Catch a Viscount
Defying the Duke
To Marry Her Marquess
The Devil and the Debutante
Devil by Daylight
My Heart Forever

THE HEART OF A SCANDAL
In Need of a Knight—Prequel Novella
Schooling the Duke
A Lady's Guide to a Gentleman's Heart
A Matchmaker for a Marquess
His Duchess for a Day
Five Days with a Duke

LORDS OF HONOR
Seduced by a Lady's Heart
Captivated by a Lady's Charm
Rescued by a Lady's Love
Tempted by a Lady's Smile
Courting Poppy Tidemore

MCQUOIDS OF MAYFAIR
The Duke Alone
The Heiress at Sea

SCANDALOUS SEASONS
Forever Betrothed, Never the Bride
Never Courted, Suddenly Wed
Always Proper, Suddenly Scandalous
Always a Rogue, Forever Her Love
A Marquess for Christmas
Once a Wallflower, at Last His Love
Endlessly Courted, Finally Loved
Once a Rake, Suddenly a Suitor

THE READ FAMILY SAGA
A Winter Wish

MEMOIR: NON-FICTION
Uninterrupted Joy

DEDICATION

To Jenn
My friend. My editor. My hero. I know you've got me.
And for that, I'm eternally grateful.

PROLOGUE

The Viscount St. John's Kent country seat
Alfriston, East Sussex
1820

SHE'D LOST HER GLASSES.

In fairness, Miss Anwen Kearsley was always losing her glasses.

It was why when she'd been but a small girl in the nursery, her mama had taught Anwen to have 'proper places' where she always put them so that they weren't lost. And she did. She kept them: next to her bed. On her vanity. Atop the center bookshelf in the nursery. Atop the center bookshelf in the library. On the mantels in the parlors.

This time, she'd gone and lost them on the floor of the Tunstall Forest.

Anwen sighed.

Everything had been going so well…until she'd reached branch eight. It'd been at the gnarled, thick branch where she'd paused to assess the distance between herself and the ground…when her spectacles had toppled clear off her nose, and land…*somewhere*.

The way she 'saw' it, she'd but two options: climb back to the ground and attempt to locate her spectacles.

Or, climb higher to ensure she could never be found in this latest round of hide-and-seek she now played with her siblings, and then have the entire brood of Kearsley's help her find the missing pair.

Anwen glanced down.

The forest floor, however, remained a murky brown blur, below.

Yes, no need to rush down. In fact, if she climbed just a wee bit more, she'd have such a distance between herself and the ground, her sisters would never find her all the way up here.

With that, Anwen grabbed the next branch.

She immediately paid the price for her greediness.

Anwen gasped, as her feet went out from under her. She curled her fingers, and tightly clung to that lifeline.

She squiggled her feet…searching for—and blessedly finding—a tiny perch for the tips of her boots. That slight ledge Mother Nature had fashioned of the aged bark allowed her aching arms a brief reprieve.

Panting from fear and her efforts, Anwen fought to keep her panic at bay.

At least, she'd not made it all the way to the top. Not one to let even a small success go unappreciated, Anwen gave thanks that she'd not made it all sixty feet to the top.

At least, she was a mere—

Anwen took another glance at the ground and lost her balance.

It'd been as inevitable as losing her spectacles that day.

As the footing fell out from under her, Anwen cried out. Her hands shot up, grappling for—and catching—a sturdy green-brown branch.

She remained dangling above the Tunstall Forest floor.

Her heart slowed to a pace that would prevent it from pounding right out of her chest but remained at a cadence befitting a young woman one slack grip away from breaking her neck.

Anwen pulled herself up—or attempted to.

She tried again.

Her efforts proved in vain. Nay, not in vain. Not really. She'd managed to create beads of sweat on her brow, that now trickled down her forehead…and into her eye and instantly stung. Now, her up-close vision that didn't give her trouble became blurred.

"Splendid," she muttered.

You couldn't have stayed in place. You couldn't have been content where you were.

Biting down hard on her lower lip, Anwen continued wiggling and squirming.

Her grip slackened, and her pulse resumed pounding in her veins, in her ears, and in her throat.

Leaves rustled below.

Not the smooth, rhythmic sway of the emerald, green leaves still vibrant and full of life in June, but rather the crunchy remnants of their leafy ancestors that had come before.

Her heart sank.

She'd been found.

Not that she shouldn't be well-accustomed to being found first by her siblings.

Anwen was always caught first.

Such was the way for young ladies with less than stellar vision. Or as the case for Anwen—dismal. And she should be grateful. She did, after all, require help.

This time, however, was different because this time, she'd been absolutely determined to be the last Kearsley standing.

"*Anwen?*"

Alas, she didn't need hearing to know who'd found her.

Her arms straining, Anwen adjusted her grip as best as she was able.

"Yes, it is me." She'd not been found by a Kearsley, after all—someone close to it—her brother's best friend, Lord Landon, who'd also been like another brother to all the Kearsley girls.

"What are you doing, Anwen?" Lord Phineas Lesar, the Marquess of Landon, called incredulously.

"Oh, I don't know," she drawled. "Just…hanging about."

Anwen's levity proved brief. She lost her purchase.

She cried out as the earth—or the branch. She was after all in a tree.—fell out from under her feet.

Her descent proved a short one.

She landed a grip on a smaller branch just under her previous purchase.

She would have breathed a sigh of relief, but the force of her weight bearing down on the limb wrenched the muscles in her shoulders; the pain was excruciating, and yet, she'd not landed head-first on the ground, and with a broken neck, so she welcomed that small price to pay for, well, *living*.

Through her panic, she dimly registered Phineas cursing, and then the further rustle of leaves—this time from below—as the young, agile marquess pulled himself into the old birch.

Relief swarmed her senses. Anwen was going to die. As a member of the Cursed Kearsley family, it was as preordained as the setting sun and tides. But it wouldn't be this day.

"Thank God, you're here," she panted, out of breath from her exertions.

"My father would say, my arrival is more a product of the Devil's work than the Lord's," he said, amusement tinging his voice, which had grown increasingly closer.

"Your father is bacon-brained," Anwen muttered, breathless from her efforts.

Phineas' chuckle came close, *so* very close.

"Among other things too polite to say in the presence of a lady and sister," he drolly added.

Sister.

Anwen shifted and squirmed, fighting to retain her hold.

Given the way her muscles and ligaments screamed in protest to the feat she'd asked of them this day, Phineas' not inaccurate description seemed rather inconsequential. They *had* been like siblings. So why should his statement rankle this time?

She tucked the annoyance into the back of her head to stew over later.

Biting her lower lip, she tightened her grip. "A bit more haste if you would, Phineas," she gasped.

He was near. So near. She reminded herself of that, talking herself through.

And then it was too much.

Capable of emitting nothing more than a little squeak, Anwen lost her hold.

She fell, her stomach dropping all the way with her, and then she was—

Caught.

"Oomph."

Anwen collided with something as hard as the ancient trunk, but also a good deal warmer.

"Got you," Phineas rasped, sounding as pleased as he had when he'd managed to snag a raisin and a nut in the midst of a rousing game of snapdragon.

Phineas wrapped an arm hard about her waist and anchored her close—so close she felt the muscled plains of his flat stomach and biceps. Anwen's heart did a strange jump. Since when had Phineas become so... *muscular*.

And worse, since when had she become the manner of lady *noticing* any man's—but especially, her brother's best friend, Phineas—muscular frame?

This time, that organ in her chest pounded erratically for some reason other than fear, but no less terror-inducing.

She shrank back.

"Worry not," he said with a smile in his voice. "You're safe," he promised, all the while misunderstanding the reason, she'd recoiled from him. "I have you."

With an ease and grace she'd never not envy, Phineas maneuvered them into the nook of their enormous hiding spot: her tucked in the corner, and he perched with his legs straddling either side of the gnarled and hardy branch like he was some circus acrobat poised to do a flip.

Her heart still thundering, Anwen sat with her back pressed against the trunk, face to face with a grinning Phineas.

I have you...

When he'd spoken in that solemn, steady way, she believed had he promised she could fly like a bird from the uneven perch she'd found herself on and soar high into the sky.

I have you...

That three-worded vow murmured in his smooth, pleasing baritone, played over and over in her mind.

Phineas' smile faded and he searched his gaze over her face. "Anwen?"

"Yes?" Her voice emerged as an embarrassingly high squeak.

Then, he touched her cheek, palming it in his big palm.

Oh, dear. This is not good. This is not good at all.

She swallowed hard.

When had his hand become so big, as well? Those strong,

powerful digits were the ones belonging to an equally powerful man.

Phineas spoke again in that strong, melodious baritone, "What is it?"

What was it? Was there a right way to describe fingers that were so very tender, yet strong, and…

Concern creased Phineas' brow. "Anwen?"

He isn't talking about the feel of his hand, you nitwit.

Say something. Say anything, you ninnyhammer.

Anwen tried to speak but her tongue felt all heavy, and she couldn't remember the way to make her lips move to form words.

"I've never seen you afraid," Phineas continued.

She'd been afraid any number of times in her life. Again, if she'd been capable of words, those were ones she'd have spoken.

None of her past fears, however, seemed as perilous as her having realized Phineas was a man, and she was suddenly a young woman *aware* of men. Nay, not men—but Phineas, the Marquess of Landon. And worse, she'd gone and found herself all tongue-twisted with him.

Phineas stitched his blond eyebrows into a single line. "Anwen?"

She managed to find her voice, but nothing more than a single word—his name. "Phineas."

His long, clear-eyed gaze fell to her mouth. Something darkened those startling blue irises.

Anwen's heart raced.

Mayhap she wasn't the only one this day to notice, in a new light, someone who'd always been there.

He frowned. "Spider."

Why was he frowning?

Then, his words hit her.

Anwen followed his gaze—a gaze that had most certainly not been on her mouth—to the enormous, blackish-brown spider sporting a big, bulbous shiny abdomen, that'd chosen to set up home on the neckline of her dress.

Anwen screamed to bring the trees down—or, as the case would have it—herself, and Phineas.

Phineas' deeper shout drowned out her startled cry as they went hurtling for the earth, in a fall that seemed endless.

This is how I die, then. She and her sisters had always wondered at what demise awaited them as Kearsley's. At last, Anwen learned how she'd meet her end; by breaking her neck after a graceless fall from a tree.

Anwen squeezed her eyes shut tight. She only wished it'd been something a lot less painful.

She dimly registered the marquess snatching her close and then, with the same ease with which he'd previously saved her, Phineas reversed their positioning.

He hit the earth first, and Anwen came down so hard atop him, the force of their collision sucked the air from her lungs.

They lay there in a tangle of limbs. And Anwen with her face buried in Phineas' chest, came to another startling discovery—he smelled, rather *nice*.

More than nice.

Anwen breathed deep of his smokey scent, a subtle hint of orange blossoms, bay leaves, and bergamot.

She froze.

Which meant, if she could still smell, then *she* must be alive.

Warmth poured off Phineas' hard, well-muscled frame, which must mean—

Anwen pushed herself onto her elbows and brightened. She'd die, but this particular tree wouldn't be the one to take her down.

"We *both* live!" And to verify as much, she wiggled higher up and placed her palm in front of Phineas' mouth so she could feel the soft sough of his breath.

Phineas groaned.

"Did you hear? We are *alive*, Phineas!"

"Only barely," he muttered.

She wiggled her way up higher on his frame.

With a contented little sigh, she rested her cheek against his hard chest, and just…lay there. The two of them stayed that way, and it felt so very right being in his arms—as it always had when he'd hugged her at various points over the years. But this time? This time felt somehow different.

Eventually, Phineas angled his head up to look at her. "What were you doing up there?"

"I think it should be fairly obvious, Phineas: I was hiding."

"Ah." His luscious golden tresses she'd have traded both littlest fingers for, caught in the slight gust of wind Mother Nature had surely created for the benefit of highlighting his glorious head of hair.

"Nasty governess?" he ventured.

"Game of hide-and-seek; I'm determined to not lose this time," she added that last part under her breath.

She was always losing.

As if in perfectly dreadful cue came the noisy approach of a Kearsley crashing through the forest.

"I heard something this way," her younger sister Delia cried breathlessly, from somewhere nearby. "It is Anwen!"

"Oh, hell," Anwen muttered. "They're going to catch me."

Phineas pressed a fingertip against his lips. "No, they're not," he whispered.

In one fluid motion, Phineas set Anwen on her feet and leapt up. "*Run*," he mouthed, and with his other hand, he took her fingers in his, and tugged her along.

They set a quick pace, and as they trampled through the forest— Phineas with a slight limp, and she being pulled along by him.

Frowning, Anwen dug her heel in and forced him to stop. She'd not have him further harm himself because of a silly game she played with her siblings.

He cast a glance over his shoulder. "What?"

Folding her arms at her chest, she glared at him. "You're hurt."

Her sisters, whose voices had grown further away, came closer once more.

"…this way…hear her…"

Phineas scoffed. "I'm not. And I'll be damned if you scaled that tree, survived a fall from it, only to be found by your sisters."

Anwen went all soft inside.

This was the moment, then. The ones from her romance stories, where women were suddenly thunderstruck by love. She'd previously taken those scenes for implausible moments, dreamed up by an author, and exaggerated for the reader. Only to discover, in this wooded forest, the poets and authors had it right all along.

She tamped down the breathy sigh fighting to escape.

Phineas winked and caught her hand in his again.

Her palm instantly tingled, and a thousand butterflies fluttered in her belly, and she stared riveted at the sight of their joined fingers: his large and strong where hers were smaller and softer, and yet how very perfect they felt together.

He leaned down, his mouth drawing nearer.

Anwen's lashes fluttered, and she tipped her head up to receive her first kiss.

"*Run*," Phineas whispered against her ear.

Run?

She came crashing back to reality as hard as if she'd taken another tumble from the old oak behind them.

Together, hand-in-hand, she and Phineas took flight.

Phineas steered them over to the bank of a nearby babbling river, and each found shelter behind the trunks of a pair of oak trees.

Anwen dipped her head out just as Delia and Daria stepped into a clearing some five paces away.

"It had to be Anwen," Delia was saying. "I recognized her scream."

Delia scanned their woodland playground.

"She may be dead," Daria murmured in her eerie flat tones. "The curse."

"Hush," Delia chided. "Do not say that," the younger twin commanded, fear ripe in her voice.

"Death is inevitable. Now, come," Daria took Delia by the hand. "I think she is this way."

Anwen ducked her head back behind her oaken shelter, but not before she caught Delia's troubled gaze locked on a thick row of bramble.

A triumphant grin tugged at Anwen's lips. Once, years earlier while picking blackberries, Delia had gotten herself caught in the thorns of one of those bushes. From that day forward that plant had become "Bramble, that vulnerable heel of the Delia Achilles".

Phineas couldn't have selected a better hiding spot had Anwen described it, and he himself created it.

She looked to Phineas. They shared a smile. He slowly touched a fingertip to his lips again.

"Perhaps she is somewhere else," Delia spoke haltingly, interrupting that silent exchange between Anwen and Phineas, and pulling Anwen's attention back to the twins' debate. "I...do not think we should go this way, Daria."

"Because you do not like thorns and blood." The nearly indiscernible modulation of the younger girl's voice conveyed frustration.

"Does *anyone* like blood and thorns?" Delia shot back.

Daria.

"I do," Daria echoed Anwen's silent thoughts.

Their other sister, Brenna, called out and effectively ended the debate. "She is this way!" Brenna cried.

Anwen's gaggle of sisters took off in a flurry; the crunch of brush and twigs growing more and more faded, and then, but for the song of a lone robin, only silence filled the forest.

As Phineas did a sweep for the Kearsley's hunting them, she freely studied him.

How had she never seen him before now?

How had she failed to note the way the summer sun had left his unfashionably long hair a dozen different shades of gold and blond? Or the power and strength of a hand that had chuffed her under the chin or tickled her or wiped her tears too many times to count over the years.

He remained oblivious to her scrutiny, or the great shift that had occurred between them—or at least, in the way *she* now saw him.

Touching another finger to his lips, he caught her and headed to a felled log for greater cover.

He staggered, and the two of them came down hard for a second time in another tangle of limbs, with Anwen landing atop him, and this time laughing as they fell.

"Shh," he whispered, between his quiet gasps of amusement.

"*You* 'shh'." She swatted at his chest.

When suddenly, he went absolutely motionless.

Anwen looked up. "What is...?" Her question trailed off.

The harsh plains of Phineas' face formed a pained mask. His eyes which usually glittered with levity had gone dark as she'd never seen them. And in an instant, the earlier joy she'd had playing hide-and-seek with him at her side, faded.

Her gut clenched.

Of course. The fall.

They'd both come crashing down from a great height with her landing hard against his chest, now twice.

And here, all the while he'd been in pain, she'd been playing games with her sisters.

"You're hurt," she furiously recalled.

"I'm—"

"Have you broken anything, Phineas?"

Before he could answer, she proceeded to run her hands over his shoulders and forearms and searched him for serious injury.

"And you've experience with identifying broken limbs?" he asked, his slightly strained voice containing a wealth of amusement.

"Indeed," she said, not bothering to pause in her evaluation. "Daria fractured each forearm on separate occasions, and her ankle another."

"And *you* were the one to identity and make the formal diagnosis."

This time, she looked up. "It isn't that difficult."

"Ah, of course." Phineas inclined his head. "As you were."

Ignoring that sarcastic twist to his words, Anwen resumed her examination. Having verified his arms hadn't suffered any fractures in the fall, she shifted her attention to his lower limbs.

She pressed her fingers along the part of his leg just above his knee, and Phineas stiffened.

Anwen stopped and looked quickly up. "Do you have pain here?"

"No!"

She frowned. *His* usually smiling lips were compressed into a pained line. "You're lying."

"I'm not," he said, *too* quickly.

"Oh, stop being so proud," she said under her breath.

"What was thaaaa," Phineas' question dissolved into a high-pitched squeal as she touched his upper thigh.

"You *are* hurt," she said, casting an accusatory glance his way.

"That's not what you said," he said, entirely too hastily, and attempted to back away.

"Then if you know, you don't need me to repeat myself. Now *stop*," Anwen said more emphatically.

She proceeded to massage his thigh.

All his muscles jumped under her touch, and a low, agony-filled groan filtered into the peaceful quiet of the lush and fruitful forest.

"Shh," she chided. "You are going to give us…" Anwen glanced up, and the rest of her chastisement died a swift death.

Phineas' handsome patrician features were strained, and yet he studied her through unblinking blue eyes that radiated a different kind of heat.

Her heart thumped.

Her hands shook, and those trembling digits ceased their previous massage of Phineas' leg and remained frozen upon him.

For she recognized all too well that glint in Phineas' gaze—The Look. Certainly not from any actual experience, but rather one she'd read enough of on the pages of the gothic novels she lost herself in to identify it in the flesh. It was a look she'd sighed over and dreamed of and hoped to know when she made her debut… only from Phineas—charming, dashing, roguish Phineas.

He slid a steady, penetrating, stare over her face, and it was as though he saw her for the first time, in a new light, in the same way, she saw him.

His gaze lingered on her mouth.

Her heart kicked up a wilder beat.

For she also knew from her history of reading, what followed, The Look.

The Kiss.

He is going to kiss me.

Anwen fluttered her lashes, tipped her face up, offered her mouth to him, and waited.

And waited.

And, well, as The Kiss invariably came fast and furious and without a hint of hesitation, she peeked up at him.

"Do you have something in your eye, Anwen?"

Something in her…?

Phineas continued to study her. Only, it wasn't The Look but rather a look—one of brotherly concern from a man who was decidedly not her brother; a discovery she'd only just made in this moment of madness.

Then, his question registered. As did his absolute obliviousness to *her*.

Anwen drew back quickly. "Yes," she yelped. "I…ah…have something in my eye."

And as she'd never had a flare for artifice as her younger sister Delia did, she reminded herself to blink wildly.

With a frown, Phineas took her face in his hands, smushing her cheeks, in the same way her baby sister did whenever Anwen held her.

His eyes brightened. "I've found the culprit."

"Yewhave?" she asked, lips still compressed by his big, strong, and very warm hands.

"Indeed."

Given the less-than-romantic way in which he held her, she rather doubted *that*.

Phineas released her.

Then, with an infinite gentleness, he swept the pad of his thumb under her eye.

"An eyelash," he said, displaying his finger.

She drew back and squinted. "I don't see—"

"Be still or you'll lose it," he scolded, and she promptly ceased her squirming.

He brought that lash to rest on the edge of her nose.

Anwen peered at the tip of her nose, going cross-eyed in the process.

"Close your eyes," he instructed. "You're supposed to make a wish."

Anwen closed her eyes.

Make a wish.

Over the years, she'd made any number of wishes upon lost lashes, and with coins she'd snuck from her brother Clayton's rooms, and then, in turn, had thrown into wells.

She'd wished for second rounds of dessert. She'd wished for her favorite desserts. She'd wished for some peace and quiet from her younger, noisier siblings. But those were the wishes of a girl. Today, having seen Phineas in a new way, marked a shift; a change in her from girl…to young woman.

"Ready?" he murmured, his warm breath that bore a hint of the chocolate she'd likely have been wishing for in previous wishes, caressing her face.

She swallowed around a knob in her throat and managed an unsteady nod. Then, he lightly blew; that slow, deep exhalation wafted over her skin.

"Open them."

Anwen's lashes fluttered, and she touched two fingers to the spot his breath had previously kissed. "Is it…"

He made a flourishing circular sweep with his hand. "I'm happy to say the lash is gone, and your wish, destined to come true."

Destined to come true.

Her heart did a somersault.

As they ducked back down, they fell into a companionable silence. Her siblings' shouts as they searched for Anwen came in the distance, and the child's game that had once seemed so very important mattered not at all.

Unable to take her eyes off Phineas, she gazed longingly at him.

"Well?" Phineas urged. "What was the wish?"

He waggled his eyebrows in that way he always did when he was looking for a third helping of desserts from Cook. It never failed to make her giggle. Until now. For if he did, if he knew the truth, that the wish she'd made this day would be to live long enough to be Phineas' wife, then, he'd have without a doubt turned tail and run.

"You've got me even more intrigued, Wynbug," Phineas persisted when she still didn't say anything.

"If I tell you, it won't come true."

"Very well." He inclined his head. "I shall cease and desist, as I'd not ruin your wish, and we all know there's nothing more powerful than an unspoken wish."

Alas, he wasn't a Kearsley. As such, he couldn't know, what she did: a curse was far greater in strength than any mere wish. And as a Kearsley, her only destiny was a cursed one.

CHAPTER 1

11 Years Later
London, England

MISS ANWEN KEARSLEY DIDN'T WANT to visit her mother's fortune-teller, and not because she didn't believe in the preternatural.

After all, a foredoomed woman, from a cursed family, who'd both read about—and on occasion—witnessed the ill-fated of all the Kearsley's to come before her, couldn't *not* believe. Rather, she didn't want to know, because once she knew, then there'd be no *un*hearing that information.

Alas, sandwiched on a curve-backed sofa with two of her sisters, in the formal drawing room of Madam Pomfrets, watching the mother of their Kearsley brood pace, the same couldn't be the said for the woman who'd given them life.

"She is usually always punctual," the dowager viscountess troubled her hands as she paced before the bench containing three of her off-spring. "I don't recall her ever being late."

"One would think our dear mama is actually eager to find out about our ends," Anwen muttered.

Their mother paused only long enough in her pacing to throw a wounded look Anwen's way. "Madam Pomfret does not just prophecy death."

"No, I'm sure that is true," Anwen allowed.

Her mother smiled.

"The woman's undoubtedly had a number of clients, who were

not part of a cursed family, and will live perfectly long, eventful, full lives—unlike your children," she added, bringing a swift death to her mother's previous smile.

"Oh, phooey with all Anwen's usual worrying," Delia said from her seat at the opposite end of the sofa.

"I'm not always worrying," Anwen said, with a frown.

"The sun is shining," the younger woman continued happily. "That is certainly a good omen and I, for one, would welcome some cheerful news."

"People die on sunny days all the time," Daria pointed out in her haunting tones.

Precisely.

"Either way, this isn't the day we're dying," Daria murmured.

That was fair.

"This is the day we find out *how* we die."

Their mother's groan covered the rest of Daria's gleeful declaration.

"I daresay that is the first I recall Daria ever modulating her tone," Delia, her Shakespeare loving sister said from behind her volume of Lady Macbeth.

"No, it isn't," Anwen muttered. "She uses it any time someone mentions anything related to death."

For Anwen knew her sisters better than she even knew herself sometimes.

As their mother went on to lecture Daria on Madam Pomfret's expansive skills and services beyond reporting on matters of the afterlife, Anwen stared wistfully at Daria, with something that felt very much like envy.

Where most feared death, Daria revered it. In fact, since she'd been a child of six, the only thing to truly bring Daria's lips tipping up had been mention of the afterlife, and thoughts of people getting there.

Not Anwen.

Anwen had witnessed her father's death, and when one witnessed a person take their last and final breath, well, the memory of that stayed with them.

Unbidden, that very memory whispered forward like a slow-rolling London fog that blanketed a street and stole away all warmth, and Anwen's ability to so much as blink.

...Papa, wasn't that funny? Why did you stop laughing? Papa? Papaaa?

Anwen briefly squeezed her eyes shut, and when she opened them, they landed on Daria's perpetual black skirts of mourning the girl never went a day without wearing. Nay, there was nothing grand or great or amusing about death, but rather a sadness and finality at that loss. Anwen would be content to never see a black garment again. Because all they did was mark a loss and serve as a reminder of it.

And it was why, she wanted absolutely nothing to do with her mother's fortune teller or her sister's fascination with death and dying.

She exploded to her feet, and her mother and her sisters stopped conversing about...whatever it was they'd been talking about when Anwen ceased paying attention to them.

"Given, Madam Pomfret is clearly very busy," Anwen said, hating the slightly reedy quality of her voice, but hopeless to contain it, "might I suggest we return some other t—"

"No!" Daria exclaimed.

"We are not leaving," the dowager viscountess said, her soothing tones better fitting a mother reassuring a child at Gunter's ices.

Of course, they weren't leaving. Their mother would never dare abandon an appointment she had with the great Madam Pomfret.

Anwen nudged her sister on the shoulder. "You don't want to be here either, Delia. Tell her this is ridiculous," she whispered.

"I didn't want to be here because I was reading and didn't wish to stop," Delia turned a page with a flick of her finger. "I'm now reading *here*."

And also, content to stay, await the illustrious Madam Pomfret's appearance so that the old woman could offer her prophecy for the end of Anwen's, and her other attending sisters', deaths.

A muscle rippled along Anwen's jaw, and, restless, she stomped over to the window overlooking the streets below. As her sister had pointed out earlier, the sun shone brightly from a magnificent blue, cloudless sky. Smartly dressed couples walked arm in arm.

Others held the leads of ornamental pups better suited for a lap than a walk.

Those strangers, each going about their business, without a thought about what the awaiting future did—or in Anwen's case—did *not* bring. And it was not as though Anwen hadn't come to accept her inevitable lot—she had. Neither, however, did it mean she wished to have all the details spelled out before her so she could spend her days worrying about that moment.

Alas, her sisters, they were obsessed. Her mother, too. Why, even her brother Clayton had been, until he'd fallen in love, married, and had children to distract him.

Anwen, though? As an almost thirty-year-old spinster, she didn't have love or marriage or children with which to distract her. Nor would she ever have those things.

She'd been born needing spectacles and with mousey brown hair whose greatest distinction was a patch of white she'd been cursed with, and despite a lifetime of her parents professing her beauty, it hadn't been long before she realized society didn't agree—it didn't agree, at all.

Her sisters? Now, they were each beautiful and unique and interesting in their own way and right. They hadn't spent a lifetime searching for their own identity. They still had hopes of experiencing those things Anwen would never know before she perished.

From within Madam Pomfret's perfectly polished crystal windowpanes, Anwen caught the approach of her mother.

Splendid. Having finished lecturing Daria, she'd now turn her attentions on Anwen.

Determined to cut her off at the pass, Anwen faced her. "Is it not enough I'm here? Must you dictate that I smile through the appointment, as well?"

"I did not *dictate* that you come." Her mother infused more than a touch of defensiveness into her tone. "It was more a *suggestion*."

"A suggestion?" Anwen quirked an eyebrow. "'I demand you girls finally accompany me, or else'?"

A pink blush filled the still youthly dowager-viscountess's cheeks.

"I did add 'please'," she pointed out, with a suitable degree of sheepishness.

Always loving, and devoted, it was nigh impossible to remain angry at their mother. Sighing, Anwen made to look outside again.

"Anwen," her mother continued, with such a quiet earnestness it stayed her. "Did I ever tell you about when your father and I first met?"

At that abrupt shift in discourse, Anwen hesitated.

When she'd been a small child, she and Clayton had covered their ears and eyes whenever their parents had been romantic or even talked about anything romantic in front of them. When Anwen had at last been old enough to appreciate love and romance and think of her parent's love story, it'd been too late. Her father had died, and Anwen hadn't wished to cause her mother pain with thoughts of her late husband.

"No," she finally said, softly.

"Your father and I moved in *very* different social circles," she began.

"You would have."

"Yes, you know how your grandparents were," her mother said, a smile in her voice.

The dowager viscountess's late parents had been stodgy and stiff, while the Kearsleys? Well, the Kearsleys—not unlike Anwen's siblings—were wildly eccentric and vivacious and *loud*.

"Given that, when I made my Come Out, your father and I never crossed paths." Her mother paused.

"Until at an event hosted by the Duchess of Mallen. The dowager duchess and I had grown up on neighboring estates and were the best of friends. We drifted apart only because she had her debut before mine, and then she married."

Drawn into her mother's story, Anwen turned around.

"The first event Lydia hosted was a great ball, which included hundreds of guests. She did not discriminate as your grandparents did, and as most lords and ladies still do."

Her mother's gaze grew distant, and Anwen knew the moment she'd become lost in her own telling; drawn back into the memories of a distant time, she still spoke of, as if they were as fresh as yesterday.

"My parents were in a dither. Our family's longstanding connection to the duchess's and Lydia's status dictated we attend, and yet, in addition to the most respectable families, it also included some of the more scandalous ones, as well."

"Like the Kearsleys," Anwen supplied.

"Like the Kearsleys," her mother confirmed. "In the end, we attended the duchess's ball. As the hostess, Lydia managed to spirit me away from my mama. The duchess fancied herself something of a matchmaker. That night, she couldn't contain herself. She explained she'd found just the suitor for me. She was going on and on…" A wistful smile teased at her mouth. "And I was barely listening, because from across the ballroom, my eyes collided with his, and it was like…"

Anwen hung onto that unfinished thought.

"Magic," the dowager viscountess whispered. "Everything and everyone melted away. The orchestra and the set they played, faded. He strode across the ballroom and then stopped before us. He didn't await an introduction or request one. He said: 'My name is Norton Kearsley. I'm destined to die, but before I do, I would spend the rest of my life bringing you the greatest joy'."

Anwen's heart tugged at the meeting her mother painted so vividly.

The dowager viscountess rested her palms upon Anwen's shoulders. "And your father did know so much happiness because of the family we made and had. I want that for you, too."

As had Anwen. And yet…

"It is different, Mama."

Her mother had fallen in love with a Kearsley, but she'd not known the weight of the curse that followed those who bore the name.

"Because I'm only a Kearsley by marriage?" her mother astutely pointed out the very thoughts Anwen had let go unfinished. The dowager viscountess shifted closer. "The thing of it is…your father? He knew he was eventually going to die, but Anwen? He was determined to find joy before he did."

She opened her mouth to say if her mother wanted her to focus only on joy and living, then she'd be best not to force them to come to Madam Pomfret's, where they were certain to receive news of their deaths.

A silence descended over the room, the first of its kind that Anwen ever recalled in any household where Kearsley's had assembled. As one, each Kearsley woman turned and looked to the person who filled the doorway.

Filled the doorway. It was a funny thought given the diminutive size of the woman whose presence commanded notice.

This was their mother's renowned augur?

Over the years, Anwen had considered the mad prophetess her mother paid weekly visits to. Anwen had envisioned a towering, ancient, wild-haired, heavily wrinkled woman with gnarled hands, and mayhap an eye patch covering one of her glassy eyes.

Just a smidge over five feet, and several years younger than Anwen, the flaxen-haired Madam Pomfret was but a handful of inches taller than Anwen's youngest sister, Eris, and thin as a whisp. And yet, fill the doorway, she did.

Her features were soft, and her gaze sharp, as she did a sweep of all the gape-mouthed Kearsleys—except Anwen.

From her spot at the window, Anwen attempted to make herself as small as possible—a feat that as a bullied wallflower, shunned for her streak of white hair and spectacles, she'd honed. There was an art to hiding in plain sight: drab dresses. Don't don jewelry. And *avoid* eye contact. *Always*, avoid eye contact.

"Madam Pomfret!" the dowager viscountess gushed. There came the slight creak of the oak floorboards as she went to meet the prognosticator. "It is most wonderful to see—"

"You." The seer's quiet murmuring cut across the rest of that effusive greeting, and another hush descended upon the room.

Do not look up. There were two other young women present whom she could be speaking to. Likely was speaking to.

After all, Anwen had made herself so very, very small, and she was the most non-descript of the Kearsley girls and—

"*You*," Madam Pomfret repeated, and this time, Anwen couldn't help herself. Reflexively, she looked up and her gaze clashed with the young woman watching her.

Her, as in Anwen.

Anwen's stomach dropped.

Madam Pomfret nodded.

Still desperate enough to hope, Anwen glanced wishfully about. Daria stared enviously back. Even Delia had parted with the pages of her beloved Shakespeare long enough to cast a jealous look Anwen's way.

With all the same thrill undoubtedly known by those off to meet their executioners, Anwen returned her stare back to Madam Pomfret. This time, silent, the seer gave nothing more than a small nod; a nod confirming what Anwen had already deduced.

Anwen's belly sank another inch, and she dug her toes sharply into the soles of her slippers. "Me?" she silently mouthed, pressing a hand against her chest.

Madam Pomfret nodded once. "With the streak of white."

Well, *that* was pretty unequivocal.

Without waiting to see if Anwen followed, the fortune-teller turned and left.

Anwen stared after. Hope reared its head once more. Perhaps she'd tire of waiting for Anwen to join her. Perhaps—

Her mother gave her a more than modest nudge. "Go, Anwen."

"I want to go," Daria said. "Let me go in her stead."

"It doesn't work that way," their mother insisted, not so much as glancing over at her stolid daughter. "It is Anwen's turn."

But Anwen didn't want to go. She was content *not* knowing answers to questions her mother was determined to have answers to. Her feet twitched with the urge to flee, and she sprung forward on the balls of her feet to do just that.

Her mother caught Anwen's hands in her own, stopping that flight before it started.

"Anwen." Her mother spoke with a quiet earnestness. "You assume all Madam Pomfret only speaks to her clients about their demises. But that is not the case. She prophecies so much. You will see that. Now, go."

Go.

Go.

Turn, run, flee. Toward Madam Pomfret? Or away from the fortune-teller. Everything was swiftly becoming scrambled in her mind.

As if she'd sensed her resolve flagging, Anwen's mother gave her hands a firm, but supportive squeeze.

"You will be glad you did," her mother predicted.

With that vote of confidence from the dowager viscountess and the envious stares of her younger sisters following Anwen, she quit the room. She looked left and then right down the corridor, but for the hum of a heavy quiet, empty of anyone and anything.

For a brief moment, she considered the path that led to the small foyer they'd been shown a short while ago. But something, with an inextricable draw, a powerful energy that pulled her the other way, deeper down the hall to the last room in the hall.

Anwen looked inside, already knowing she'd find the seer there. Silently, the young woman motioned for Anwen to join her, and strangely, there was no great urge to flee; nothing compelled Anwen back the other way. Rather, a quiet peace called to her, and she followed that sensation, all the way over to the circular table where Madam Pomfret sat.

Anwen looked about, taking in her surroundings.

With its pretty pink upholstered chairs and equally pretty pink silk wallpaper and the pale blue buds overflowing their pretty pastel porcelain vases, the parlor may have been any young lady's parlor.

Her gaze locked on a small bronze frame just over Madam Pomfret's shoulder, and Anwen wandered over to inspect that painting of two young sweethearts; a lady in enormous white ruffle skirts perched upon a swing, and a handsome beau who arched over her shoulder; his expression adoring.

Of all the renderings she expected a seer might sport upon her walls: a dark, turbulent storm, angry Greek gods and goddesses, a romantic tableau of two lovers had not been one of them. In fact, one would never know the room in question belonged to London's most feared fortune-teller.

In fairness, not *every*one feared her. Most who employed her services revered her. Certainly, most of the young ladies and older ladies, and ladies somewhere in between as Anwen was, came to this place for glimpses into what would be a hopeful, happy future.

Not Anwen.

Anwen had the misfortune of already knowing what fate awaited her.

"Would you like to sit?"

That gently spoken question jolted across her disordered thoughts, and Anwen jumped. She turned back and found Madam Pomfret patiently staring.

Even as Anwen's heart thumped a fast, angry beat, she forced a smile. "Do I have a choice?"

"One *always* has a choice," the seer corrected.

"Only, that isn't altogether true." That wasn't at all, true. Why, Anwen hadn't even truly been free to decide to attend or, in her case, not attend, the appointment.

"Isn't it?" Madam Pomfret asked.

"If people truly had control over their fates, then what is the good in having you tell us what our future holds?" She paused. "That is, unless, you believe a person has the opportunity to stop future events from happening?"

"The future cannot be stopped." The seer shattered Anwen's brief hope with the immediacy of her answer. "Whatever one's fate, it is destined to happen."

Her heart clenched painfully, and she made herself flash another wry grin through that contraction. "Then, I'd be remiss if I failed and pointed out that reality flies in direct contradiction to each person having a choice."

"Our destiny is set. But life? It presents so many different paths, and those paths forward are not preordained. They just eventually all arrive at the same destination." Madam Pomfret steepled her fingers together and peered intently at Anwen over the tops of them. "And the course we take? That, Anwen, we ultimately have complete control of, and in this, despite our *eventual* fate, the choices belong to us."

Anwen spoke haltingly. "In taking certain paths, can one's destiny be…delayed."

"Fate is your future. It does not, however, know anything of time, as we think of it in this world, Anwen. There is no specific continuum it adheres to."

She considered that a moment.

"If you tell me you don't wish to sit at my table, Anwen, you will be free to take your leave," Madam Pomfret said matter-of-factly. "I do not discuss my readings with others. The dowager viscountess therefore will remain none the wiser as to whether you have your fortune told or not."

She didn't want to be here. So why then, did she hesitate a moment more, then drift over to the other end of the table where Madam Pomfret patiently waited?

Perhaps because, after years of avoiding it, she'd finally come 'round to wanting to get the business of her dying over with. Or mayhap it was that her mother's fortune-teller had a way about her that was both inviting and soothing.

Anwen pulled out the dark oak seat opposite Madam Pomfret and sat. The moment she slid into the stiff folds of the armless, hall chair, Madam Pomfret reached across the table.

Anwen hesitated. The seer's hands were of like-size as Anwen's. They were also un-callused and soft-looking. Somehow, despite the dread knocking around Anwen's breath, *something* inside compelled Anwen to lower both palms into the fortune-teller's.

Madam Pomfret gathered Anwen's left hand between both of her hands.

She emitted a nervous giggle. "Does one pay extra for each hand?"

Her attempt at jest fell on deaf ears. Madam Pomfrets face remained set in an unreadable mask.

"Relax," Madam Pomfret ordered.

Relax? Oh, yes, because any lady about to find out about her death was the sole of tranquility.

Anwen swallowed the knob which had formed once more in her throat and splayed her fingers wider. The seer trailed her three middle fingers over those on Anwen's right hand. A heat and volatile energy which emanated from within the other woman's digits. Anwen recoiled and reflexively yanked her hand back and hid it under the table.

"When you are ready," Madam Pomfret murmured, holding her palms upright. "We will begin slowly."

Closing her eyes, Anwen focused on steadying her fast-beating heart. Finding calm in the absolute quiet and stillness, Anwen opened her eyes and offered the seer her right hand.

"Your right hand, it is your dominant one that you use for turning pages in books and tweaking your sister's ears."

Anwen's brows shot up. "You know all that?" She really was good.

Mirth played with the corners of Madam Pomfret's lips. "Neither is a testament to my readings. You had a book in your hands when you arrived that you gave over to your mother, and I have a younger sister of my own whose ears are oft in need of tweaking."

She winked once.

Anwen and the seer shared a smile. And just like that, Madam Pomfret managed the feat Anwen had believed impossible when she'd set out this morn—she set Anwen at ease.

"Shall we continue?"

Anwen nodded.

"Some soothsayers disagree on the need or benefit of reading both palms. The truth is, one cannot fully understand a person or what the lines portend without studying the lines of *both*," Madam Pomfret said, and took Anwen's hands in hers.

"Your dominant hand," she slightly lifted Anwen's right one. "Will give me a look into your past and present life," Madam Pomfret brought Anwen's left palm up. "Whereas from your non-dominant one, I can glean your future."

"Everyone has three lines," the seer explained, and with her index finger, she traced the creases in question. "The top one here is your heart line." Madam Pomfret moved to the next. "Below that is your headline. Next," she touched the third, "your lifeline," she murmured.

Under the table, Anwen's feet curled so tight her entire arch ached. She made herself relax. Or told herself to. Over and over.

Relax. Relax. Relax.

The soothsayer closed her eyes, and then rested her right palm, upon Anwen's. From the other woman's fingers came more of that mesmeric warmth that managed to chase away the fear permeating her being.

Madam Pomfret opened her eyes and continued as if there'd been no break in her telling. "Some people, however, have four lines." She glanced up. "You are one of those people."

"And...which one is that? A death line?" She chuckled weakly.

"There is no death line, Anwen. Our bodies are but temporary vessels. When we die, our physical body perishes but our soul lives on, eternal. There is a birth, death, and rebirth unto a different form."

It was a different thought on life, death, and dying. Or at least, one so very different than that which the vicar who'd spoken at her father's funeral, and Anwen found a welcome peace and beauty in that alternative view.

"No, this one is the fate line."

Wordlessly, Madam Pomfret looked to Anwen.

Anwen nodded.

The fortune-teller immediately returned all her focus to Anwen's left hand. "You suffered great loss."

She had. The entire Kearsley family had. It didn't, however, take a seer to see that.

Anwen stayed silent as the other woman focused intently on the lines she'd just moments ago explained. "You saw that loss unfold before your eyes and your heart suffered its first break."

A chill slithered up Anwen's spine. Mother had likely shared the details of that day with Madam Pomfret.

Madam Pomfret whose eyes remained closed while she slid a finger along one of those lines. "It is not long and curvy, and as such, you are not one who freely expresses your emotions and feelings."

As the eldest sister, Anwen didn't—and had never had—that luxury.

"Were this line here, wavy," Anwen leaned closer to get a better look at what the seer spoke of, "it would denote many relationships and lovers, but an absence of serious relationships. But there is no movement, which signifies...loneliness."

"Sharing a household with a mother, five sisters, one brother, a sister-in-law, nieces, nephews, and another babe on the way, makes it rather difficult to be lonely," Anwen said wryly.

"Ah, but even amidst a crowded room, a person can feel all alone."

As a wallflower, Anwen well-knew no truer words had ever been spoken. Unable to meet the knowing seer's eyes, Anwen made herself stare still at her palm.

Madam Pomfret continued.

"You suffered another heartbreak." The seer's brow furrowed deeply. "This time, a different loss."

Anwen went absolutely motionless.

"A…gentleman." The fortune-teller squeezed her eyes tight and squinted. "Dashing and golden like the sun, but unlike the sun and the earth, masses swirl around him."

Golden like the sun.

Dashing.

There couldn't be a more apt descriptor of the man who'd held Anwen's heart—Phineas, the Marquess of Landon. And unlike Anwen who found herself as lonely as an owl, Phineas was the proverbial housecat—a social being, he was bombarded with interest from all.

The gentlemen wished to be him.

The ladies wished to wed or bed him.

Amidst that cacophony of people vying for his attention, well, he'd never note Anwen standing there.

He never had.

"This loss, you feel keenly, every day," Madam Pomfret said softly. "You've loved him your entire life."

Every muscle within Anwen tensed tightly, and drawing breath became an impossible chore through her now constricted throat.

"We…" Except, there was no 'we' where Phineas was concerned. "He does not know I'm alive." Only that wasn't true. "At least, not in the way—"

"Be silent," Madam Pomfret interrupted without inflection. "Or you will interrupt the flow of energy and end the reading. "He sees you. There is a forest…and trees, so many trees. You run. You do not wish to be found but your pursuer… persists."

Another shiver overtook Anwen. The fortune-teller may have been aware Anwen had witnessed her father's death, but the woman could not know about that long-ago game of hide-and-seek in the forest.

Suddenly, Madam Pomfret stopped. An entranced smile formed on the woman's lips.

"Love," she whispered so softly, Anwen strained to hear, but hear she did. "There is so much of it; a great, all-consuming love."

Anwen's pulse picked up. She'd despaired of ever herself knowing the splendor and wonderment to be had in that emotion.

"You will know great joy. Laughter." Madam Pomfret cut off abruptly. Her black eyebrows stitched together in a line of deep concentration. "You are hiding. Again." The previously relaxed plains of her delicate features turned to granite.

"Someone is calling for you…but you ignore it," Madam Pomfret's tone grew more frantic. Each of her words quickly tumbled into the next and blended with Anwen's harshly drawn breaths. "There are even more trees. *Different* ones. Birch. They are older with diamond fissures. Now, a storm. It threatens. It rustles those trees. Their bases are rugged and dark and broken."

The fortune-teller's eyes remained closed, and she swayed ever so slightly, back, and forth. Back and forth, like one of the branches of those slender silvery birches she spoke of, shaking in the tumultuous storm.

Suddenly, the seer opened her eyes; her eerie gaze collided with Anwen's.

A rush of cold traipsed along Anwen's back; it raised the gooseflesh on her arms. Her teeth chattered, and all the earlier warmth that had passed from the seer's hands to Anwen's transformed into a frosty chill that penetrated all the way through to her soul.

She made to pull her hand back, but Madam Pomfret retained a death-like grip upon her.

"The sky unleashes its fury," Madam Pomfret intoned; her eye sightless, and turned inward on a vision only she could see but that Anwen would one day live.

"The tempest rages. There are tears. Yours. Others? It is unclear." The seer rasped. "Violent rain. Streaks of lightning. Death," she wailed, her voice creeping louder and louder. "The death of hope, happiness, 1—"

And there it was.

Anwen gave her palm another yank, just as Madam Pomfret freed her fingers, and Anwen's went recoiling back. With her heart pounding hard, she drew her palm close to her chest.

As if the vision had robbed the woman of life and energy, the young soothsayer slumped over the table.

Anwen jumped up from her chair so quickly, the spindly armless chair went tumbling back. Only, she remained trapped there; suspended, with her feet frozen to the light oak floor.

She'd known what information she'd likely receive this day, but something about hearing it, and finally being armed with the knowledge of how she'd someday meet her end, had her teetering on a precipice.

Madam Pomfret blinked slowly several times, and then that dazed glint in her brown eyes lifted, and in its place, was a return to the seer's previous calm.

"I…do not suppose this great lightning storm will happen when I'm an old woman?" she ventured, with a hope she didn't know how she managed to muster.

Madam Pomfret hesitated.

Anwen saw the soothsayer's indecision as clearly as the other woman had seen Anwen's future.

Her heart fell.

"I am not always right," Madam Pomfret offered that most fragile of assurances. Not a lie, and also an evasive answer.

"But you usually are, and you saw me falling," Anwen said softly.

The seer nodded. "Va."

Yes.

I want to go. I want to leave. I wish I'd never come.

But she didn't break down weeping or run from the room as she wished. She held on tight to her pride.

Anwen took a slow, unsteady breath, and then nodded. "I thank you for this. It is best to be prepared for when it happens."

There that sounded steady and sanguine.

"Anwen," Madam Pomfret called to Anwen before she could

leave. "You are right. It is best you be prepared," she agreed and took a step towards her. "But not that you prepare for the start of your new beginning."

"The start of my new beginning," she echoed wistfully. "Perhaps that is why you are called soothsayers."

"Soothsayers do not give false assurances. We were given our name as being those who speak the truth. And the truth? It is never something to fear, Anwen." She joined her at the door, and took her hands back into hers, lightly squeezing. "The best preparation, the *only* preparation you should make is to live your life to its absolute fullest. Do not spend your days imagining your next life. Find, take, and make joy from every moment this life has granted you."

And from the misery and grief and regret, sprung light at the empowering words spoken by the soothsayer.

Yes, her end would come and come soon…but before she did, Anwen had every intention of doing exactly what Madam Pomfret had urged—find, take, and make joy from every moment life granted her.

And there wasn't any time to waste.

CHAPTER 2

London, England

OVER THE YEARS, PHINEAS LESAR, the Marquess of Landon had spent a fair share of time hiding: usually while keeping company of lonely wives whose indifferent husbands unexpectedly returned home. However, at that precise moment, Phineas Lesar, was hiding again. And was he neither too proud to do so or admit it.

And, he was hiding in the last place his aunt, also his godmother, or, for that matter, anyone else would look for him.

Standing at the edge of the floor-to-ceiling length window, and with his back pressed against the window, Phineas squinted through the slight gap in the moth-eaten curtains, the heavy velvet better suited for the dead of winter than the height of the London Season. Alas, empty pockets made new trappings in a household less of a priority.

Phineas stole another look. The outrageously pink carriage emblazoned with that grand, golden ducal crest of his aunt's late—and thankfully, dead—husband. Sure enough, it remained parked precisely as it had been for the better part of fifteen minutes.

Suddenly, the door exploded open, startling a curse from Phineas.

The Duchess of Fife, Phineas' benevolent, if domineering aunt, cane in hand attired in her notorious fuchsia skirts, and wearing her usual slow, humorless smile stood at the entrance of Phineas' office.

"Caught," he muttered.

She pointed the tip of her ornate gold tulip-headed cane his way.

"Caught, indeed." She pushed the door closed behind her; cutting off the one path from which Phineas could escape.

He briefly contemplated the big bay window.

"*This* is where you've been hiding." Folding her arms at her chest, so that the cane she didn't *need* to use, but did for aesthetic, dangled over her other elbow. "It's quite clever of you, you know."

He did a flourishing little sweep of his arms as he bowed. "Why, thank you. Any praise from you is high praise, indeed, dear aunt." And quitting his spot, he headed over to his desk, seating himself, and establishing ownership of if not their exchange, this office.

"I had my servants check all your usual haunts: Forbidden Pleasures. The Devil's Den. The Hell and Sin Club. Why, with your reputation of not starting up an affair with a former mistress, I'd even made inquiries into those women's households as you don't have a new lover yet." She paused. "You don't, do you?"

Phineas inclined his head. "I do not." He didn't, but he wouldn't have told her, even if he did.

"Shocking," she said, sounding eminently bored and mildly disgusted.

He resisted the urge to fight with his too-tight cravat. Something in knowing she'd kept abreast of all the women Phineas bedded and his habits where lovers were concerned, was enough to set even him, a seasoned rake, to blush.

His aunt wasn't done. She continued wandering over. "I had my servants check Covent Garden, Drury Lane, Haymarket, the Olympic theatre, the Lyceum. All to no avail."

Good God, she really *had* scoured the whole of London—just as he'd expected she would, and also why he'd set himself up at home.

She stopped before him so, that with Phineas seated, he'd no choice but to look up.

Suddenly regretting the vantage he'd given her when he'd carelessly set himself up at his desk, he angled his head back. "I trust it is most important business that has brought you here."

"Indeed," she said, not taking the bait he left with his sarcasm ripe response.

Having long since abandoned hope of getting rid of her this day,

Phineas gestured to the lone leather chair at the foot of his desk. "Would you care to sit, aunt?"

"Would you like for me to stay?"

"Do I have a choice?"

"Do *you* think you have a choice, Phineas?"

"Never."

"You've sense enough to realize *that*, at least." She smiled and, at last, sat. Her smile proved fleeting. "Your butler attempted to turn me out," the duchess shared.

"I trust you handled poor Georges."

She chuckled. "*Poor* Georges is still searching for the pet cat I carried inside."

"Came with a diversion, did you?"

"Would you expect anything less?" she countered.

"I'd expect nothing more."

"As I said, it took me long enough to find you." She moved a steady, incisive gaze around the room, before turning her censorious focus back on Phineas. "The office," she murmured to herself. "Of course. With your books and ledgers, why one would never dare think you'd hole yourself up here, of all places. Next time try taking up rooms at the Albany. It'd make it harder for me to see you."

But not impossible. After all, Phineas' late mother's sister was dogged and determined, and, if she so wished, could have likely convinced the trustees who ran that place to lift the ban on women in the exclusive apartments.

His astute aunt's gaze missed nothing. She slid that assessing stare over the green upholstered queen oak armchair she now occupied, and the empty spot where its sister pair had been.

"Forced to sell the other leather armchair, I see. You pissed away everything away your father left, didn't you?"

"Not the drapes, so there is *that*." He flashed a grin...that went unreturned.

"You would have been better selling that comfortable one you're enjoying. Perhaps, then, if you had a miserable seat beneath your lazy arse, you might rethink the behaviors that have gotten you where you are."

"Is this why you've come?" he drawled. "To discuss my furnishings." Attempting an air of equanimity, Phineas reclined into the deep, cozy folds of his desk chair.

"I'm no longer supporting you, Phineas."

He was glad he'd already been leaning back and had a chair under said 'lazy' arse for that kick-in-the-teeth news she'd given him. It'd been inevitable. That didn't matter. Still, hearing her say as much, having her state her intentions to withdraw the last support he had to rely on, left a pit in his stomach.

"Do you want to know why, my boy?" she asked quietly.

He forced a grin. "I expect whether I wish to know doesn't matter. That you intend to tell me, anyw—"

"You're a wastrel, and you are not getting any better."

"I was correct, then. You intended to tell me anyway," he said dryly.

Only, there came no rapid-fire retort or further recriminations, just...a sad, quiet disappointment in the eyes that now studied him, which somehow proved worse.

The irony wasn't lost on him. His father had detested him until Phineas fashioned himself in the marquess's image. His aunt abhorred him for being *like* the brother-in-law she'd hated. Not unlike high-stakes and wagers, Phineas had been destined to lose in every way in life.

Still close-lipped, his Aunt Betty stood, and for a moment he thought he'd managed to run her off.

Except, she continued her silent march over to a portrait someone had hung entirely too close to the mantel of the fireplace. Soot stained the canvas's edges and had long since distorted the family of three captured in that rendering: Phineas, a boy of four, smiling an enormous smile.

The icy late Marquess of Landon who'd never do something so plebian as crack a hint of his frosty expression and have it recorded for all time. And then, the woman who lovingly cradled Phineas upon her lap—his mother. Where father and son looked back at the artist, the late marchioness's gaze remained downward. The artist had perfectly captured the devoted glimpse; she'd been caught taking of her son.

With a sad little shake of her head, the duchess drew her attention from the portrait and put her focus back on Phineas.

He didn't ask. He didn't even need to. He knew what she intended to say before the words even formed on her lips.

I am my father's son.

"You are your father's son. Your mother would be disappointed in what you've become."

"What I've become?" He curved his lips up in a half-grin. "Don't you mean, what I've always been? After all, I've always been his son."

She gave him a censorious up and down glance that contained an even-for-him humbling amount of disdain.

"Yes, you were," the duchess said, regrettably. "It was a sad day when he began paying you attention."

Age ten. Phineas recalled—and would forever recall—the exact moment. It'd been the last time he'd seen his mother who'd been sent away to their estates at the edge of the sea in Suffolk. Her screams and sobs reverberated in his mind like a distant echo; the sounds of her pleas, mingled with Phineas' own, as they'd begged the marquess to let her stay.

...I will not be soft...I promise I will not be soft...just let her stay...

Hiding his hands behind his back, Phineas balled them tightly, painfully, in a bid to drive out memories he didn't allow himself to think on and hadn't thought of in years. His aunt and godmother *would* resurrect those reminiscences. Undoubtedly as punishment for being the nephew and godson, she so disapproved of.

Even with her denunciation over the years, however, she'd still given him financial support. Now, she'd pull even that away.

"I want you married."

The smile froze on his face; a rigid uptilt of his mouth's muscles that felt strained and pained.

"Need I point out, it isn't for lack of trying on my part." Over the years he'd courted any number of.

She snorted. "Are you referring to your half-hearted attempt at winning Lady Beatrice's affections? Or the time you courted that gaming hell girl."

"Miss Cleopatra Killoran," he clarified. Born on the streets and raised inside the Devil's Den, one of the many clubs Phineas frequented, she'd arrived for a London Season. With her deep pockets, a sordid past, and want for a titled husband, she'd made sense as a potential future marchioness. Only… "The lady is *now* Mrs. Cleopatra Thorne," he felt obligated to acknowledge.

"*Mrs.* Thorne," his Aunt Betty muttered. "It is a sorry testament to the state you're in, boy, when a gaming hell girl rejects the opportunity to be a marchioness, in favor of marrying another gaming hell owner. At that, a former baker's son."

He frowned. How did she know that particular detail?

The duchess emitted a little snort. "I know everything, dear godson. *Everything.*"

Now, *that*, he believed.

Desperate to be done with this quarterly meeting, Phineas withdrew his watch fob and consulted the timepiece. "Enjoyable as this conversation has been, I've an appointment I'm already late for."

"Of a sudden, you're concerned with being on time for meetings?" she drawled.

Of a sudden, he was concerned with getting the hell away from this one, which had already carried on far longer than he needed or wanted.

"Of all the pieces you've sold through the years," she said softly. "My sister's favorite tiara. All her jewels. Her paintings. Her embroideries. Her books. You kept *his* watch."

Had she looked at him with more of the previous disdain and regret, it would have been easier to take than this aching sadness.

"Back to the reason for my visit," the duchess finally said.

"Is that what we're calling this, dear aunt?" he asked, infusing a hefty dose of sarcasm into that query.

"I've been far more patient with your antics than I should have been—far more patient than anyone else would have. I'm doing something I should have done long before this moment—as of today, the allowance is gone, Phineas."

Today.

The smile on his mouth froze. She'd threatened to do so before, but he'd either managed to talk her out of it or she'd had a change of heart.

He'd managed to survive and stave off debtor's prison these years, because of his devoted aunt and godmother. He should have trusted her goodwill would eventually run out. He'd just not expected—or allowed himself—to think of that day.

"Not so flippant now, are you, dear boy?"

And worse, she was…enjoying this.

"I trust this has something to do with your new—"

She narrowed her eyes on him, and Phineas swiftly readjusted course. "Suitor."

Lover. The man was her lover.

"I'd advise you to leave Sir Lloyd out of this," she said warningly.

Ah, Phineas had hit the nail over the proverbial head with that one.

"Of a sudden, you're of a mind to withdraw support for me. That only leaves all the more for him. How…convenient," he said, unable to keep the bitterness from his voice.

And here he'd been happy his eccentric aunt who'd endured a horrible marriage should have found happiness with a fellow who treated her well. His aunt's recent relationship with a man ten years her junior and ten years Phineas' senior, Phineas should have only expected her magnanimity would come to an eventual end. The direness of his circumstances, however, had prevented him from entertaining that unwelcome possibility.

"Lloyd has pointed out to me that I've been overindulging you—to your detriment."

"Sir Lloyd who possesses an even wilder, wickeder reputation than mine?"

His aunt refused to take that bait. "You take nothing seriously. You spend the majority of your days at clubs—at that, not even the respectable ones—gambling away funds you do not have. Would you like for me to go on?"

"That really isn't necess—"

"You spend your nights with whores and mistresses and actresses. Why, it is a wonder you haven't rotted your cock off with the legion of women you've bedded."

His face went hot. "It's hardly a legion," he muttered.

She jabbed the end of her cane Phineas' way. "The end of the Season," she said flatly. "Though I shouldn't I'll give you until the end of the Season to get yourself married, and if you don't…"

The duchess let that linger there as the clear threat it was. One, he'd sizably wager was because despite her stern showing this day, had always been soft where Phineas was concerned—certainly softer than he deserved.

"Debtor's prison," he said. "Mayhap even run off the Continent."

Her graceful features, just beginning to show the faintest hint of wrinkling at the corners of her eyes, wavered.

"Likely, I'd be headed to Australia," Phineas murmured. Such a reminder of the possible fates awaiting him had never failed to bring her around to continuing her support.

Alas, this instance should prove the exception.

"Then, perhaps you should get to the business of sorting out your finances and finding yourself a respectable bride to keep you in check." His godmother thumped her cane on the floor, for emphasis. "Sir Lloyd said I've been too soft on you."

Phineas silently cursed the bachelor.

Eager to get this meeting over with, Phineas headed over to the door and drew the panel open. "Thank God for Sir Lloyd's good guidance," he said dryly.

His aunt, however, had never been and would never be one to let someone show her out before she decided.

"By the end of the Season, Phineas," she warned. "If I don't see you reformed and married to a good, upstanding lady, or any and all support you receive from me, is at an end."

Phineas' stomach muscles clenched, and he made himself prop a shoulder against the doorjamb in a bid at casual indifference. "You do know what they say about rakes."

He and his aunt spoke at the same time.

"They make the best husbands."

"That dangerous but too commonly received notion, that a reformed rake makes the best husband," Phineas finished over her.

His aunt snorted. "Quoting Samuel Richardson, dear boy? There is hope for you yet."

"Because I've quoted a fellow who had a firm view on women's roles and lamented their boldness?"

"That you even know that is and of itself commendable." She seemed still determined to see the good in him. "Furthermore, the fact you've read anything at all, and did so enough to remember passages is proof testament of there being some good in you. The same could never be said for your father who likely didn't even know the proper way to hold a book. God rot his soul," she muttered that last part to herself.

"You give me more credit than is deserved."

"Let us hope not for your sake," she said. "Now, I believe you said you have a meeting?"

Phineas stared dumbly at her, and then yanked out his timepiece. *Shite.*

She released another one of those little snorts. "No meeting, is there? I'd wager it's a trip to one of your clubs."

"That's a wager you'd win," he said with a lazy smile. "After all, you know me."

Her eyes grew sad. "Yes, yes, I do." And with a last, lingering look, she left.

A short while later, as the Duchess of Fife predicted, Phineas guided his mount to a stop outside one of his many clubs. He tossed the reins to a waiting servant then bolted up the five steps and through the famous black door that was immediately held open by a finely clad servant.

Phineas did a quick sweep of the crowded room; every table packed with patrons and the steady roll of indistinguishable murmurs of the meetings taking place. His gaze landed on the circular mahogany table at the center of the room.

The Viscount St. John, Phineas' oldest and closest friend, sat, with an untouched glass of brandy near his left hand, while, with his right, he consulted his timepiece.

Phineas lifted a hand in greeting and quickened his place to the table. "God, I need a drink," he muttered, as he slid into the leather armchair opposite the viscount.

"You are late." St. John slid his own drink across the table, and

Phineas promptly accepted the brandy, and downed nearly half in a single pull.

And if that wasn't a metaphor for the way their friendship had always been, Phineas didn't know *what* was: the viscount, good, and honorable, and generous enough to give the jacket off his back, and Phineas, who'd next to nothing but a smile to his name, and unashamed to take whatever those around him were willing to share.

"My dear aunt paid a visit, and wouldn't be turned away," Phineas said.

"Ah." St. John inclined his head. "That bad?"

"Worse."

"Care to talk about it?"

Talking about his circumstances and the reliance he had upon his aunt's generosity wouldn't solve anything. "That is the very *last* thing I'd like," Phineas muttered.

"The reason I've asked to meet," the other man began, as a servant appeared with a new sifter. St. John waved off that offer, and only after the young footman left, did he continue. "Sylvia, as you know, is expecting our next child, and we are headed to Alfriston tomorrow morn."

Ah, this meeting began just like the two similar ones they'd had before it.

"You needn't have taken time out of your schedule, of course, I'd be honored to serve as godfather to this one, as well." Though God help him, for the life of him, he couldn't fathom what in hell would bring St. John or his wife to instilling that important responsibility to *Phineas*, of all people.

"Yes, well, thank you. But I took that favor as being understood."

Which implied St. John would ask…a *different* favor of him.

"Let us hope it's not for funds as you'd be better served asking Scarsdale," Phineas jested.

Married, and in possession of a fortune, powerful parents who didn't want to kill one another, the earl was by far the more stable friend to put a favor to.

"Nothing as burdensome as that, Landon." St. John followed that assurance with a laugh; one Phineas would have marched over to the betting book in the middle of the room and staked a fortune—if he had one—was forced.

He stared over the top of his drink at the man he'd been friends with for nearly the whole of his miserable existence. "What is it, St. John?"

"Tomorrow, I'll be retiring to the countryside for Sylvia's confinement."

"Yes, I believe we have covered that part."

"And," St. John continued. "There is the matter of…"

Phineas stared at the viscount, and when it became apparent the other man wasn't going to finish that thought, Phineas nodded, in a silent urging for him to continue.

"My sisters."

Frowning, Phineas did a sweep of the exclusive, all-men's club. If any women were going to invade the sanctity of this place, it would be one of the six Kearsley ladies.

"Anwen," St. John clarified.

Anwen Kearsley? Bespectacled and bold, but certainly not the most brazen of the sisters that he'd have wagered would be—"*Here?*"

The viscount blinked slowly, and then understanding lit his eyes. "You think I brought her here?"

"I don't think you'd manage to '*bring*' a single one of your headstrong siblings anywhere. On the other hand, I *would* expect any one of them to bring you 'round to escorting them 'round the globe if they wished it."

St. John sat forward quickly. "And therein lay the problem," he said, dropping an elbow on the table.

Something in his friend's tone, gave Phineas a healthy pause.

"Sylvia and I are leaving," the viscount explained. "However, my sisters, this time, will remain behind in London. There is the matter of Anwen."

A warning shiver started up Phineas' back. "And what matter is that exactly?" he asked, prodding his friend along.

"Given Anwen's circumstances, my mother feels it would be dire for her to miss the Season."

"And what circumstances are those?"

"Have a care, Landon." St. John gave him a sharp look. "I know you're the jesting sort but making light of the fact Anwen hasn't had any marital prospects is crossing a line."

This would be the one-time Phineas *hadn't* been making light of a situation. "St. John, your sister hasn't married because the lords in London are a sorry lot of dimwitted fellows who can't appreciate a clever lady like Anwen."

His friend gave him a peculiar look.

"What is it?" *Now.* A voice in Phineas' head added in a silent emphasis.

The glimmer in the viscount's eyes receded. "I'd ask you to look after my sisters in my absence, particularly Anwen."

"*Look* after them. Yes, but," dread tickled at the back of Phineas' mind, "what exactly does this entail?"

St. John stared at him, and then ever so slowly nodded.

Lost, Phineas shook his head.

Again, St. John nodded.

Then the other man's meaning hit him. Phineas began to shake his head again, then stopped. "Egad," he recoiled. "You want me to…*to*…" He couldn't even bring himself to finish the thought. It was far too heinous.

He needn't have bothered.

"I'd ask you to attend the same events as my mother and sister." St. John reached inside the front of his jacket. He withdrew a small, folded page, and slid it across the table at Phineas. "These are them."

Phineas glanced at the white vellum sheet.

"You'll find there a list of those affairs my mother has already accepted invitations to."

He scanned the object in question but made no move to take it.

"I'm hardly at the top of the most respectable lists," he pointed out. "Why…why, all these events your mother and sister will be attending are ones I haven't received invitations to in more years than I can remember." And thank God, for that.

"That's already been taken care of," St. John, killer of hope, said. "My mother has put in a personal request to those hostesses. You can expect invitations to be arriving any day." Because both the dowager viscountess and St. John would expect nothing more than Phineas' capitulation. They'd a faith in him he certainly didn't deserve.

A panicky laugh built in his chest. "Thank you."

"You're most welcome."

"And…this you take is the less difficult of asks?" Phineas downed the remainder of his drink. "Jesus." Though Phineas, had never been the praying sort before now, the Lord and Savior's name emerged just that—a prayer.

"I know you are not one usually given to attending respectable events,"

Phineas lifted an eyebrow. "*Usually*?"

Guilty color filled St. John's cheeks. "Very well, *ever*. If there was any other option, you must know I wouldn't ask you to place yourself in a position you do not wish to be in." He turned up a palm. "But Scarsdale is married and…"

Ah, so this is why Phineas had been chosen.

"And there is no one else," Phineas supplied for him. Scarsdale, the third friend in their trio had gone on and married several years ago.

"There is no one I'd trust more," St. John clarified, paused, and then added, "*And* there is no one else."

Phineas scrubbed a hand over his face. First his aunt, and now *this*. If that weren't the bloody perfect top on this day. The duchess demanded his marriage to a respectable lady on her list. In having Phineas watch over his eldest sister, St. John would stick him at all those affairs, Phineas had previously avoided like a plague.

Mayhap 'tis for the best. It'll be like killing two birds with one stone: he saw to his duties as best friend, and at last, secured a wife while doing so.

Phineas grabbed the bottle, filled his empty glass, and then emptied it for a second time. He grimaced as the liquid burned a fiery path down his throat. "Very well."

St. John's shoulders sagged in palpable relief. "Thank you."

Phineas waved off that expression of gratitude. "Did you think I'd decline your request?" he asked curiously.

The viscount's lips curled up in a slow smile. "Not for a moment."

"Well, that makes two of us," he lied. As St. John barked out laughing, Phineas filled his glass for a third time.

This one, however, he pushed across the table at his friend, then Phineas helped himself to the rapidly emptying bottle. "Shall we drink to your impending fatherhood?"

"Alas, my family awaits." St. John consulted his timepiece then returning it to his jacket, the viscount stood. "Given the undertaking you've agreed to, I trust you require that liquid fortitude far more than myself."

Phineas would toast to that.

The moment St. John took his leave, Phineas turned to the task of getting himself good and soused. By the fourth brandy, dread at his newly assigned role as 'Protector of the Kearsleys' remained. After his fifth, some of the bleakness began to fade.

After all, in the scheme of the Kearsley sisters, Anwen had certainly proven the least mischievous and naughty of the lot. Granted, they were *all* naughty—just to varying levels. And by the time Phineas drained the last drops from the battle, he'd gotten around to the idea that mayhap this wouldn't be so bad.

CHAPTER 3

ASSESSING HER REFLECTION IN THE pure gold leaf angular floor mirror and flanked on both sides by her two best friends, Lady Faith Rutherford and Lady Marcia Waters, Anwen Kearsley had but one thought: This was never going to work.

At Anwen's left, Faith shook her head; that slight movement sent her black coiled curls bouncing. "This is *not* going to work."

Faith appeared to be of a like opinion.

Anwen's shoulders sagged.

Marcia slipped closer and linked her arm with Anwen's. "*I* for one think you look splendid."

Anwen eyed her reflection dubiously. The trousers Faith had pilfered from one of the shorter men who worked inside the clubs belonging to her husband, Lord Rutherford, clung too tight to Anwen's hips. The black wool coat did little to hide the curves of her breasts.

"I'm not saying she doesn't look splendid," Faith protested. "*Of course*, she does. I'm saying, she doesn't look…" She gestured to Anwen's neckline. "*The part.*"

When Marcia only stared puzzledly back, Faith threw her arms up. "A man," she exclaimed. "She doesn't look like a man." Faith slid her incisive stare Anwen's way, once more. "She doesn't even look like a boy."

The three friends went silent, and each resumed their study of Anwen with critical eyes.

Any other time, Anwen, London's longest-running wallflower, would have *welcomed* the problem of being seen as *too* womanly.

But her entire plan of entering the Albany exclusive gentlemen's suites, however, hinged upon Anwen passing only as a 'young man'. After all, the apartments at the Albany barred women from entering their *hallowed* halls.

Anwen wrinkled her nose. Notorious rake, Phineas, the Marquess of Landon *would* be so contrary as to suddenly close up his townhouse and set himself up in a place where ladies were prohibited. He, who'd a scandalous reputation and a book-long history of liaisons with countless widows and women chose *this* time to quit his residence in favor of the infamous hotel suites.

Faith's eyes brightened, and she shot a finger into the air. "I have it." She sprinted over to her French carved walnut armoire, tossed the doors open, and withdrew an emerald, green muslin cloak from inside.

Faith dashed back over. "There!" With a pleased smile, she tossed that garment around Anwen's shoulders, obscuring her form.

"Splendid," Marcia said dryly. "No one at Albany's will dare pay another glance at her wearing a woman's cloak."

Faith gave a roll of her eyes. "This isn't for Albany's." She paused. "It is to ensure we can leave and venture out in a carriage without attracting *notice.*"

"Ahh," Anwen and Marcia said as one.

Notice, as in…Faith's husband, the enigmatic Marquess of Rutherford. Clever friends were worth their weight in chocolate.

Only… "What about when I exit the carriage and head for the marquess's suites?"

Faith instantly folded her arms around Anwen and dropped her chin atop her shoulder. "It is a dark, moonlit night. The majority of the men in those apartments will still be out at their wicked clubs."

Anwen caught the skin of her cheek between her teeth and troubled that flesh. This was madness. But what other choice did she have? If Anwen wanted to have a sliver of the dream she'd always carried in her heart before she died, then this was the only way forward.

"Or," Marcia rested her chin atop Faith's hand that still rested on Anwen's right shoulder.

"Or?" Anwen asked hopefully. Perhaps one of them had an actual solution.

"Or, we don't have to do this," Marcia said quietly.

Her friends let Anwen sit in silence of that suggestion. They'd support her, either way. Whether she continued forward with her plan to have some time with Phineas before she died, or if she scrapped it altogether. Either way, they'd keep the secret of this night.

Anwen stared at her cloaked, bespectacled image reflected back. She'd never been bold like Brenna, or fearless like Daria. Or as feisty as Eris. She'd never had a head for science and mathematics like Cora, or able to recall and recite a Shakespearean sonnet with the zeal and passion of Delia.

Nay, in every way, Anwen had never been exceptional in any way and forever been...*ordinary*. There'd never been anything exceptional about her. It was likely why there'd never been a suitor or interest from the gentleman she'd loved since girlhood. Why, the gossips hadn't even bothered to cut their teeth on her for being the longest-lasting wallflower. Her life was whirring past, and soon, she'd have never done anything scandalous, daring, or bold—*until tonight*.

"Anwen?" Marcia spoke gently.

Anwen smiled. "I am ready."

Faith's eyes brightened. "Huzzah! We are doing this, then." She sprinted to the armoire like one who feared Anwen might change her mind and fetched two more cloaks. One she handed to Marcia, and the other she tossed over her own shoulders.

Faith reached for the brass door handle.

"You're husband?" Marcia asked for the third time since she and Anwen arrived.

"I've already told you," Faith said, escorting them from the room. "This is Rex's Day to work these hours at the club. If we do not do this now, we'd have to wait until next week."

Together, they made their way below-stairs, and to the grand marble foyer, with but two sconces lit.

Faith cast a glance over her shoulder. "I'd already coordinated for our driver to wait," she whispered.

"Dare I ask where you're going?"

That low, silken question startled a collective shriek from the trio, and they spun. The Marquess of Rutherford stepped from the shadows.

Dark, dashing, and previously dangerous, Faith's husband assessed them through inky black lashes.

Faith gasped, and then flew over. "You are home!" she cried and launched herself at him.

The marquess caught the diminutive marchioness in his arms and spun her in dizzying circle that left Faith's cheeks flushed a cheerful cherry red. When he'd brought them to a stop, Faith caught his face between her small, gloved hands, and gently kissed him.

"Trying to distract me, I take it, love?" Lord Rutherford slowly lowered her, so she slid down his body with a deliberate, and seductive slowness.

Faith pouted. "Are you suggesting I anything but love your embrace, dear husband?"

The marquess placed his mouth close to the ear Faith had full hearing from and whispered something that caused Faith's lips to drop a fraction, and a sigh to slip out. Then Lord Rutherford flicked his tongue out to tease the shell of Faith's ear.

Anwen blushed at witnessing the intimate display between the desperately in love pair. She needn't have worried. The handsome couple spoke as if they two were the only souls left in the world, and there was such an intimacy, both a physical and emotional connection shared between the couple, Anwen found herself equally compelled to boldly watch or look away.

The marquess said something that deepened the color on his wife's cheeks. Faith shook her head. He whispered something else, and this time Faith swatted her handsome husband on the sleeve. Lord Rutherford pulled his attention from Faith and looked Anwen and Marcia's way.

"Miss Kearsley, Lady Marcia," he greeted, with a belated, but impressively deep bow. "A pleasure, as always."

Anwen and Marcia promptly sank into matching curtsies, and a sudden, awkward silence descended over the corridor.

Faith's husband proved the one to break the quiet. "Going out, I see," he murmured. His gaze lingered a moment on Anwen's boots, and she automatically drew her cloak closer about her person. "No response?" he drawled.

It hadn't sounded very much like a question. Even so, in a bid to go unnoticed, Anwen kept herself from saying as much.

"It didn't sound like a question, Lord Rutherford," Marcia however, said the quiet part aloud for all of the friends.

Faith frowned. "It wasn't." She gave her husband's arm a light pinch. "Lord Rutherford knows we have plans for the evening."

"This is true." The marquess propped a shoulder against the wall. "A visit to the theatre, I believe you said. I did *not*, however, realize said plans included one of you ladies being dressed in gentleman's clothes." He directed an entirely too astute glance back at Anwen's ankles. "Which leaves me...intrigued, to say the least."

Oh, hell and double hell. Anwen drew deeper into her clothes.

"Pulling at your cloak doesn't help, Miss Kearsley," Faith's husband remarked with a sardonic twist to his voice. "The problem lies, *ahem*, elsewhere."

Anwen and her friends mechanically followed his downward focus back to the boots and hint of trousers still damningly revealed.

"Oh, hush, dearest," Faith chided, giving him a gentle tap. "It hardly matters what she wears."

"No," the marquess agreed with his wife. "It doesn't. It *does*, however, suggest you three are up to some clandestine business that merits such a disguise, and the last time you were up to such antics—"

"We ended up married," Faith cut him off.

Lord Rutherford collected his wife's hands in his and brought each to his mouth, one at a time, for a kiss. "A greater fate than I could ever dream of," he said huskily, and with none of his usual dry humor, and filled only with love and warmth.

Faith's eyes went all soft, and at Anwen's side, Marcia sighed.

And Anwen was undoubtedly the worst sort of friend because her heart hurt with envy. That is what Anwen yearned for, and had always wanted, *with Phineas*. She'd long since ceased hoping he'd feel such devotion for her.

Faith stretched up on tiptoe and made to kiss her husband's cheek. The marquess turned his head quick so Faith's lips collided with his.

Faith giggled, and then sank back on her heels. "You wicked man," she whispered, affectionately. "I love you."

"And I you."

Faith put her focus back on Anwen and Marcia. "Shall we, ladies?" With that, Faith came forward and looped her arms through one of theirs.

They made it no further than a pace.

"Halt."

Anwen's heart fell. Of course, it wouldn't be that easy.

"We could always pretend we didn't hear him," Marcia whispered.

"I heard that, Lady Marcia," the marquess drawled.

Had Anwen *really* expected Faith's devoted husband would just turn a blind eye to his beloved wife sneaking off in the dead of night?

"What I *didn't* hear," his voice came just past their shoulder, and they jumped.

No man should move so stealthily.

"What I didn't hear," he repeated, "is precisely where you're sneaking off to with Miss Kearsley dressed…" He cleared his throat. "As she is."

With a shared reluctance, each young woman turned and faced him.

"You do not need to know," Faith insisted.

"On the contrary, love. If you believe I'll not give a second thought to you galivanting about London, alone, then you don't know me."

Faith remained mutinously silent.

Anwen swiveled her gaze back and forth between frustrated husband and tight-lipped wife. Loyal as the day was long, Faith would never break Anwen's confidence. Just as Anwen wouldn't and couldn't be responsible for placing any strain in her friend's happy marriage.

"It is for me." Anwen took a step forward. "She is doing this for me."

The Marquess of Rutherford fixed an intent stare on Anwen. "For you?"

Shrewd and penetrating and darkly inquiring, Anwen understood why all of London feared him. His stare alone compelled a person to look away. And yet, this was Faith's loving husband, and such a man was not one to be feared.

She stepped forward, out of and away from the comforting folds of her friends and looked the marquess square in the eyes. "For me," she repeated.

The marquess folded his arms at his broad chest. "I'm listening."

"You don't have to tell him anything, Anwen," Faith said on a rush.

Anwen ignored her and continued to meet the marquess's gaze directly. "I'm visiting the Albany."

Behind her, both Marcia and Faith groaned.

Anwen and Lord Rutherford ignored them.

"The Albany," he restated.

She nodded.

He sought clarification. "As in the all-men's apartment which bars women from entering?"

Anwen nodded again. "The very same. Which is a rather silly rule."

The marquess proved unrelenting. "Why?"

Anwen frowned. "Because women really should be free to—"

"Why do you intend to enter the Albany?" the marquess cut her off, impatiently.

"Oh." Obviously, that's what he'd been asking about. "Er…"

"Rex!" Faith swept over and took Anwen by the arm. "You do *not* have to answer him."

"I'm going to pay a call on Lord Landon," Anwen said as if her best friend hadn't even spoken.

A brief silence met that pronouncement. "And I trust there's a reason you cannot speak with Lord Landon at a more respectable hour and in a," he looked pointedly at Anwen's trousers peeking out, "*different* way."

"He doesn't attend the same affairs."

"No, that much is true," Lord Rutherford allowed.

"He's generally at his wicked clubs…like the one you own." A thought slipped in, and she perked up. "I don't suppose—"

"You are not entering my clubs." The steely lord put a swift death to that idea. "Again," he added for good measure. "Having innocent ladies about is bad for business."

Innocent. That slight distinction didn't escape her notice.

Suddenly, his eyes grew narrow. "What is the nature of business you have with Lord Landon? Has he behaved in a way that is less than gentlemanly?" His eyes darkened. "Are you…in trouble?"

In trouble? As a Kearsley, she'd been born with a cloud following her. Then his meaning took root.

Anwen gasped. "No! He wouldn't…" Rather, he wouldn't with her. There'd been any number of other women he'd bedded. But never a respectable, virtuous lady. He didn't dally with innocents.

Annoyed on Phineas' behalf, Anwen tipped her chin up. "He's my brother's best friend, and he has been a friend to me over the years." That much was true. Even as she'd yearned for more from him, the one constant had been his friendship. "I've known him nearly my entire life, and he isn't the scoundrel you and society take him for. He is loyal and supportive and—" Faith's husband continued to contemplate Anwen with that incisive stare, and she made herself stop that rambling defense of Phineas. "I'm not in trouble. It… isn't like that," she finished weakly.

"And how exactly is it, Miss Kearsley?"

How exactly was it, indeed?

"Do not answer him," Marcia called over.

A hysterical giggle bubbled in Anwen's throat. How exactly did she sum up her intentions for Phineas?

"Rex, *stop* badgering her." Faith's adamant demands fell on deaf ears.

"Miss Kearsley?" Lord Rutherford persisted.

"I want him to help me," Anwen said.

"Help you, how?"

"Rex!"

They ignored Faith's protestations.

"I want him to help me attract notice so that I can find a

husband." It was the same lie she intended to feed Phineas, and as such it felt safer to give twice.

Lord Rutherford continued to examine Anwen in that discriminating way.

"It is Adam Smith's law of supply and demand," she finished dumbly.

"Adam Smith?"

She nodded. "The economist and philosopher," she explained when Faith's husband only continued staring at her.

The Marquess of Rutherford said nothing for a long while. Anwen and her friends exchanged nervous glances, and Anwen prepared for the marquess to order her back to her mother's household for the night.

Then, Lord Rutherford tossed his head back and roared with laughter. Anwen and her friends stared at him, and then at one another.

"Faith, is your husband all right?" Marcia ventured.

"I…" Faith puzzled her brow. "Think so?" That slight uptilt turned Faith's words into a question and conveyed all the young woman's doubt.

"A–Adam Smith," he rasped, between great big laughs.

"Have you heard of him?" Anwen asked hesitantly.

The marquess dusted the mirth from the corners of his eyes. "I'm quite f-familiar with his works as applied to business. I've not, however, ever known it to be applied to courtships and marriage."

Anwen bristled with indignation. "And why can it not be also applied?" She crossed her arms at her chest.

Lining up alongside her, Faith and Marcia folded their arms, perfectly matching Anwen's pose.

"Oh, it most certainly can be, and it absolutely must be," the marquess acknowledged, after he'd reigned in his amusement. "You should have stated your intentions for Landon much sooner. The marquess being made to do anything respectable? This is too good to not be supported."

Anwen brightened. "You'll let us go, then?"

Faith's eyes lit like her husband had handed her the moon.

"I'm going to do far better than that, Miss Kearsley." The Marquess of Rutherford flashed a half-grin. "I'm going to *personally* escort you to his apartments."

With that pledge, a short while later, they were on their way: Anwen, Faith, Marcia—and Faith's husband, along with two armed guards atop the carriage.

The moment they arrived; Lord Rutherford exited the carriage. He reached a palm up to Anwen, handed her down, then looked back inside at the two remaining women seated there.

"You are to remain here." The marquess directed that at his wife.

He reached under his jacket and withdrew a gun from the waist of his trousers. "Jax and Jackson will stand guard. This is for you."

Faith leaned down and dropped a kiss on her husband's lips. "You are the very best of husbands and men."

A rakish grin curved hard lips. "You can remind me all the many ways later."

The dark of the night and the dimness in the carriage did little to hide the blush that spread across Faith's cheeks. Then, together, Anwen and Lord Rutherford started for the exclusive hotel.

Despite the ungodly hour, they were promptly greeted by a rotund and short, liveried butler with sparse black strains of hair he'd smoothed across an otherwise bald, shiny pate.

Without a word, Faith's husband furnished a card. The stolid butler, dipped small, deep-set eyes a fraction, and skimmed the identifying name emblazoned upon that small scrap.

In an instant, Anwen and the marquess were granted entrance into a foyer with dark hardwood floors and clean lines that merged modesty with sophistication.

"Come," Faith's husband murmured, and motioned for her to follow.

As they fell into a matched step, she felt a rush of giddy excitement. "It is that easy?" Anwen whispered.

"There's not a part of every club or establishment I don't own or, in some way, have connections to," he said, with more of a matter-of-factness than arrogance.

"How do you know where to go?" she whispered.

He held a finger against his lips, silencing her. "It also behooves me to know the exact whereabouts of the men deep in debt to me."

Deep in debt to him.

Which meant, Phineas was one of the insolvent men who owed the marquess.

She well-knew Phineas' propensity for wagering. After all, he'd been the one to teach Anwen how to play Vingt-et-un, faro, and hazard (among others). But hearing the proprietor speak of the hole Phineas had gotten himself by gambling made it real in ways that it had previously only been hearsay from the pages she'd dismissed as gossip.

Anwen and Lord Rutherford didn't say anything the rest of the way. The marquess brought them to a stop before a paneled door.

Without uttering so much as a word, he pointed to the oak slab separating Anwen from Phineas, and mouthed, "Here."

Here.

Anwen continued to stare at the entrance of Phineas' rooms, and the first stirrings of doubt crept in. What if Phineas wouldn't agree to help her? Yes, they'd all but grown up together, and he'd been a friend, but what if he'd only done so out of a sense of loyalty to Anwen's brother, Clayton? What if that same devotion didn't, however, extend to Anwen?

Her stomach twisted.

Or worse, what if he were repelled by the idea of spending time with Anwen, in the way she sought? Then, there'd be absolutely no way of having even these smallest memories of him to carry with her when she perished. And it was truly a mark of just how pitiable she in fact was, that she wanted them, anyway.

The marquess leaned down. "Have you changed your mind?" he whispered so faintly against her ear, she may as well have imagined the words he spoke. "If so, you need just say the word and I'll immediately escort you back to the carriage."

Anwen shook her head. "I want to do this." She *needed* to do this. It was her last chance to have even this small, pretend moment with Phineas.

Faith's husband gave her another long, hard look.

"I'm ready," she said in hushed voice.

The marquess reached into the front of his black, wool jacket, and brandished a gleaming key.

Anwen's eyebrows went flying up. "*And* you have *keys* to your client's rooms?" she blurted, and then promptly slapped a hand over her mouth.

Lord Rutherford gave her a sharp look. "Quiet," he mutely ordered.

Frantically, she looked left and then right, more than half expecting guests and servants to come streaming out to prevent a break-in of their hallowed establishment.

"You have keys to your client's rooms?" she asked again, this time in a whisper.

"And I have keys to my client's rooms."

Despite herself, despite knowing the man beside her was in fact the husband of her best friend, a shiver traipsed up Anwen's spine. For that cool confirmation from Lord Rutherford served as a reminder that he wasn't just Faith's husband. He was also the ruthless, dangerous gaming hell owner… whom Phineas was in debt to.

Before her resolve deserted her, Anwen plucked the key from the marquess' fingers, jammed it in the lock, and let herself inside. The inky black of a room doused in darkness met her eyes. Anwen blinked several times to adjust to that dim lighting and stepped inside.

Lord Rutherford immediately pulled the door closed with a nearly imperceptible click, so that Anwen found herself alone in Phineas' apartments, with the ringing sound of silence in her ears the, otherwise, only company.

Then, she heard it.

A bleating, not unlike the goats she and Cora loved to care for during their summer visits to the countryside. And something in that endearingly imperfect snore coming from behind the emerald, green velvet Habarteen hangings that flanked the sides of the enormous four-poster bed chased away the last of her reservations.

Shoving her hood back, Anwen loosened the ties of her borrowed cloak and wandered deeper into the room. She reached Phineas' bedside and took in the gold watch fob he was never without. That etched timepiece rested at the very edge of the walnut nightstand.

Phineas' right forearm remained the only part of him exposed out the side of the bed hangings. In sleep, his long, slender fingers stretched towards his watch fob, as if setting it down had been the last thing he'd done before he'd collapsed into the Mornine mattress, and grabbing it as soon as he awakened, proved the first thing he planned to do.

Another shuddery snore cut across the quiet. Anwen jumped and swung her gaze to the crack in the makeshift curtains draped around the frame of the bed. Phineas remained slumbering, with the soft-spun yarn of the Witney blankets pulled over his head.

Anwen shrugged out of her noisy muslin cloak and set it on the bottom of Phineas' bed, and still, the marquess did not stir.

He'd always been a sound sleeper.

But he'd never snored. She would know as her room had been next to her brother's.

Somewhere over the years, that had changed, and as Anwen hovered there beside his sleeping form, she was struck by the realization that time had changed him, and oh, how she wished she could discover all those big and small transformations.

Anwen, determined to finally set her plan into motion, caught the thick edge of the bed hangings and drew them open.

Wholly oblivious to her standing over him, Phineas continued quietly snoring.

She perched herself on the edge of his mattress. "Phineas," she whispered.

Only another one of those gusty exhalations met her attempts at waking him.

She tried again, catching his arm through the coverlet, and giving a gentle shake. "Phineas."

A loud unmistakable snore proved her only answer.

Sighing, Anwen folded her arms at her chest and frowned at his still-draped frame.

You're not going to make this easy, are you?

But then, he'd always had an intuitive way of avoiding polite affairs. Perhaps in sleep, he'd sense to know trouble loomed, she thought wryly.

"Phineas," she repeated for a third time and tugged at the wool and cotton coverlet, then instantly froze.

Her gaze remained locked, trapped, and happily so upon the bare expanse of his chest.

In the course of her life, she'd seen him without his shirt on countless occasions when he'd been a boy and Anwen snuck upon him swimming in the lake with Clayton and their other friend, Charles Hayden, the Earl of Scarsdale. But then, she'd been more interested in sneaking off to watch and wish she could join in that fun. Certainly, she hadn't thought twice about the fact he'd been naked.

But this? This was different. Now, she was all grown up, and his chest wasn't the scrawny one of a young lad.

Look away. Look away. It was bad enough she'd snuck into his private apartments. Observing him while he slept, well, that was certainly a sin dark enough to bar her from those pearly gates. And Lord forgive her, in this instance, rooted to the floor, she had a hint of why the weak traded their souls.

"Phineas." This time his name emerged as a soundless utterance.

What in hell? This was Phineas. Yes, she'd loved him nigh on forever, but neither was she one of those simpering misses who made a cake of herself over him either.

Giving her head a firm shake, she set her jaw and, leaning over him, she then touched his shoulder; the heat of his delicately bronzed skin briefly froze her. Except for her heart. That organ hammered furiously against the walls of her chest.

Two years earlier, she'd accompanied her sister, Daria, to the Royal Museum where they'd visited a collection done by Daria's friend, Lady Bolingbroke. Anwen had stood in silent awe of a statue of an unknown man, chiseled in stone by the baroness. Anwen had been so very certain there could be nothing more magnificent, and certainly not any mere mortal.

In this instant, she appreciated just how wrong she'd been. This finely built Phineas may have very well been that divine work of art come to life. The light matting of tight golden curls covering his bare chest, however, marked him a very real, and exquisite man.

Unbidden, and her sole reason for being here briefly forgotten,

Anwen reflexively caressed her fingers over Phineas' arm. Even in sleep, his biceps bulged. His sleek triceps jumped under her touch.

Suddenly, he shot out a hand and caught Anwen firmly by her wrist.

She emitted a little squeak, that faded to a breathless gasp as Phineas, in one effortless motion, brought her under him, and had her framed between his propped elbows.

"Mmm," he purred, and with still-closed lids, he had the look, sound, and unpredictability of a rugged lion just roused from its rest.

Oh, God, and hers was a silent entreaty to that all-powerful creator above.

And then, he touched his lips to her neck.

"So soft," he sluggishly praised. He ran a bold, possessive hand along the curve of her hip. "I'm dreaming."

Anwen's lashes fluttered shut.

Nay. I am.

Anwen brought her arms up and twined them about his neck. "Phineas," she whispered against his ear, silently begging for his kiss.

His chiseled body tensed against hers. In what appeared a laborious chore, his lashes lifted. His sleepy gaze locked with hers, and then there came a slow, dawning recognition.

Because of course.

Of course, she'd believed he'd awakened, and all the while he'd been asleep, imagining she was someone else. That burned in a different way, Anwen yanked her hands back and dropped them uselessly to her side.

"Hullo, Phineas." With all the dignity and pride, she could manage, she mustered a smile. "It is…me."

CHAPTER 4

HULLO, PHINEAS. IT IS ME

With that greeting, whispered in the huskiest contralto he'd ever before heard, Phineas found himself dreaming.

For laying naked in his bed, with a young woman under him, her supple body pressed invitingly against his naked one, there could be no denying, he'd landed himself in the most delicious of dreams he'd no wish to awaken from.

Only…He no longer slept.

His head still foggy from sleep and the heavy amount of spirits he'd helped himself to that evening, Phineas slogged his way past his dazed head.

And then, he registered the familiar form under him. *Not* familiar because she'd been a past lover or lady he'd lain with. Rather, for the big, joy-filled smile and even bigger brown eyes behind wire-rimmed spectacles he'd pushed back onto the bridge of that gently sloped nose.

Phineas swallowed hard.

Nay, he'd found himself trapped, in a bloody nightmare, because no decent gentleman went about, either in a sleep state or wake one, with thoughts of having a best friend's sister under you in bed. Not that he'd ever been accused of being an honorable sort. He hadn't and he wasn't. Only, for society's correctly drawn ill-opinion of him, even Phineas had scruples enough to not go bedding St. John's eldest sister.

He squeezed his eyes shut. *One, two, three-wake up. One, two-three, wake up.*

Phineas employed that same strategy he'd used to get himself awake from nightmares as a boy when his mother had been sent away by the late marquess.

He forced his eyes open. It hadn't worked then, and it didn't work now.

Anwen smiled more widely; a deservedly sheepish one that dimpled her left cheek.

"Phineas," she greeted again, with the same carefree ease as when their paths crossed during his visits with St. John.

"*Anwen?*" he croaked.

She wiggled a hand free of the unintentional trap his arms had made around her and gave a little wave. "The same."

Phineas recoiled, and, clutching at his sheets and coverlet, he scrambled away from her, all the way to the other side of the bed.

Too far.

He came down hard on the wood floor; the soft wool and cotton blanket did little to blunt the fall.

Anwen ducked her head out from the curtain and stared over the side of the bed. "Are you hurt?" The question hadn't even fully formed on her lips before she began moving closer.

Blanching, he shot a hand out, warding her off. "D-Do not."

The bed linens promptly slipped through his fingers and dropped…as did Anwen's wide-eyed gaze.

With a hoarse croak, Phineas grabbed at the downed fabric, swiftly drew it up into place, and proceeded to scramble across the floor, backward on his arse. "N-No closer," he choked.

He should have known better than ordering a Kearsley about. Why, he may as well have issued an invitation to join him on the floor. For that, was precisely what the saucy minx did…and with a friend, no less.

His back collided with the plaster wall, which effectively put a halt to his retreat.

She stopped over his prone form, and he craned his neck at an awkward arch to see her and truly had his first glimpse since he'd found her in his bed.

And swiftly wished he hadn't.

For her nighttime visit, she'd donned a too-tight lawn shirt that did nothing to conceal marvelously full breasts and a pair of snug-fitting trousers. The black wool hugged every single curve, from her generously flared hips to her surprisingly muscular calves. Hers were limbs crafted by God to wrap around a man's—

He groaned.

Anwen folded her hands at her chest, plumping breasts that certainly required no assistance there, and drawing Phineas' gaze back to previously unnoted details: the dusky outline of her areolas; taut nipples that pressed tellingly against the fabric of her shirt.

The devil was determined to punish him this night, for all Phineas' past transgressions. Phineas swallowed. Or, rather, he tried to.

And failed.

Smothered by another fit of coughing, Phineas jerked his focus a touch higher so his eyes could meet Anwen's face.

She scowled.

Good, a frown was far safer than that winsome smile she'd worn when she'd been under him.

"You're frowning?" he asked. "*You?*" Incredulity brought his voice creeping up.

Her scowl deepened.

"I'm disappointed in you."

"In *me*? I'm the one responsible for that sentiment this night, and not, let us say, you who has snuck into my private *suites*." That last word exploded from him with a sharp hiss.

The lines at the corners of her mouth deepened. "You'd think you would at least ask as to the reason for my visit."

He opened his mouth to remind her that visits were mutually agreed upon appointments, while this early morn intrusion decidedly was not, but stopped suddenly.

Why is she here? A voice whispered at the back of his mind.

An insidious thought slipped in and supplied Phineas with an answer: some bounder had noted and taken advantage of Anwen Kearsley's innocence. A visceral rage snaked through him; a deep, seething fury so great it darkened Phineas' vision, and briefly blinded him.

A growl worked its way up his throat. "Who?" he seethed. He'd remove the bastard's limbs and feed him his own fingers.

Anwen stared at him.

"Who is the man that hurt you?" he asked on a barely controlled whisper.

"Who hurt me? No one."

Phineas' shoulders sagged with palpable relief.

She wrinkled her adorably pert nose. "What is it with men believing any time a lady is in trouble that a man is responsible?"

"Because they invariably are." Then, something she said gave him pause. "Which other man was of a like opinion?"

She hesitated.

"Anwen?"

"Yes, well, you see…"

"No, I don't see anything, which is why I asked for clarification."

"I have sense enough to not travel alone in the dead of night, and, as such, enlisted the support of my friends." She went silent.

"Your friends being…" he prodded, already knowing. God help him, he knew.

"Marcia, the Viscountess Waters."

Some of the tension eased from his frame. Of course, Waters' wife. Waters who happened to be another one of Landon's closest—

"And Faith, the Marchioness of Rutherford," Anwen added that other name as an almost afterthought. Then she went close-lipped.

"Anwen?" he urged.

"Yes, well, we were departing for the night when Lord Rutherford happened to discover us sneaking out, and he was gracious enough to escort me here."

"Here," he echoed.

Anwen nodded and then pointed across the room. He followed that long, still-bobbing digit.

"Here, as in outside my rooms?"

Anwen nodded. "He has a key," she added.

Naturally, the ruthless bastard would.

Thoughts of the powerful gaming hell proprietor standing on guard outside these very suites proved the effective dram in dousing Phineas' unholy hunger of Miss Anwen Kearsley.

Anwen wrung her hands together. "Can we talk?"

"We've been talking." He issued that terse reminder through clenched teeth.

"About the reason I've come here. You see," she took a step closer, "I—"

"Back up, and then turn around."

Anwen stared back through those impossibly huge, brown eyes.

"So that I may dress, Anwen," he said impatiently.

Her gaze dipped a fraction to his bare shoulders. Understanding replaced the earlier confusion in those expressive irises of hers. "Ahh, yes, of course." She retreated several steps and then presented him with her back.

Muttering under his breath, Phineas stomped over to the garments he'd shed hours ago, back when it'd been a simpler time; back when his aunt had cut him off, and his best friend had asked him to watch over his sister.

Watch over her.

The viscount would have been better sending the entire Royal Guard and a Bow Street fleet.

"And still, that probably wouldn't have been enough to keep her secure," he muttered under his breath.

"What was that?" Anwen asked, angling her head.

"Do *not* turn around," he barked and hastened to finish pulling on enough garments so that he wasn't bare-assed before St. John's beloved sister.

"May I n-now?"

"Yes."

Anwen faced him, once more.

In his lifetime, Phineas Lesar, the Marquess of Landon had stumbled upon any number of naughty ladies, seeking out his even naughtier company. But here, inside his rooms at the exclusive Albany marked a first for him—and according to the legend of the bachelor's residence, now the only known second time a lady— after Lady Caro Lamb—had invaded the men-only establishment.

"*Doubtlessly* it would be a Kearsley," he muttered.

"What would be a Kearsley?" Anwen asked.

"That would dress herself up as a pageboy, sneak inside the Albany, and hide herself in my rooms."

"I'm not hiding here."

Which begged the question… "What *are* you doing here?"

"I'm in need of assistance."

"And this was not the kind of assistance that could wait for, say, a more respectable hour…and place?"

"Hardly," she scoffed. "It's far easier sneaking past all the men and servants living here, than attempting a private moment in my family's household, with all my sisters about."

"I'll drink to that," he muttered.

Which reminded him… the situation—being alone in a bachelor's residence with his best friend in the world's younger sister—certainly called for a drink.

"I'd rather you were sober," Anwen called over, as he went to pour himself a drink.

Phineas didn't break stride; rather, he went straight for a bottle of brandy.

"I'm sober," he said, as he made a tall—he thought better of it—a *very* tall glass.

"But you already stink of spirits, and you'll be even less clearheaded."

Stink of spirits? He bristled. Furthermore… "I'm perfectly clearheaded." *Enough.*

He tossed back a sip.

Anwen continued to eye him dubiously. "It didn't appear that way. When you saw me, you had a queer look I'd never before seen from you."

A look like he'd wanted to tug down her trousers, so he could better appreciate her curves, bare under him and his touch.

Phineas took another, bigger, sip of his drink.

Hell, I'm going straight to hell. That was, of course, if the eventual fate of his soul hadn't already been settled long before—which it decidedly had.

"Phineas, please," she asked softly, in a slightly pleading way he'd never before heard from her. And for the first time in his life, he discovered himself wanting and able to put someone else's needs before his own.

"What is it, Anwen?"

She beamed, then glanced about so quickly her spectacles tipped to the very end of her nose. With a smile, she pointed…and he followed that long, gesturing digit over to the cane back fireside chair. "It would be easier if you sat?"

"Easier for who?" he drawled.

"For me."

He'd wager the very last of his funds that with whatever she intended to say, a seat would be best for both of them.

Drink in hand, Phineas settled himself on the gold and cream striped Louis XV chair and waited.

And continued waiting, while Anwen stood there with a furrowed brow and looking as lost as Phineas had often been attending lectures in his university days.

"Anwen?"

She jumped. "Adam Smith!"

He stared at her.

The troublesome minx cleared her throat. "He is—"

"I'm familiar with Adam Smith."

She brightened. "Indeed?"

He nodded.

"Then, you're aware of his philosophy on supply and demand and—"

"Anwen," he cut in. "Have you come here to enlist my support in a matter of business? Because if that is the case, given the state of my finances, you'd be best looking elsewhere." He made to rise.

"I need you to make *me* in demand," she said on a frantic rush before he could get to his feet.

And he, Phineas Lesar, the Marquess of Landon, charmer, who always found the right thing to say, was failed by words. Flummoxed, he tumbled all the way back into the folds of his seat and remained fixed there. Mute.

Anwen grimaced. "I'm making a mess of this."

They agreed on one thing this night.

She began to pace. "Diamonds are rare, which is why ladies of unrivaled beauty are referred thusly. I, am not a Diamond," she spoke with a matter-of-factness and without a hint of one seeking out compliments.

He scowled. Annoyed on her behalf, and at her, for that low opinion she possessed of herself.

"You are beautiful, Anwen," he said, curtly.

She stopped abruptly. "You're only saying that because you're my brother's best friend."

He *shouldn't* be saying that because he *was* her brother's best friend. As such, he let her to her incorrectly drawn supposition.

"Ladies who are not possessed of grand beauty must attract attention in different ways, through their musical accomplishments, of which mine are limited. Through their family's most elevated bloodlines, but my eccentric ancestors and living family have earned a reputation for being oddities.

"If I were to receive attention from London's most celebrated, inveterate bachelor and rake, then my…supply will go down, and my demand will rise. Lord Rutherford suggested I lead with that," she finished lamely.

He scrubbed a hand over his stubbled chin. "*Of course*, he did." The hard-hearted proprietor must be laughing even as Anwen and Phineas spoke.

He and Anwen continued studying one another. She, with her flushed cheeks and a bashfulness he'd never before witnessed from her. Hell, that he'd never before witnessed from any one of the Kearsley sisters.

"You want me to pretend to court you?" he finally said. Phineas wouldn't do it. He couldn't do it. He certainly didn't want to do it.

Anwen eyed him like he'd sprouted a second nose, and at that, a hooked one, with warts on the end. "Whyever, would I want you to do *that*?"

"I…The pretend courtship has proven effective?"

"Perhaps in romance novels." She paused and eyed him curiously. "Do you read romance novels?"

"*No!*"

Anwen frowned. "You needn't sound so adamant. I'd have found it more admirable were you not so close-minded to that very important genre."

"Is this what you've sought me out in my private suites to discuss, Anwen?" he said dryly. "To debate *literary works*?"

She brightened. "At least, you'll not disparage them. Most men… most *people*, do. But classifying them as literary works—"

"Anwen," he said warningly.

"Oh, yes. That is right. No."

No? He puzzled his brow.

"That is 'no' to your earlier question."

And were his neck with a noose around it and a correct answer dependent upon saving it, he couldn't recall what in blazes the last question had been.

"No, I don't want you to court me," she said impatiently.

She was impatient. *Her?* Since when?

He shook his head attempting to clear his mind. So that wasn't what she was asking? Phineas should be wholly relieved. Why, then, did he feel this peculiar…letdown?

"All of society, everyone, remarks on you and everything you do. I'm invisible, Phineas," she said. "You are the opposite of that."

"Do you mean, I'm visible?"

She didn't take that wryly tendered bait. "As such, your even being *near* me, will at last force their attention my way. Then, they will wonder why you're coming 'round. I do not want *you* to court me," she repeated, again.

"Yes, I believe you've said as much," he said, tersely.

She brought her narrow but strong shoulders back. "I want you to show me how to make myself visible all on my own so that *someone else* will court me."

Someone else.

He should be relieved.

Phineas growled.

Over my dead body.

She was the baby sister of his closest and best friend in the world, which likely also accounted for the more than mild irritation her declaration roused inside at her mentioning pursuing some other chap. For he hated the faceless man in an instant.

"No."

Anwen cocked her head. "I didn't ask you anything."

She hadn't needed to. "To your being courted. No. Absolutely not."

Anwen laughed. "Phineas, I'm not a child."

"You can't be more than—"

"Twenty-seven."

He stopped mid-sentence. "Indeed?"

Anwen nodded, that slight movement sent her spectacles tumbling to the bridge of her nose once again, and she pushed the wire rims back into place.

"I even have white hair," she said, pointing to the strands in question.

"You've had those since you were sixteen."

She sighed. "Just another Curse of the Kearsleys."

He scoffed. "Hardly. They add an air of…interest to you."

"An air of interest?" Anwen snorted. "La, sir, you'll turn my head. Matrons and mothers have white hair, not…" she slashed her arms up and down, gesturing to herself, "*younger* women."

"Ah, but you're wrong." His gaze slipped over those white locks that leant an ethereal, almost other-worldly look to her.

"The sailors rescued by Leukothea, that savior of Odysseus, and the ancient goddess of the sea would disagree," he murmured. "Those warriors of old would be as arrested by that streak as they were of Leukothea." Had he truly never before noticed the mesmeric quality of those strands?

Her enormous brown eyes unblinking, Anwen studied him. "Are you…comparing me to a Greek goddess?" she whispered.

Unbidden, his hand came up, and in a gesture that wasn't at all brotherly, but one he couldn't keep himself from, Phineas ran several fingers over that silken soft patch of white. "I…believe I am," he said softly.

Odd, he'd felt her hair before; there'd been the time she became tangled in a button on his coat sleeve, and he'd been forced to snip those locks free. He'd even brushed her curls once when he'd been a boy of twelve and she a girl of six who'd ordered him to run a comb through her tangles. But both times, he'd been just a lad, too young to properly appreciate the smooth, richness of Anwen Kearsley's tresses.

Her lips—a perfect upside-down cupid's bow—that lent a deep pout to that flesh, quivered. And God rot his soul for being the bounder he'd always been, found himself riveted, his attention diverting back and then forth from her plaited dark brown hair, to her mouth. All the while, his fingers remained in a frozen caress of those curls.

Only, her mouth trembled, demanding his attention, demanding things no best friend of a brother should ever consider.

Anwen burst out laughing.

Blinking, Phineas came back to the moment.

She rolled her eyes. "You're only saying that because you are a charming rogue."

"Ah, but I wouldn't charm St. John's sister," he pointed out.

I wouldn't charm St. John's sister. I couldn't charm St. John's sister. I shouldn't charm St. John's sister

He reminded himself of that great code of friendship, over and over.

Another frown formed on her lips, and Phineas hurried to interrupt her. "You don't need a suitor, Anwen."

"I agree."

Good, that settled the—

Anwen lifted a finger. "I *want* a suitor." She paused. "A husband to be exact."

He frowned. "And…have you settled on a certain gentleman to fill the role?"

That way, he'd have a name so he could kill the gent. This was, after all, *Anwen*.

"Yes."

Splendid. *Liar.* Phineas wanted to kill the bastard even more.

Anwen studied him, with more of that rare hesitancy. "Well?"

He opened his mouth to deliver a swift rejection of her request, and yet…She was St. John's sister, and she had come to Phineas for support.

"Phin—"

"I'm thinking," he cut her off and resumed his ruminations.

The viscount had explicitly asked that Phineas watch over Anwen, to which Phineas had already agreed. After all, he'd have laid down his life for the other man. Who was to say what she could or likely would do to snag the fellow's affections—at that, a bounder whose name she deliberately withheld?

"Phin—?"

"Still thinking," he said curtly.

What was more, if Phineas did agree to this mad idea she'd hatched, he could eventually wheedle the identity of her secret suitor.

Then, Phineas could kill him.

He shook his head. Nay, wait. Then, Phineas would be able to ascertain whether the gent was worthy of Anwen—which he, of course, wouldn't be, because, well, she was Anwen Kearsley. Then, he *would* kill him.

Also, since St. John had explicitly asked that Phineas watch over and after Anwen, that assignment already required Phineas to attend the same social functions as the eldest of his sisters. Why did that feel like an afterthought consideration?

Anwen tugged at his sleeve. "Phin–?"

"I'll do it."

She froze; her fingers rested on his shirtsleeve; the lawn material did little to dispel the feel of her hand or the warmth emanating from deliciously long digits, fingers all but made for wrapping around a man's l—

"You'll do it?" Anwen asked breathlessly.

Aye, he wanted to do it. Always a sinner, never a saint, he ached to take her fingers, and guide them—

She launched herself at him, twining her arms about his neck, even as the rapidity and force of her zeal sent the chair tipping back, and toppled he and Anwen.

They came down hard. Her forehead bounced against his chest, and he immediately brought a palm up to keep her neck from whipping back. Their fall knocked her spectacles free, and Anwen stared at him with dazed eyes.

"This has become something of a habit for us," he said, hoarsely, and searched a hand about—and found—her glasses.

For this wasn't the first time he'd had her atop him in this way. A memory trickled forth; one that he'd kicked sand and ash and dirt, and built bricks upon, to make himself forget because she'd been a girl, and he, well, he was himself. *But now, she's all woman,* the devil inside whispered.

Willing those wicked voices in his head to silence, Phineas returned Anwen's spectacles to their proper place. From around those circular rims, Anwen continued to stare in that dazed way, blinking slowly, and then wildly.

He frowned. His lustful musings forgotten. "Are you hur—*oomph*?"

Anwen hugged him tight enough to squeeze the air from his lungs.

"I am so grate…" she prattled happily as if they sat discussing their arrangement over tea, not with her draped sensually over his chest.

And he proved the most unscrupulous of rakes; settling his palm along the flat of her delicate back, he grazed his fingertips over the swell of her buttocks.

He blanched and swiftly yanked his hand free. What in hell was he *think*—?

"Will you come tomorrow?" she asked softly.

"Come?" he croaked. He *wanted* to come now.

Hell. I'm going to hell.

In fairness, Anwen unknowingly led him down the path of sin as effectively as Eve with her apple.

"I thought Hyde Park." Several creases furrowed Anwen's brow. "But mayhap it is best to begin at my household, as Clayton is not present, and your visiting will immediately draw the attention of the *ton*."

As if she'd settled the matter for the both of them—and mayhap she had—Anwen pressed her palms against his chest and shoved against him.

"*Oomph*." The air left him on another swift exhale as she hopped to her feet.

"You will not regret this, Phineas!" she exclaimed, her bright, innocent eyes giving no indication she'd caught a hint of his wayward, lust-filled musings.

She let herself out, like a whirlwind, and as the click of the door resonated in her wake, Phineas lay there.

Not regret this? I already do.

CHAPTER 5

THE FOLLOWING MORNING, PHINEAS DID just as he'd promised—he visited Anwen. Or rather, he paid a visit to *all* her sisters. And Anwen's mother–dear Mama–she was present, too.

A swell of laughter to rival that of a boisterous crowd at Covent Garden roared from the breakfast room. A still very much invisible, Anwen lingered outside and took in the tableau. Her mother and sisters all sat on the same side of the long, rectangular mahogany table built specifically to accommodate the sizeable Kearsley family, while Phineas occupied the square-backed mahogany Chippendale chair in the exact middle between the assembled Kearsleys.

With a grape between his thumb and forefinger, Phineas stared intently, through squinted eyes at the dowager viscountess. Without breaking focus, he arced his hand several times and then launched the tiny piece of fruit across the table.

Anwen's mother caught it effortlessly in her mouth.

Her sisters' cheers erupted around the breakfast room, and they stomped their feet in noisy approval. And if Anwen weren't so miffed at her first stolen day with Phineas having been commandeered by her entire family, she would have sighed at the sight of the high-spirited gathering.

Why, Phineas even had the always grim-faced *Daria* smiling.

But Anwen *was* miffed. When she'd envisioned the time she'd have with Phineas before she died, her imaginings and plannings only ever included just the two of them, not an audience of her Kearsley kin.

Alas, Anwen remained as invisible as she'd always been, and where she didn't give a fig that the *ton* barely knew she breathed, that Phineas didn't see her standing there caused a sharp pain deep inside.

Then, through the misery, his gaze shifted, and his eyes met hers. He smiled widely, and the sadness instantly ceded, replaced by a giddy lightness.

"Look!" Phineas exclaimed. "It is Anwen."

Every last Kearsley turned as one, so a sea of stares landed her way.

Anwen's heart lifted. "Hull—"

Phineas cut her off. "Catch, Anwen." He launched another grape, this time, with an impressive throw, all the way across the table, and to the entrance of the doorway, and—

Plunk.

Anwen started and went cross-eyed as that cylindrical missile hit her square in the forehead. The purple grape fell forlornly at her feet.

A new chorus went up; this one disappointed groans and moans.

"That was pathetic, Anwen," Eris bewailed.

"I'm sad to say I must agree with Eris," the dowager viscountess lamented.

Anwen gave her a look. "*Mother.*"

Her traitorous mama slipped sheepishly down in her seat.

"You must play, Anwen." Brenna urged, with a clap of her hands.

"She already did," Delia said, from behind the copy of *Romeo and Juliet* she'd resumed reading upon Anwen's interruption of the gameplay.

"And did a terrible job of it, hence mother's critique," Cora added.

Anwen turned a frown in her direction.

"What?" Cora gave her shoulders a defensive, little shrug. "Phineas tossed the grape, and you were to open your mouth to catch it, neither of which you did. As such, reporting on your failure is mere, science."

"Science, indeed," Anwen muttered. She did a sweep of the room taking in the empty to nearly porcelain plates before she finally settled her stare on Phineas' which contained but a few crusty remnants of the toast he took in the mornings. Or, in this case, the toast he'd *taken*.

Why, everyone must have concluded breaking their fast some time ago.

Anwen's frown deepened. "The servants have already been dismissed?"

"You usually break your fast first, and given you've been missing the whole morning, I expected you'd already done so," the dowager viscountess remarked.

Suddenly very aware of being on full display before her sisters, Anwen brought her shoulders proudly back. "I have not."

"Are you unable to make yourself a plate, Anwen?" Eris asked, with a wide-eyed guileless Anwen didn't believe for one moment— not *one* London moment.

"Not at all," Anwen said, through a tight-teethed smile.

In fact, she did so daily, but that was neither here nor there. Her mother should have at least cared that Anwen might wish for some assistance from a servant.

"The marquess has business to attend this morn," the dowager viscountess said to the room at large.

Phineas had business, which meant he'd spoken about his day's plans with Anwen's mother and sisters, while Anwen had waited with breathless anticipation to speak with him about anything and everything.

The Kearsley ladies released a collective groan.

"Now, now," their mother chided. "We've outings of our own planned, and governesses waiting. Come along, my dears." The dowager viscountess clapped her hands once, and each of her daughters took to their feet, with Eris the slowest to follow suit.

"Lessons," the youngest of the Kearsley girls lamented. "You hate me, Mama. You truly hate me," she muttered but dutifully offered Phineas a parting wave.

He returned a jaunty salute and Eris fell into line before filing from the room.

Knowing she was being as petulant as a child, but unable to stifle that response, Anwen stomped over to the white-painted, four-door Buffet de Chasse and collected herself a dish.

"Thank you for stopping by, dearest Phineas," Anwen's mother said affectionately when the marquess reached her at the doorway.

He offered a deep, flourishing bow. "It is a joy as always, my lady."

Going up on tiptoe, the dowager viscountess bussed his cheek and bustled off.

Anwen proceeded to shovel eggs and bacon and more bacon onto her plate.

Another mother, *any* other mother, or matron, or woman at all, would have never dared depart before their gentleman caller. Not Anwen's mother. Nay, because Anwen's mother knew very well she needn't fear Phineas behaving in an untoward way with Anwen.

She gritted her teeth and added another two strips of bacon to her overflowing dish. Because Phineas would never—Anwen jammed another piece onto the mound of meat on her dish—*ever*, dare desire a woman like her. Plain, indistinguishable, imponderable, inappreciable ole' Anwen.

She turned to go, thought better of it, and added more bacon.

Phineas stood there, staring bemusedly at her.

"What?" she snapped.

"Are you certain you don't want any more bacon?" he asked, straight-faced.

Frowning, she followed his pointed gaze to her plate. Her cheeks went hot, and, swallowing a curse, she plucked another piece from the sideboard, this strip of well-done meat she stuck between her teeth.

Phineas roared with laughter; that rich, fulsome expression of jollity which made it impossible to ever be cross with him, and despite herself a grin tugged at her lips.

Not that you have a right to be angry, the silent voice of reason in her head, reminded. *You are all but stealing a courtship from him.* An act of deception that was both pitiable and dishonorable...and desperate.

And yet, that was it exactly. With death all but breathing down her nape, she'd a heightened sense of panic and pressure to *live,* and that included this lifelong yearning for a man who had never seen her standing there.

Unable to meet said gentleman's eyes, Anwen stepped around him and headed for the table. She set her dish carefully down on the Italian lace tablecloth and availed herself to the chair she usually occupied, the one right beside where Phineas had occupied while he'd hurled grapes at her kin.

If she'd come down more quickly, she could have had the seat beside him. Yes, her sisters and mother had all been present, but at least she would have had that time with him, close to him. Pathetic. Absolutely path—

Anwen felt Phineas' presence there, still. She made a show of grabbing a white linen napkin. Then, giving it several snaps, she set the scrap upon her lap.

Why is he still here? Why, when he had other places to be and business to see to?

She stole a peek across the breakfast room, and then, at the sight of him, promptly wished she hadn't. Attired in a sapphire wool waistcoat, fawn trousers, and a loose snowy white cravat, and leaning with one shoulder dropped against the doorjamb, Phineas oozed rakish repose. This suave, golden-haired, Greek-God-like being, proved the reason ladies happily tossed aside their reputations.

Foregoing a fork for her fingers, Anwen grabbed a piece of bacon and took a large bite. "You're still here," she said around a huge mouthful.

"Should I not be?" he asked playfully.

Even with the distance between them, she caught the twinkle in his brilliantly blue eyes.

Anwen carefully swallowed, then answered. "My mother indicated you had business." She waited for him to share more, to *say* more, but he remained tight-lipped. He'd shared details about his day with Anwen's mother and sisters, but not her.

It soon became apparent he intended to say nothing more. "And you've put in your appearance for the day," she said, unable to keep her bitterness from creeping in. "Thank you for... that," she finished lamely.

"And I've put in my appearance for the day."

Funny how a mere echo of words she herself had uttered should cut more painfully when spoken by this man. Miserable, Anwen grabbed a forgotten apple on the table, took an enormous bite, and then promptly wished she hadn't. The sweet fruit became an effort to chew, and an even greater chore to swallow.

"You're upset," he said softly.

She looked up.

Phineas pushed away from the doorjamb, and then, with languid, unhurried steps, he approached. "Why don't you sound or look pleased about my being here, Anwen?"

Because she wasn't pleased.

"I've paid a visit, as you requested. Wasn't that what you wanted?"

This hadn't been *what* she'd wished for, but rather, a real visit… with him and her. And to avoid saying as much, Anwen took another big bite of the succulent fruit.

Phineas availed himself of his previously vacated seat, and, with his larger-than-life presence, turned the mere mahogany chair into a throne. "Hmm? If you wished to see me, then why were you so late to rise?"

"I didn't say I wanted to see you," she said on a rush.

The twinkle in his eyes indicated he'd detected the lie there. Oh, God. Her toes curled tightly. *What else had he seen? What else did he know?*

"I didn't believe you'd come this early," she mumbled.

"Because I'm not a man of my word," he asked, tweaking that hated strand of white that had pulled free of her coiffure.

She swatted his hand away. "Because you don't like to arise early."

"This is true. Why did you want to see me, Anwen?" he asked, with an uncharacteristic seriousness.

And she did what anyone who'd landed themselves in the spot she had would do—she lied.

"I…needed to speak to you."

He stilled. "About?"

"I've been thinking," she said, fiddling with her skirts. "And, well, I know you aren't one to attend polite affairs…"

"I don't."

"Yes, yes."

"No, no," he teased, and gently, teasingly flicked the tip of her nose.

Anwen cleared her throat. "It is just, given I'm trying to make myself visible…"

"To the secret gentleman whose identity you will not share?"

She nodded so quickly, her spectacles slipped. Before she could push them back into place, Phineas saw to the task himself, in an endearingly sweet and intimate little act that pulled a soft sigh from her lips.

He stared peculiarly at her. "You were saying?"

Anwen no longer had any idea. Every rational thought had fled her head. Then, it came back to her. "The Marchioness of St. Cyr," she blurted.

Phineas glanced about for the noblewoman in question.

"She is not here," she said, stating the obvious, and recalling Phineas' attention. "She is hosting a ball, this evening, and I think… that is, I *believe* it would be a good idea if you attend Lord and Lady St. Cyr's gathering, as everyone will be there. The *ton* always looks forward to attending because there are fireworks in the evening, and…" *I'm rambling. I'm rambling and I can't make myself stop.* "And if you dance with me, then," *I'll know what it is to be held in your arms,* "people will know I exist," she finished lamely.

He made a dismissive sound. "That's preposterous, Anwen. *Of course*, people know you exist."

She shook her head. "They don't. Not really. I may as well be invisible."

Phineas sat in silence with that information, and then, catching the underside of his upholstered chair, he turned it so he and Anwen faced one another.

"Do you know what I think, Anwen?" he quietly asked.

She shook her head.

"I believe any man whose attention you have to work to attract is an addle-brained twit, who certainly doesn't deserve you, and he is *definitely* not worthy of you."

You are. "He is," she said huskily.

His eyes darkened. "I heartily disagree." He brought a lone

knuckle up and ran it down her right cheek. Her eyes slid briefly shut under that slightest of caresses. Something in the air shifted; it crackled like the earth right before a lightning strike, and she forced her heavy lashes open.

Phineas stared at her, with the oddest expression. His mesmerizing eyes remained locked on Anwen's face. He leaned in, just as she did. They both lingered, remaining that way a moment, before angling their heads closer, ever closer and then they stopped, just a fraction away. Their mouths but a breadth apart.

Then, he touched his lips to hers, and it was as if that kiss freed them.

He slanted his lips over hers, in a fierce, hungry meeting, that she surrendered herself all too happily to. Whimpering, she crept her arms about his neck, and kissed him back, with all the love and longing she'd forever carried for this man.

With a low, growl of approval, Phineas plucked her from her chair and deposited her on his lap so she sat spread-legged across his middle, and her skirts hiked about her hips, her core pressed indecently against the flat ridge of his stomach. A heat both wicked and wonderful pooled between her legs, and she moved her hips rhythmically in a bid to get closer to him.

Phineas gathered her buttocks in his strong, competent hands and pressed her closer. All the while, he massaged and squeezed that flesh. A shamelessly ebullient moan spilled free of her lips, and he swept his tongue inside.

She met that exploring, heated flesh with the tip of her own in a dance that felt so very natural, so glorious, that were she to be struck down now by that fated bolt of lightning, she'd go onto the hereafter happy and content.

Phineas curved his right palm around her nape and angled Anwen's head, deepening the kiss. She met every bold lash of his tongue with a ferocity of her own. His kiss, she'd dreamed of knowing. This moment, she wanted to last forever.

He tasted of coffee and cinnamon and brown sugar, and she would never not taste those items without conjuring the memory of him.

Phineas drew his mouth away, and she wanted to keen with that loss, but he only shifted his worshipful attention to the sensitive point of her neck where her pulse pounded. He lightly nipped at her flesh, like a stallion she'd once witnessed marking a mare as his, and Phineas' was a brand Anwen was all too happy to wear.

For he was all she'd ever wanted.

He continued to suckle at that overly sensitized spot on her neck. Gasping, Anwen arched her back and reached her fingers back to grip the table and hold herself upright. All the while he worshipped that skin, his powerful hands gripped and ungripped her buttocks.

A sharp crack cut across the discordant rhythm of their ragged breathing and jolted them apart. Dazed by desire, and her mind muddled from Phineas' embrace, Anwen blinked slowly and attempted to sort out the source of that tinkling explosion.

She glanced down at her porcelain plate she'd inadvertently sent tumbling. Upon the floor, tiny shards of shattered porcelain, now mixed with the remnants of her untouched bacon and eggs.

Anwen turned her gaze up to Phineas. "I…" The words froze on her lips.

Phineas looked at her, horror dripping from every beautiful plain of his chiseled face. With stiff, clumsy movements, he set Anwen on her feet and jumped to his own. His rugged cheeks turned an unhealthy shade of white. He pointed at the floor.

Anwen peered down at the scattered remnants of her repast and frowned. *What—?*

"Your…" Phineas frantically jabbed his wavering index finger. "Your… *skirts*," he whispered furiously.

Anwen followed his frenzied gesturing. She gasped and swiftly pushed her still slightly rucked skirts back into their proper place.

She glanced up.

If possible, Phineas had gone several shades whiter.

He's…going to be ill.

Mortified shame threatened to swallow her, and Anwen prayed for that fate. Anything to be spared the utter horror in his revealing eyes.

"Yes," he croaked, and with still quaking digits checked his timepiece. "Er…yes, well, business. Mine…that is, I have business, as you recall. Do you recall that?"

She stared dumbly at him.

"My b–business?" he stammered.

"I don't know what it is, if that is what you're asking." she ventured.

"No. Not what it is. Just that I have it. Do you remember that, Anwen?"

"You did mention it."

"Yes, because I have it…*business*," he said, his voice creeping up an octave. He scrabbled with his cravat. "Anwen." Then, without waiting for a goodbye, Phineas made an awkwardly wide path around her, and fled as fast as if the serpent-headed Medusa had come to life before him.

Forlornly, Anwen watched him bolt. After he'd gone, she swiped an empty platter from the table and proceeded to pick up the broken pieces of her plate.

How could a moment go from being the most magical to the most humiliating, in an instance? A particularly sharp sliver bit painfully into the bad of her thumb, and she welcomed that discomfort and the distraction it brought.

Anwen added the last sliver of dropped bacon to the dish she'd used as a makeshift dustbin, and she glared at her once favorite breakfast meat which had spoiled her embrace with Phineas.

Never again.

Certainly not to eat bacon, and, by Phineas' nauseated response, definitely not to ever again know his kiss.

CHAPTER 6

ℐT WAS A WELL-KNOWN FACT that Phineas Lesar, the Marquess of Landon, would rather take his chances surviving the Black Death than a night at a respectable *ton* gathering. He'd rather pluck his nails out than be made to so much as put in an appearance at the tedious affairs. Lord and Lady St. Cyr's annual ball proved no exception.

In fact, he'd given some real, serious thought of bowing out, and sending 'round his regrets'–not, however, for his usual reasons.

Nay, at that very moment, seated on the faded and fraying gold velvet-upholstered bench of his carriage, Phineas couldn't bring himself to get out of the conveyance, make his way up those stone steps, and through the double doors to the festivities taking place in the pink stucco mansion.

He'd kissed her.

He'd kissed *Anwen*.

He'd kissed Anwen Isadora Kearsley's.

St. John's sister.

His best friend's sister.

And not only that, but he'd also reveled in that hungry, fevered embrace. Phineas spent the day alternately dreaming of the feel of her bare, lithe legs draped around him, and the feverish way she'd moved against him, and flagellating himself for his desirous musings of Anwen Kearsley. Lord have mercy on his soul, how could he see her again, and not think about the sweet hint of apple on her breath, or the satiny softness of her generously rounded buttocks?

Groaning, Phineas dropped the back of his head against the wall and thumped it slowly so he could bury the thought of Anwen. And how badly he'd wanted to continue that embrace, and how, if it weren't for her errant plate's flight to the ~~flower~~ *Floor*, he would have done not only that but more. He would have slipped a hand between her legs, and teased her with his fingers, and—

Phineas knocked his head harder.

She is Anwen. St. John's sister. Phineas had taught her how to skate and spit and skip stones. All those reminders together should be enough to kill his lust.

They weren't.

Rap-Rap-Rap "My lord?"

"Not yet," he called for a fourth time since poor Williamson had inquired about Phineas' plans, or as the case would have it, lack of plans, to exit the coach.

Enough. Phineas sat up and gave his head a firm shake. *You're being a deuced dolt.*

Since when had Phineas become such a paragon as to castigate himself over a mere *kiss?* Yes, the recipient of his attentions that morn was in fact, St. John's sister. But it'd only been a kiss. Her lips and nape, and nothing more. Why, in his lifetime, he'd kissed countless women in that same way. What's more, he'd done scores of things more scandalous, more wicked, more outrageous than a mere kiss.

And neither did a single one of those embraces haunt your thoughts and memories as Anwen's had.

Stop!

At last reigning in his thoughts, Phineas opened the door and jumped down. His driver made to scramble down from the bench, but he waved him off. "You've made the climb from that box enough times that I'll not have you do it again, ole fellow," Phineas said. "I shan't be long."

Get in. Dance with Anwen. Twice. Act as if everything is normal, for it is. Then, get the hell out.

Reciting that list in his mind over and over again, Phineas headed for Lord and Lady St. Cyr's residence. A pair of white-clad footmen with gold epaulets stood sentry on either side of the stark, gleaming white, wrought-iron doors. In perfect sync, each servant drew an intricately sculpted, carved panel, open.

A short while later, Phineas found himself at the front of a since-ended assembly line. All the noble guests who'd previously occupied the spot he now stood, vied for space amidst the crowded, high-ceilinged ballroom.

Phineas scanned the faces of Lord and Lady St. Cyr's guests, all the while looking for the sole person who accounted for his presence at this infernal affair. His gaze alighted on Anwen's mother, the dowager viscountess, sans daughter, who stood near Lady Rochester. The two regal noblewomen laughed and gestured as they spoke, just the two of them. No, Anwen.

Dismissing the pair, a restless Phineas turned his search elsewhere, on to the lords and ladies assembled on the dancefloor currently performing the dainty steps of a quadrille. He looked among those partners completing a turn, for a hint of Anwen and the undeserving chap who'd managed to secure a set with her. A growl started in his chest and worked its way up his throat.

Anwen. Where in hell are you?

And the only thing accounting for this restive need to find her was because the sooner he located her and danced with her as she'd asked, the sooner he could get the hell out of here.

Then, from the corner of his eye, a faint gleam caught his notice. And Phineas went absolutely still, as, at last, he found her.

Not dancing, not conversing with any fop, or dashing fellow, nor sipping ratafia. Rather, perched upon one of two dozen or so gold chairs, otherwise, nearly empty which had been reserved for the wallflowers and slumbering matrons who'd sought a rest from the night's revelries.

A spectacle-less Anwen sat discreetly wiping the lenses of her glasses upon the side of her dress, a satin gown, trimmed in crystals and pearls, of a hue somewhere between the color of sunshine and spun gold. Candlelight from the giltwood and crystal chandeliers overhead played with the beading of Anwen's dress, lending its wearer an otherworldly incandescence.

Mayhap it was because he'd kissed her and lived the day with the memory of it, or mayhap he'd gone mad, or mayhap both, but as she returned those wire frames to their usual place upon her nose, it was as if Phineas himself, could, for the first time, more clearly see.

Caught in a trance, he drank in the sight of her. A row of diamonds had been sewn along the edge of Anwen's plunging, organza neckline as if some seamstress who clearly knew nothing about anything had believed that glittering embellishment necessary for its wearer to attract attention. But Phineas saw and feared he'd never not see her in this way—an ethereal princess, whose rich chestnut and chocolate-shaded tresses made an earthly coronet of curls about her head.

If he were any sort of friend to St. John, Phineas' first order of business should be to pluck out his own eyes, but then, he'd not be able to snatch the eyes of the other fellows around him who dared to gaze upon her.

A black, unreasoning jealousy took over. He'd spirit her away from the cads around them. Phineas took a step towards Anwen to do just that, then stopped as their exchange from earlier that day whispered forward.

"...If you dance with me, then people will know I exist."

"That's preposterous, Anwen. Of course, people know you exist."

She shook her head. "They don't. Not really. I may as well be invisible."

Phineas drew back, as the truth him square between the chest. Why...why, she'd been correct. The gents present *didn't* see her. The sorry lot were in greater need of spectacles than the lady herself. And where moments ago he'd been ready to rip all the dandies' heads off for daring to eye Anwen Kearsley, now he wanted to shred those same fools apart for not having noted her.

Steeling his jaw, Phineas stomped the remainder of the way. "Penny for your thoughts," he murmured.

Anwen gasped and whipped her head up so quickly, she promptly grabbed at the back of her neck. "Phineas," she said breathlessly. "You're...here."

"And did you think I wouldn't be?"

"Given the ball has already been in progress for three hours, I'd begun to have my doubts."

He dropped into the vacant chair on Anwen's left, and for the first time in all his time of knowing her, an awkwardness hovered between them.

"I'm sorry," Phineas blurted.

"It is fine," she assured him. "You are here, and I didn't—"

"I meant about earlier," he interrupted, disabusing her of the reason for his regrets. *Are they really regrets?* the devil on his shoulder jeered.

Anwen continued to peer at him. She'd make him state it explicitly. That was fair. That open acknowledgment was, at the very least, what he deserved.

Phineas angled his head away from the crowd's undoubtedly prying, and rabidly, curious stares. "The kiss," he mouthed.

A shadow passed across her eyes. "You needn't give it another thought, Phineas."

He tugged his chair closer. "But I must. I…it shouldn't have happened. It can't happen. It won't happen, ever again."

Though, in this instance, he couldn't sort out whether he sought to convince Anwen or himself.

She gave him a gently rueful smile. "You needn't look so agitated, Phineas. It was just a kiss."

A relief so profound swept through him, that he suspected had he been standing it would have knocked his feet out from under him.

Just a kiss.

Yes! Hadn't he tried to tell himself as much since he'd fled the Kearsley residence? But hearing it from Anwen's lips—his mind stuttered. It'd been the wrong silent word choice, and yet, once thought, it couldn't be *un*thought. An image slipped in of her spread across his lap, and her mouth—

Anwen leaned up and whispered. "I've been kissed before, Phineas."

And there couldn't have been a greater slayer of lust than those five words: *I've been kissed before, Phineas.*

That indiscriminate, and unbounded rage of earlier flared to life once more, and briefly blinded him, as, this time, a different thought slid in; an insidious one of Anwen and some faceless, nameless man locked in a hungry embrace. And in his mind's eye, the sexy tableau he'd replayed over and over in his mind, morphed so that another fellow occupied that Kearsley breakfast chair, and Anwen sat, with her lithe limbs draped across him.

He balled his hands so tight, his nails left marks on his palms.

Why, perhaps the man whose affections she sought was, in fact, the one whose kiss she spoke of here with Phineas. He turned another searching stare out on the ballroom; this time, he combed his gaze over the gentlemen present at Lord and Lady St. Cyr's gathering. Who'd known Anwen Kearsley's kiss? Could it be——?

"Phineas?" Anwen asked; concern wreathed her question and creased her brow.

"I'm fine," he squeezed out those two syllables.

He lied through his tightly clenched teeth. He wasn't fine. Far from it. And it was because he saw her the way he might a younger sister.

Except, the wanton kiss they'd shared and the licentious thoughts that'd gripped Phineas certainly didn't constitute brotherly ones. Nor did this searing jealousy poisoning him from the inside out.

And the irony wasn't lost on him; he, Phineas Lesar, the Marquess of Landon, who'd had numerous lovers, and never once viewed a mere kiss as an intimate act, now found himself seething at the idea of Anwen with another.

What a bloody hypocrite! Even knowing as much, didn't make him despise the bounder any less.

Anwen brushed her fingertips against his thigh; those muscles bunched under even that most innocent of caresses. He glanced down.

"You can leave," she said softly.

That was the conclusion she'd reached?

"I don't want to," he said, stunned to find…he actually meant it.

Anwen laughed, that sincere and exuberant sound he recognized so very well, and just like that, the tension dissipated.

They spoke at the same time.

"I——"

"May——?"

Anwen motioned for Phineas to finish first.

"May I sign your dance card?" he asked quietly.

Her perfect bow-shaped lips twitched. "You're really going to make me display my blank card?" she asked, already handing over her pencil.

Phineas skimmed the little booklet tied about her wrist, and then signed his name in big, scrawling letters that covered the page. "There wasn't really any room for any other partners, anyway."

They shared a smile.

"We can hardly dance all the dances, Phineas."

"No, that would be a scandal, even for my standards."

Anwen studied his name a moment. "How do I know which sets are yours?"

As if on cue, the light strains of the orchestra filled the ballroom.

Phineas stood and stretched out his hand. "Of course, I'm stealing a waltz from you, Anwen."

With an adorable little snort, Anwen placed her palm in his. "Given you've seen my bare card, I daresay, we can both agree, 'stealing' a waltz might not be the most apt of word choices."

Phineas waggled his eyebrows. "Ah, but it merely affords me another waltz to steal." His teasing words drew another one of her musical laughs.

"I'd expect nothing less," she said.

And he wanted nothing more.

As Anwen placed her fingertips upon his arm and allowed Phineas to lead her onto the dance floor, he marveled at how being joined with her, in this way, felt ...oddly right.

Phineas squired Anwen through a throng of colorfully clad guests, who parted like a rainbow divided. He brought them to a stop in the middle of the black and white tiled dance floor.

The moment the orchestra launched into a charmingly celestial waltz, Anwen spoke. "I told you," she said so quietly, he very nearly didn't hear her.

He furrowed his brow.

Anwen clarified. "People notice you, and because of that, they now see me."

Phineas followed her gaze to the audience now watching them.

"They aren't watching me, Anwen," he murmured. For there could be no disputing every man present was thoroughly bewitched by her. "They have eyes for only you." He swept her in a wide, sweeping arc.

Anwen released another snort. "If *that* were the case, my dance card would be full, and I wouldn't be London's longest-standing wallflower."

How could she possibly be a wallflower? Had there not been a single man with sense enough to see the gift she was, to get down on a knee, and promise her the world? He'd always admired Anwen for her sparkling wit, spirit, and cleverness. But how had Phineas failed to appreciate her beauty?

Until now.

"*I* see you," he said quietly, then guided them into another deep, sweeping circle.

Anwen's lips parted, and his gaze locked on the slight gleam of moisture upon her slightly fuller lower lip.

"I see you, Anwen," he repeated. "And…other men," more worthy men; ones who were not rakes, but instead, respectable; gents who weren't best friends with her brother, "they will not be able to help but do so." Phineas drew her closer and leaned down. "You must promise me something, Anwen."

She stared at him with huge eyes.

"You'll not bind yourself to some bounder." *Like me.* "You must not settle for anything less than a man who loves you with all his soul and who treats you like you are his only queen."

"There is no one like you describe," she whispered achingly.

He pulled her even closer. "Do not settle for less. If this… gentleman whose favor you seek cannot appreciate you for the gift you are, then do not wed him."

They didn't say another word.

They didn't have to. But then, with this woman, silence had always come as easily as speaking with her.

Until, at last, the music came to a stop. All around them, the other sets of partners brought their hands together in a polite clap. Phineas and Anwen, however, remained motionless, their eyes locked upon one another.

A shadow fell over them and effectively shattered the moment. Benedict Adamson, the Earl of Wakefield stopped before them.

"Miss Kearsley." The tall, wiry gentleman sketched a bow that managed to angle out Phineas. "Would you do me the honor of partnering me in a set?"

A muscle twitched at the corner of Phineas' eye. The pup would brazenly intercept the lady on the dance floor. Or mayhap it was just a mark of the dark-haired fellow's notorious perspicacity.

"I…" Anwen stammered. Her confused gaze went from Phineas to Wakefield, the card on her wrist, and then back…to *Wakefield*.

Phineas' muscles went taut to the point of pain.

"Of course, my lord," she said, and Phineas retreated a step, as the notoriously honorable earl reached for Anwen's card. With a gasp, she made to yank it back, but Wakefield proved persistent.

The gentleman went silent; his eyes took note of Phineas' hugely scrawled name, and then a taciturn Lord Wakefield availed himself to Anwen's pencil. He scribbled on her card…and marched off as quickly as he'd come.

Only when he'd gone did Phineas return his attention to Anwen. An uncharacteristically silent Anwen, whose gaze remained fixed on her dance card, and where, in the tiniest of letters, Wakefield had managed to squeeze on a line marked for a waltz.

Wordlessly, Phineas offered Anwen his elbow. Everything was going to plan—that was, to *Anwen's* plan.

So why, as Phineas escorted the lady over to where her mother still stood conversing with Lady Rochester, did he feel oddly bereft inside?

CHAPTER 7

THE FOLLOWING MORNING, WHILE HER boisterous siblings raised their voices to make themselves heard over one another at the always lively breakfast table, Anwen sat in silence. Lost in her own thoughts, she was all too content to remain there and not join in the spirited discussion taking place among her Kearsley kin.

With the tip of her fork, Anwen distractedly pushed around a particularly fluffy piece of scrambled egg. Nay, she'd never not see the breakfast food and think of him, or the way he'd pulled her onto his lap, and ran his hands all over the skin he'd bared to his touch.

Anwen's heart hammered, and she went hot all over.

"You must promise me something, Anwen…You'll not bind yourself to some bounder…You must not settle for anything less than a man who loves you with all his soul and who treats you like you are his only queen…"

"Anwen?" Her sister Cora's concern-laden query brought Anwen's remembering to a screeching halt. "Are you feeling unwell? Your cheeks, they are all flushed."

Every single set of eyes landed on Anwen. Even Delia, lowered her edition of *Macbeth* a moment to check on her eldest sister, then she returned to her reading.

Daria's eyes expanded the slightest bit. "Perhaps she has a fever?"

Under the table, Anwen curled her toes sharply. "I'm f—"

Their mother interrupted. "I say, you *are* incredibly red in the face," she said concernedly. Ignoring Anwen's protestations, the dowager viscountess quit her seat at the head of the rectangular breakfast table and dashed to Anwen's side.

"As I predicted," Daria said for a second time in that toneless way. "A fever."

"Mother," Anwen said, again ignoring her younger sister's postulation, "I am more than f—"

"More than feverish?" the dowager viscountess cried. She slapped the back of her palm against Anwen's forehead, as she once more cut off her eldest daughter's assurances. The dowager's frown deepened. "You *are* hot."

A collective gasp filled the room…with the exception of a sangfroid Daria.

"As I said, fever," the inexpressive girl pointed out yet again.

Anwen threw her hands up. "Oh, for heaven's sake."

"She is appealing to God now," Brenna, her bookish and entirely too clever to share in the same histrionics of their other kin, remarked.

Anwen shot her a look. "Your acting leaves much to be desired," she muttered.

Brenna winked, snagged herself an apple, and sat back in her chair to take in the show. At least *someone* was enjoying this.

"If not illness…" Cora remarked. The science-minded girl grabbed the notepad she always kept close at hand and studied Anwen the same way she pondered her various subjects and experiments. "Then what else could account for flushed cheeks?" She scribbled some notes in her little leather journal. "And," she looked up, and gestured to Anwen's dish, "a lack of appetite?"

Yes, mortification at being caught thinking about the passionate embrace she'd had with Phineas, at the very breakfast table her family sat so bucolically around, *would* do that. Anwen slunk into her chair and resisted the urge to squirm.

Eris pointed a finger in Anwen's direction. "Look!" the little girl cried. "She is *collapsing* in her seat."

Cries and shouts abounded.

"General weakness," Cora said, over the din, and jotted something else in her book.

"I'm not weak," Anwen snapped.

"Irritability," Cora murmured to herself.

"We must fetch Dr. Carlson," Mother wailed.

The bewigged footman closest to the door took a step to do his mistress's bidding, but Anwen shot up a staying hand.

"I do *not* need a doctor, Ezra."

His features strained, the stout servant vacillated between the occupying mistress of the house and Anwen.

"Go, Ezra," Anwen's mother urged. "Make haste."

The footman took a step.

"Do not, Ezra," Anwen countered, halting him in his tracks once more, and he'd the look of one completing an intricate dance.

"Do not forget, Cora," Brenna said, "Madam Pomfret indicated Anwen would be smote by lightning, *not* a fever."

"Ahh," Cora murmured, and as if their bluestocking sister had sagely proffered actual scientific evidence to be factored into Anwen's diagnosis, Cora frantically scribbled another note into her pad.

Their mother brightened. "That is correct." She cast a beaming smile the footman's way. "There will be no doctor required this day, as Madam Pomfret is never wrong about her predictions. We'll save Dr. Carlson for that day."

"But, wouldn't that mean," Daria intoned, "when that day does, in fact, come?"

Which it would.

"That a doctor's efforts would be futile? If Madam is always correct, Anwen will have no hope."

The dowager viscountess frowned. "I…"

"Ahem."

Anwen and the rest of the Kearsleys looked to the source of that welcome interruption. The family butler, Mr. Georges bowed.

"A gentleman has arrived,"

Phineas!

Eris clapped her hands. "Phineas!"

Anwen's heart galloped madly, and breathless anticipation filled her.

The old, white-haired servant cleared his throat. "That is," he continued past Eris's interruption. "A gentleman visitor has arrived to see Miss Anwen Kearsley. The Earl of Wakefield."

All eyes flew to Anwen as Georges managed the seemingly impossible—silencing the Kearsleys.

The Earl of Wakefield? Anwen's heart sank.

Her sisters began speaking over one another in a frenzy of whispers that droned like a swarm of bees.

"…I knew after he waltzed with her…"

"He *waltzed* with her…?"

"…walked onto the dance floor after one set to…"

"…It was in the gossip pages…"

"…Now, I must begin reading the gossip…"

Anwen's head swam. Placing three fingers at her lips, the dowager viscountess reigned her daughters in with a piercing whistle.

They instantly fell quiet.

"The Earl of Wakefield, did you say?" Anwen's mother asked.

Mr. Georges extended the small silver platter in his hands. "Yes." More silence met that announcement. Poor Mr. Georges again cleared his throat. "I…took the liberty of showing His Lordship to the drawing room."

Anwen's sisters came alive all at once.

"Anwen!" Brenna squealed.

Cora snapped her notebook closed. "Now, I know the reason for your flushed cheeks."

A forlorn Eris looked about. "Is Anwen getting married?" she asked the room at large. "I don't want her to marry the Earl of Wakefield and move away until I marry and move away. I will miss her, too, much."

As her family converged upon her, Anwen's head swam. She was drowning.

"It is just a visit," she said weakly.

Her mother helped Anwen to her feet. "Benedict Adamson is such a nice boy," she extolled. "A very nice boy."

"And he arrived with flowers," Mr. Georges interjected with the familiarity only a lifelong servant could.

Anwen's mother beamed. "Flowers!" She steered Anwen towards the doorway. "Off you go."

The same way she might launch a toy ship, the dowager viscountess gave Anwen a light, little shove on her back, and propelled her forward. Suffocating, desperate for air, Anwen found herself sprinting away from the sea of Kearsleys.

It is just a visit. Furthermore, Anwen should only be grateful for any attention shown her. Only it'd never been about the attention from just anyone. Rather, it'd been about receiving interest from a certain someone.

Anwen stopped at the entrance of the drawing room.

A certain someone who was not, nor would ever be, the always-somber fellow before her. His hands clasped behind his back, Lord Wakefield stood, looking out the long, floor-length windows. The lace drapes had been drawn and fastened at the gilded bronze tie-backs, and the sun's rays streamed through the crystal windowpanes.

With Lord Wakefield's attention otherwise occupied on the streets and scenes below, Anwen took an opportunity to study him. Of an impressive height and build, and sporting sun-kissed blond hair, Lord Wakefield possessed a striking handsomeness that would have set any sensible lady's heart aflutter. At that, he proudly donned spectacles which leant him a greater era of sophistication.

Spectacles! When Anwen so often lamented on being one of so few, outside of the elderly, to sport those useful and necessary frames, here was a suitor who also wore them. So why couldn't her heart have jumped, when he'd boldly met her on Lady St. Cyr's dance floor? Or when he'd taken her in his arms and expertly waltzed her around the ballroom? Why couldn't she be overjoyed and breathless at his being here to visit, now?

Her gaze slipped to the exquisite bouquet he'd set down on a nearby marble console table. Only, she knew. Her heart would only ever belong to Phineas. It was why when Lord Wakefield came with an extravagant showing of flowers, she still yearned for even imagined scraps of affection from Phineas.

"Are they not to your liking, Miss Kearsley?"

Anwen's gaze flew from the flowers to the owner of that low, rumbling baritone. Through long, blond lashes, Lord Wakefield looked unnervingly back. That unswerving stare, coupled with his severely sharp cheekbones, and hard, powerful draw leant an almost air of maleficence to him.

Then, he flashed the slightest and wryest of smiles, that briefly displaced his somber demeanor. "The flowers," he clarified.

"No!" Anwen rushed over and joined the earl at the window. "They are lovely," she said, reaching for them.

And they were. Pale yellow and pink roses, mixed with yellow daisy poms and baby-blue delphinium that together put her in mind of the English countryside. A yellow organza ribbon to match the fabric of Anwen's gown the evening prior had been twined about vibrant blooms whose sweet, fragrant scent filled the air.

"You were frowning," the earl remarked.

Lord Wakefield proved both direct *and* tenacious. Had Phineas spoken those *same* words, they would have been teasing.

"Is that a question, my lord?" she asked carefully.

"An observation."

This man, on the other hand, she knew largely through his relationship with their shared friend, Marcia, now Lady Waters. That was, of course, he'd been a friend to Marcia. After Lord Wakefield revealed his love for the young viscountess, that friendship had been fractured.

Unnerved by the quiet, and desperate to give her fingers a purpose, Anwen drew the lush flowers close and inhaled their sweet, heady scent.

A maid hurried forward.

Grateful for the young woman's interruption, Anwen handed the bouquet over. "Would you be so good as to see them placed in water, Alice?"

"Yes, miss." Alice dipped a curtsy and scurried off so that Anwen and Lord Wakefield found themselves…alone.

Though in truth, with both the earl's stoical silence and the dismissive way in which he'd returned all his focus to those crystal panes, Anwen could have believed *she* was in fact, alone.

"Would you care to sit, my lord?" she asked.

He ignored that offer. "I'm looking for a countess."

Anwen froze. He'd be that blunt, would he?

"Which countess exactly, my lord?" she asked lightly. "Perhaps I may help you locate her."

The gleaming pane reflected back the earl's frowning visage. "A wife," he said coolly. "I'm looking for *my* countess, to be exact."

"I know, my lord," Anwen said gently. "I was teasing."

At last, Lord Wakefield pulled his attention from whatever so fascinated him out those wide, double windows. She favored him with a droll grin; a grin that went unreturned.

Anwen and Lord Wakefield had crossed paths any number of times. She'd always taken him for a somber, serious, fellow. She'd not, however, recalled him being so very, *grim*. But then, he'd suffered a broken heart. Perhaps, when that organ broke beyond repair, it left one cold and deadened.

Having since accepted he'd no intention of taking a seat, Anwen made to join him when his next words stopped her in her tracks.

"I've decided you will make a fine countess, Miss Kearsley."

She should be horrified or shocked at that blunt…*proposal*— that presumptuous declaration, which could hardly be categorized thusly.

Despite herself, Anwen laughed. "Lord Wakefield, we do not—"

"Know one another?" he aptly finished her sentence. He winged a single haughty brow. "We've been familiar for more than five years now. We've attended the same functions. By society's standards, we would be a logical match."

A logical match. Regret formed in her throat. She'd never wanted an emotionless arrangement between herself and a suitable gentleman. She'd wanted a grand love affair with one specific man.

Anwen carefully weighed her words. She'd no wish to hurt him. As dispassionate and detached as the earl's 'offer' in fact, was, he'd been hurt deeply by Marcia's rejection, and though his heart had been engaged before, undoubtedly having his proposal rebuffed would sting any gentleman's pride.

"Lord Wakefield, despite our sharing a similar social circle, that does not mean we know one another. You do not know my interests, dreams, and desires, as I do not know yours. We've shared but a single dance, and only last night. I understand you want to secure a countess, and yet, I do not believe you'd be content were we to enter into such a cold arrangement."

His intractable jaw flexed. "May I speak plainly?"

She laughed. "And you haven't been before now?"

He ignored her question, taking it for the rhetorical one it was. "We are near in age," he continued. "You far more mature than the ladies just out on the Marriage Mart."

Her ire flared a degree. "And I should marry you then because I'm a spinster," she said flatly.

"You misunderstand me. I'm not looking for a dewy-eyed debutante. You are an intelligent woman, Miss Kearsley. You were a founding member of a lady's society who sought to improve the lot and minds of women."

Anwen started. He'd known about her work with the Mismatch Society, that league formed by her sister-in-law?

"Yes, I know that. I see and know more than most credit." He lowered his voice. "I'm also aware you've gone out of your way to make yourself invisible during previous Seasons, and I expect your efforts have been a deliberate ploy to deter would-be suitors."

Her mouth moved but no words emerged. Not a soul was privy to that long-held secret. Not her mother. Not her sisters. Not Marcia or Faith. Certainly not her brother. *No one.*

The earl approached. "Just as I know your reason for doing so, Miss Kearsley."

Anwen stiffened, and because she wasn't a coward, she asked a question of which she didn't truly want an answer to. "What reasons are those, Lord Wakefield?"

The tall earl stopped with only a pace between them. Several inches past six feet as he was, Anwen had to crane her neck back to meet his eyes.

"You have loved and longed for Lord Landon from afar," he said quietly, and without inflection.

Dread formed a cruel knot in her belly, and she reflexively folded her arms about her middle to ward off the horror spreading rapidly inside.

Oh, God. This man, a veritable stranger had somehow ascertained that most intimate secret. And more, what did he intend to do with it?

He wasn't done. "As your brother's best friend, I expect you grew up admiring Lord Landon," the Earl of Wakefield said incisively. "You see the best in him, though." He paused. "Though, given his reputation and history, I'd be hard-pressed to identify what that may be."

Fury took root.

"How dare you, Lord Wakefield," she spat. "Lord Landon is a good man, a *kind* man, and he, unlike you wouldn't dare besmirch another man's n—" At the knowing glint in the earl's hard eyes, Anwen immediately stopped that telling defense. "I…want you to leave," she said, forcing an evenness into her tone. "Now."

"Your secrets are your own, Miss Kearsley," he said, and waved his hand as if in so doing, he cleared away the scandalous words he'd spoken here.

God, he was a dog with a bone. Well, she could be just as frank.

"Are you here to bribe me, my lord? To coerce me into being your countess."

He blinked quickly, and that wild flutter of his lashes gave him an almost boyish look. "I wouldn't bribe you or any person."

She hesitated. "No?"

"And I certainly wouldn't *coerce* a woman to be my countess." He frowned. "I hope I shouldn't have to," he muttered that part more to himself. "I'd merely hoped by pointing out that your dreams of a future with Lord Landon are futile, you'd, in turn, consider…*my* offer," he finished lamely.

Anwen eyed him warily.

"I, along with my family, have been the subject of unkind gossip, Miss Kearsley," he explained.

This time, a sincerity had slipped into his quietly spoken admission.

"Discreet—" He grimaced. "And sometimes *indiscreet* whispers have circulated throughout London regarding my affections for a woman who…married another."

A frisson of pain flickered in his otherwise opaque eyes, and she didn't want it to matter. Not after the disparaging words he'd spoken of Phineas. But it did. She'd not wish a like anguish on anyone.

"I am sorry you've endured that, my lord," she said, truthfully.

His sharply handsome features grew more strained. "I'm no longer bothered by either the gossip or that rejection."

She suspected he believed that.

Sighing, Lord Wakefield removed his spectacles, withdrew a kerchief from his pocket, and proceeded to clean those already immaculate lenses. That anxious habit Anwen knew—and used—firsthand, and she felt another surprising, and unexpected kindred connection to the stony-faced earl.

Despite his icy display, Anwen suspected it was just that—a show. Whether the gentleman liked it or not, he'd revealed himself to be very human. Not unlike her, he too suffered deeply from an unrequited love.

The earl returned his glasses to his face but retained hold of the now slightly wrinkled embroidered linen he'd used to clean the spectacles.

"You say you do not know me," the earl allowed, "but something you may be assured of is, having known firsthand the misery of all that, I would never break your confidence, I would *never* subject anyone to that." He spoke with an adamancy that rang clear with his truth.

With that admission there came yet another chink in his otherwise cool and cavalier demeanor.

"Lord Wakefield, your heart…it belongs to another," she said delicately.

Her gaze went to the previous source of the earl's preoccupation: Marcia's new residence. Lord Wakefield stiffened but made no attempt to follow Anwen's stare.

"My heart belongs to no one, Miss Kearsley." He chuckled. "I've learned better than to let myself feel that fickle sentiment."

She smiled wistfully at him. "If you believe we have any real control of our hearts, then you have learned nothing."

"We may agree to disagree." This time, a sincere grin formed on his pleasing lips. The earl rocked on his immaculate heels, and that slight back-and-forth movement sent a single loose golden curl tumbling across his brow.

Funny how but one wayward strand could soften an unyielding man. Anwen angled her head and studied him anew. Whom might the earl be had Marcia returned his love?

And is this destined to be my fate? If Phineas wed before Anwen died, would she spend her remaining days like Lord Wakefield, mired in bitterness and hate?

"I thank you for your offer, Lord Wakefield," she began.

"But the answer is 'no'?"

"But the answer is no," Anwen gently added.

The earl lingered. "I have never been a romantic, Miss Kearsley. I don't know anything about romantic love. My father was an unfaithful cad who kept a legion of mistresses, and," antipathy lit his arresting eyes, "that is among the lesser of his sins. My parents certainly did not hold one another in any real regard, and though each of my sisters finds themselves in love matches, it is not a state I can personally say I believe is real."

Lord Wakefield lifted a gloved palm. "I'm aware I'm not the charming rake or rogue ladies long for, but I am a good man. I'm an honorable man. What I can promise to the woman who will be my countess is security, stability, and my fidelity. She will want for nothing."

Nothing, other than…love. And yet, at twenty-seven and well aware of the rules that guided Polite Society, Anwen wasn't so naïve as to believe that sentiment existed in most of the matches that were made. Unions were about improved bloodlines and increased wealth. Knowing that, however, still hadn't prevented her from yearning for such an attachment.

He caught one of Anwen's hands in his, and she wanted to feel a spark. She wanted to feel a tingle. Anything that might indicate another man was capable of eliciting all the feelings Phineas did.

"I'd ask that you not reject my offer outright and that you allow me the opportunity to continue my suit."

Footfalls sounded in the corridor.

"I'm disappointed to learn you've gone and broken your f—"

Anwen and Lord Wakefield looked over, just as Phineas came striding into the room.

The marquess, and the rest of the words on his lips, came to a stop. He sharpened his blue-eyed gaze on Anwen and Lord Wakefield's still joined hands. Both men, sized one another up the way gladiators of old had done the sizeable opponents before them.

Because of her.

One gentleman who wished to make Anwen his wife and viewed the other man as an encroacher upon his territory. And Phineas, who saw Anwen as nothing more than a younger sister to be guarded from any suitor.

The always-affable marquess broke the tense impasse. "Wakefield," Phineas offered a quick but respectful bow, that went unreturned.

The earl's lack of a like solicitude toward Phineas did not escape Anwen's notice. Nor by the wry smile that formed on Phineas' lips had the slight escaped him, either.

"A *pleasure* as always," the marquess drawled.

"Given we do not keep the same company, that's highly doubtful," Lord Wakefield rejoined with his usual bluntness.

Well, *this* wasn't awkward, at all.

CHAPTER 8

THAT MORN, PHINEAS HAD ARRIVED at the Kearsley residence, earlier than usual. He'd anticipated taking breakfast with Anwen, and then escorting her on a curricle ride—all because of his earlier pledge to do so.

He'd not, *however*, foreseen Wakefield, the bloody paragon, to have beat him to the bloody punch.

Though, Phineas should have. Given the fellow's brazen showing at Lord and Lady Cyr's ball the evening prior, and the two waltzes the earl had then gone on to snatch from Anwen, Phineas should have anticipated the high-minded chap would have called on Anwen, bright and early.

A young maid chose that moment to return with the artful display of flowers. By the young maid's vast, sunny smile she'd not detected the thick tension blanketing the room.

Once the girl had set the urn down near the window, Lord Wakefield turned his attention back to Anwen.

"Miss Kearsley," he murmured, bowing his head. "It was a true pleasure speaking with you this morning."

While the couple exchanged partings, Phineas stood, a silent interloper off to the side.

"Likewise, Lord Wakefield."

Likewise, she'd say?

Phineas gritted his teeth. A spirited lady like Anwen, enjoying time with the starchy Earl of Wakefield? *Not fucking likely.*

When still the uppish earl lingered, Phineas interjected. "Yes, *so* good to see you," he said, and the feigned joviality he packed into that lie, stretched six syllables into twelve.

Wakefield's face tensed.

Alas, the fellow was too proper, too respectable to ever dare meet Phineas' mordacity with mockery of his own. As silently predicted, the earl turned on his heel and left.

Phineas drew himself up onto the back of the large fan sofa. "Well, *that* was fun," Phineas said.

Anwen frowned. "Alice? Would you be so good as to fetch refreshments for His Lordship and I."

"What?" he asked after the young maid scurried from the room and Anwen turned a scathing glare upon him.

Anwen folded her arms at her chest, luring his rake's gaze to the entrancing heart-shaped bodice of her silk brocade gown. And like the callow youth of old, he'd been, lust bolted through him.

"*Really*, Phineas?"

Really, indeed. He couldn't have taken his eyes from her if mankind's existence had hinged upon his doing so.

"You were being rude."

He gave his head a shake. Wait. She'd been talking about his exchange with Wakefield.

Phineas touched a hand to his chest. "*I* was being rude?"

"You were *both* being rude." Anwen paused. "That may be who Lord Wakefield is, but it isn't who you are, Phineas."

That would be an actual first; a bet not a single soul would have placed at the White's betting book—someone believing Phineas was a better person than a bloke like Wakefield.

"He's a fine man," he grudgingly allowed.

"Not so fine as to show you a deserved respect," she said, with far more loyalty than Phineas deserved or merited. "I'm sorry he was rude to you."

He shrugged.

"He'd make you a fine husband," Phineas conceded in an admission that, given he'd rather bury Wakefield than see him in the same room as Anwen, let alone married to her, proved Phineas was more selfless than he'd credited himself capable of.

Anwen eyed him like he'd gone mad. "You believe a man who'd disparage *you* is a man I would ever dare marry?"

Perhaps he was due for a stay at Bedlam; for her fierce devotedness to Phineas, left him feeling like he soared ten feet above the ground. No one had ever seen anything worthwhile in him, and Phineas was so very tempted to encourage her unfavorable opinion of Wakefield.

If Phineas did so, she'd sever all connection before there even was a connection with the stuffy earl. Then Phineas wouldn't have to be haunted by the very thought of Anwen Kearsley in that other man's arms.

From over the top of Anwen's head, the radiant flowers called Phineas' attention. And he started discovering—he wasn't fully rotted from the inside out. For a man such as Wakefield was what Anwen deserved; a suitor and husband who showered her with gifts and fetched stars in exchange for her smiles.

But can Wakefield make her smile in return?

"You shouldn't be so hard on Wakefield, Anwen," he finally brought himself to say. "He is an honorable sort. His *father* was a reprobate, but the new earl, he built his own fortunes and improved his estates."

Unlike me.

Funny, he'd believed himself perfectly contented with his own degeneracy. Only to discover, he didn't much like himself. He didn't like himself, at all. "You should give him a chance."

Anwen searched her big, brown eyes over his face. "Is that what you think?"

Think? Yes. Want? No.

"He's a devoted son and brother," Phineas murmured.

"Is he?"

He nodded. "And clever. The smartest student in his classes back in his university days. Did impressive things improving his family's financial circumstances."

"*You* could always marry him," she said teasingly.

Tension snaked through him. "Is that what he came here to offer? Marriage?"

Anwen nodded. "He did."

He'd been expecting it. But not like this. Not this quickly. And the absolute only reason he cared was because of…of how… damned swift it was all moving. That was why. It wouldn't do. Not for Anwen. His chest moved…weirdly. Fast. Like he'd run too far and his lungs now revolted.

"Well then, Wakefield isn't as clever or as honorable as I credited." How Phineas despised the worthless bastard. "You deserve a courtship." One with the man she truly yearned for.

"After seven seasons on the shelf, I've lost the right to a full courtship," she said wryly.

"Why do you do that?" he snapped.

She drew her brows together. "What—?"

He exploded to his feet. Anwen tripped in her haste to back away. Phineas attempted to temper his fury and frustration with a deep breath—to no avail.

"Why do you act as if you are somehow to blame for society's blindness?" he hissed. "They are your inferior in every way. My God, you are a goddamned queen among them, Anwen!"

"Phineas, I'm a Kearsley."

"And what's wrong with being a Kearsley?" he demanded, more affronted than had she besmirched his iniquitous name.

Then, it hit him.

"The Curse," he said flatly. "*That* is the reason then for the sudden urgency?" If Phineas hadn't grown up with St. John, he'd have discounted her fears outright. But he had been such a part of this family, Phineas wouldn't dare dismiss that something—no matter how outrageous it may be, how fatuous.

"Of course, not," she said, a little too insistent. "I told you the other evening, I'm already twenty-seven years old and—"

"And you are afraid you'll die before you marry," Phineas interrupted.

"No, I…just…" She looked at him and sighed. "Fine. Yes. I saw my mother's fortune-teller, and she told me my end was near. There will be a great storm, and a tree and lightning," she rambled. "And I'm not certain how but during a great tempest, I'll be struck down."

Even knowing the words Anwen spoke came from some charlatan

who preyed on a vulnerable family, a terrific and overwhelming terror from briefly clouding out rational thought.

When he trusted himself to speak, he tried again. "*Anwen.*"

"I don't have the luxury of unlimited time. I am in love, Phineas!" she cried, and God help him, why did it feel like she'd splayed him wide open with that pronouncement and ripped his heart asunder?

"I'm in love, and I need to have what time I can with him."

Phineas silently willed her to share the identity of the man who'd won her heart. Even as he didn't want to know, because once he did, that nobleman would no longer be nameless or faceless. Then, Phineas would be made to see him at clubs and Kearsley gatherings and imagine him with Anwen.

"*Tell me* you understand, Phineas," she implored.

There existed but one certainty in this moment—he'd no intention of letting Anwen do anything rash nor accept anything less than a love match with a good man, because of some swindler employed by the dowager viscountess.

Phineas rested his hands on Anwen's shoulders and gave them a tender squeeze. "Anwen," he began gently.

With a fire radiating from her eyes, she wrenched herself from his arms. "Do *not* patronize me, Phineas."

"I'm not."

"But you are. Not with your words. But with your tone, and how you're looking at me now." Anwen looked around and lowered her voice. "I will die young, but before I do—"

Phineas made an interrupting sound. "Mm, mm," he said, shaking his head. He didn't want to hear it. Supporting her in her fears was one thing. Having her speak plainly about her death…

"It's true. A thunder—"

"And it's not going to happen, Anwen!" he said more sharply than he intended. Phineas took her shoulders again in his hands, this time with a greater firmness. "I'll not allow it."

And he found himself again shaken twice in this moment to discover that pledge had absolutely nothing to do with the promise he'd made St. John that he'd watch over Anwen, but everything to do with what he was feeling at this moment.

Anwen stared up at him with the widest, haunted eyes, that sucked the warmth from his body and left an icy path along his spine.

"You won't be able to stop it," she whispered.

His fingers curved reflexively before he registered that tensing. He instantly relaxed his hold…but remained frozen, unable to lower his arms. Instead, he brushed the pads of his thumbs just under the delicate puff sleeves, and over her satiny, soft skin.

The already charged air became electric as the fictitious storm she spoke of. Her eyes clouded…with desire. Or mayhap that was his own hungering reflected back in those great big pools. God, he needed to taste of her once more. Just once.

Closing his eyes, he angled his head to fill that craving.

"Phineas!"

That excited squeal jolted Anwen and Phineas apart.

Anwen looked over as her youngest sister came flying into the room and tried to put order to her thoughts.

Phineas had been a moment away from kissing her. She'd seen it in the way his lashes had grown heavy and by the flicker of hunger in his eyes. Hunger, for *her*.

He'd stared at her like she was a full-course meal, just presented to a starving man. One would never guess it. Anwen may as well have imagined it. For as Eris rushed to join Anwen and Phineas, the marquess flashed an unbothered smile.

"Why, if it isn't, Miss Eris Kearsley!"

As Phineas greeted her youngest sister, Anwen remained grateful that at least he proved collected in this instant.

He made a deep bow. "A pleasure, as always, Miss Kearsley."

"Oh, hush," Eris giggled. "You cannot be formal. We are friends." Her face fell and she grew instantly serious. "Things are dire, Phineas. Very dire."

Phineas instantly dropped to a knee. "How may I lend my assistance?"

The two proceeded to speak, and Anwen studied the unlikely

pairing between society's biggest rake, and London's most precocious child. Anwen's, heart hammered away. She remained riveted by that bucolic tableau.

How very wonderful he was with children. And how very wonderful he'd be with babes of his own. Having witnessed Phineas' love and patience with her siblings, she knew unequivocally he'd be a father who loved and respected both his daughters and son, equally.

As if he felt Anwen's stare upon him, Phineas peeked over the top of the little girl's head and winked at Anwen. Her breath caught. It was the wink. Romance novels and poets and artists all spoke about 'the look' or the hair or the smile.

They had it all wrong. For it was that lazy flutter of Phineas' golden lashes that made a lady forget her name.

A small palm touched Anwen's cheek.

"Are you sick, after all, Anwen?" her youngest sister asked worriedly.

Taking Eris's hand in hers, Anwen gently brought her arm back to her side.

"I'm fine," she said, with a forced laugh.

"That's not your real laugh." Eris looked to Phineas. At eight, Eris was nearly the same height of Anwen at twenty-seven. Stretching the remainder of the way on her tip-toes, Eris gave Anwen a dubious look.

"I don't know, Anwen. You're all red in the cheeks and breathing funny. Don't you think so, Phineas?"

She felt Phineas' stare locked upon her heated face. He caught his chin in his hand and made a show of studying her. "Now, that you mention it…"

"You're terrible," Anwen mouthed.

Grinning, Phineas gave another wink. And then, just as her youngest sister had done moments ago, Phineas touched a bare palm to Anwen's burning face.

Her breath caught. She'd been wrong. She owed her sister a debt of gratitude.

Like a man in a trance, Phineas slowly moved the pad of his thumb over her cheek.

"Do you think it is a fever?"

Both Anwen and Phineas stared at one another with matched confusion.

"Anwen?" Eris clarified; her little brow furrowed with worry. "Is it a fever?" She turned to Phineas. "Mama wanted to send for Dr. Carlson because Anwen was all flushed at breakfast."

"Was she?" he murmured.

I still am.

"Oh, yes," Eris piped in. "We thought it was fever, but then the Earl of Wakefield came, and then we suspected Anwen's cheeks were red because she's in love with him."

Phineas' features went hard. "Did you, now?"

Eris nodded. "We did."

A muscle twitched near the corner of the marquess's left eye.

Why…he couldn't be jealous, could he? As soon as the thought slipped in, it faded right out. For Phineas couldn't be envious. He'd have to regard her as a woman and not just Clayton's sister to feel that sentiment. Nay, the earl's slight from before undoubtedly accounted for that dark look.

"And what is your opinion on the earl, Eris?" Phineas murmured.

Eris pulled a face.

"Hmm? What say ye of Wakefield?" If he'd pulled his piercing stare from Anwen, he wouldn't have required a verbal answer.

"I dislike it immensely, Phineas. He wants to marry her, I suspect, but I don't want Anwen to marry because then her husband will take her away." Eris's eyes brightened. "I have an idea!"

At last, Phineas pulled his gaze from Anwen. "Do tell, Eris."

"Do *not*, tell," Anwen shot her sister a warning look.

Eris ignored her. "*You* should marry her." The little girl beamed at her own suggestion.

Phineas, however? His gloriously chiseled features froze as if he'd clapped eyes upon the gorgon, Medusa.

Oh, God.

Madam Pomfret had been wrong, after all. Anwen was destined to die. *Not* from a lightning strike, but rather from the pain of Phineas' horrified response.

And just like that, Anwen found herself praying the opposite prayer that had always been in her daily cue. Here she'd spent her life attempting to dodge the Kearsley curse, only to *now* pray the Lord spare some time to smite her where she stood.

Eris gave a tug at Phineas' hand. "Will you come with me, Phineas?"

His eyes brimming with relief, he jerked his focus back to the little girl. "Where do you find yourself journeying to?"

Eris could have answered hell, and Anwen suspected, the marquess would have been all too happy to join her.

"I am attempting to beat Captain Robert Barclay Allardice," Eris said.

Both Anwen and Phineas stared blankly at the girl.

"Captain Robert Barclay Allardice," Eris repeated, and when neither still displayed a hint of recognition, she threw her hands up. "*The* Celebrated Pedestrian of Stonehaven."

"Still nothing, I fear," Phineas said with a suitable amount of contrition in his tone.

He looked to Anwen. "What of you?" His playfully teasing tone quashed all previous awkwardness between them.

Anwen lifted her palms up. "I've never heard the name."

A sound of disgust escaped Eris. "I should have expected *you* wouldn't know, Anwen," she muttered, and with a sigh, she took *mercy* upon their woeful lack of knowledge.

"He is only *the* most impressive pedestrian *ever.*" Eris's voice grew animated as she spoke. "Captain Robert walked one mile, every hour, for one *thousand* hours over the course of eleven days."

Phineas blanched. "Good Lord, whyever would he want to do that?" he asked the question, Anwen herself had been thinking.

Eris shot a glare his way. "I'll pretend you did not ask that, Landon."

"My apologies." Phineas touched a hand to his heart. "Please, continue."

"Countless men came after him and attempted to defeat the record which he'd set. Every one of them failed. But there has been no woman who ever attempted the feat."

Ah, *now,* it made sense.

"And you intend to be that woman," Anwen ventured.

Eris jabbed her index finger in Anwen's direction and gave it a waggle. "Precisely."

Eris proceeded to go into a lengthy description of the sport, and those who'd attempted to defeat—unsuccessfully—The Celebrated Pedestrian of Stonehaven's record.

As Phineas conversed with Eris, Anwen took in the exchange.

As an older brother, Clayton had been endlessly patient and devoted where his sisters were concerned. But he had to. They were his sisters. Most gentlemen wouldn't bother looking at a child, let alone taking part in a full discourse with an eccentric, spirited girl of eight years.

Once again, more of that dangerous heat found its way inside Anwen's heart.

"You are looking all queer again, Anwen," Eris warned.

Oh, hell in a basket.

"I'm fine," Anwen gritted out.

"I don't think you're fine on a good day, Anwen. When you're sick, you're downright peculiar."

Sororicide. She was close to committing it against her youngest sibling.

Hero that he was, Phineas stepped in and rescued Anwen from further humiliation. "And how do we come into play with your footrace competition?"

Eris redirected her focus back to Phineas. "Well, you see, one cannot simply walk and win, one must practice. I need you to keep time for me."

"Aren't there enough clocks in our corridors that you can do that yourself, Eris?" Anwen asked, not bothering to keep the exasperation from her question.

Need Eris steal Anwen's time with the marquess?

Eris sent a wounded look Anwen's way. "I need it to be more exact, Anwen."

Guilt swelled in her breast. As their mother had always said: sisters before suitors. The prophecy of Anwen's impending death had added urgency to Anwen's whole 'falling in love with Phineas' and that was turning her into someone she didn't like or recognize.

"My apologies, Eris," she said softly and looping an arm around

Eris's small shoulders, Anwen drew her in for a sideways hug.

"Aww, it is fine," Eris assured her. "I know it's because you're not feeling well."

For the love of God. "I'm feeling just fine."

Anwen should have saved her breath.

"Come along, Phineas." Eris gave a clap of her hands. "Timepiece out."

He promptly had that chain in hand.

"And we're off!" Without bothering to see if he followed, Eris took off at a quick walk that resembled a sprint.

Phineas waved. "I guess I am off."

Anwen's lips twitched. "It appears that way," she said. "Thank you."

"What are you thanking me for?"

"For being so good with her. For being so patient with all my sisters." Suddenly uncertain, when for her whole life, she'd never been that way around him, she cleared her throat. "And with me."

Phineas frowned. Some indescribable emotion filled his eyes. But then, he reached a palm up and ever so tenderly brought it against her cheek.

He'd touched her any number of times. But then, she'd been a small girl and he'd been helping tend her scraped knees or other various maladies children suffered. Even five minutes ago he'd checked her for fever.

Yet never, had it been…like this. His hand, large and warm and so very tender against her cheek. Her pulse fluttered in time to her lashes.

"I wanted to…do this, Anwen."

"No, you didn't." How did she find either breath or words to speak aloud?

His lips twitched. "Very well. You know I've never been able to say no to—"

Her heart jumped.

"The Kearsleys." Phineas let his arm drop to his side.

The Kearsleys.

Of course, because Phineas had been the best of friends to Clayton. Over the course of his time at Eton and Oxford, when he'd not been away at school, he'd all but lived with the Kearsleys.

Still, that lumping of her in with the rest of the family brought her crashing back to earth faster and harder than that tumble she'd taken from that tree with him all those years ago.

"Anwen?" he asked, with so much tender concern she couldn't bring herself to meet his eyes.

Then—God, help her—he palmed her cheek for a second time. This time, his touch fleeting and all too brief.

But Anwen forced a smile, made herself look up at him, and mimicking his earlier movements, she gently patted his cheek. "You should go before she returns and scolds you for your dereliction of duties."

"Yes."

Only, he didn't go. Neither did Anwen.

Nor did she drop her arm back to her side. She remained that way, with her fingers upon his chiseled cheek; the faintest hint of growth indicating he'd foregone shaving that morn tickled her palm.

Phineas stilled but did not pull away. He remained as locked to his spot as she was to hers. Time, it stood still. The tick of the hall clock grew muted and then faded altogether. He moved a fogged gaze over Anwen's face. Confusion leaving creases upon his high, noble brow.

"What is it?" she whispered.

"I..." He gave his head a perplexed shake. "Don't know."

He took a step closer; reflexively she matched his movements and drifted nearer so but a hairsbreadth existed between them.

"Phinnnneas?" That distant shout snapped them apart.

Anwen's arm fell uselessly to her side; and of their own volition, her fingers, still warm from the feel of Phineas's skin, reflexively curled into a ball.

Eris ducked her head around the corner and fixed a glare on the marquess. "You are ruining my time, Landon."

Instantly contrite, he touched a hand to his chest. "I offer my deepest, most—"

"Stuff it, Landon," Eris snapped. "Save your fancy words for one of your many sweethearts."

His blond eyebrows went shooting up, and an adorable blush filled his cheeks. But he found his voice. "I don't have sweethearts."

"No," Eris shouted and proceeded to skip over. "But Mama said I'm not allowed to refer to them as your paramours or lovers."

Phineas strangled, then promptly choked on his swallow.

Anwen laughed, only smothering it behind her fingers when Phineas tossed an accusatory look her way. "Sorry," she mouthed.

"No, you're not," he silently rejoined.

She grinned. "No," she agreed. "I am not."

Eris reached Anwen and Phineas. The previous quick clip the girl had set for herself, tugged a number of her curls free of her plait.

Phineas gently tugged at one of those big brown coils. "And just what are you and your dear mother doing talking about me?"

Eris shrugged. "We talk about you all the time."

Phineas blanched. "Never mind," he said hastily. "I don't want to know."

The little girl flashed an impish, big-dimpled smile, leaned in and up, and whispered. "We talk about everyone," she slid a dangerously knowing glance Anwen's way. "*Every*one."

Oh, hell. Determined to spare herself from suffering any further embarrassment, Anwen jumped in, before her sister could speak.

"You'd best be getting along," she said, taking Eris by the hand, and gently but firmly directing her so she faced the same corridor from which she'd just entered. "I daresay Captain Robert Barclay Allardice doesn't spend time in idle chit-chat when he should be fast-walking."

"Never!" Eris exclaimed.

"Then you shouldn't either." Anwen gave her a slight nudge forward. "Now, off you go."

"Timepiece ready, Phineas?" the girl asked.

He displayed the engraved gold piece.

"Then, we're off."

This time, as Eris took off at her quick clip, Phineas followed, easily keeping pace at the small girl's side.

Anwen stared after the pair as they went. He said something to

Anwen's sister, that pulled a big, snorting laugh from the young girl. And then, they were gone, leaving Anwen alone.

As she trailed along more slowly behind the path her sister and Phineas had taken, the echo of their laughter filtered down to Anwen—Eris's exuberant mirth, mingling with Phineas' deeper, heartier round of amusement.

Following her meeting with Madam Pomfret, Anwen had resolved that before she died, she'd have, if even for a brief time, the relationship she'd always yearned to know with Phineas. She'd have her waltz and sit beside him in the theatre. He'd come calling on her, and they'd speak about their grand hopes and dreams and desires. When she'd set out to steal a courtship from him, she had thought only of the time she'd spend with him before she died.

Anwen's steps slowed, and she came to a faltering stop.

Her eyes slid shut.

How had she ever believed the furtive courtship she'd tricked him into giving her, one where real love did exist but remained one-sided and unreturned affection, would ever be enough?

Because you are pathetic and desperate, a jeering voice whispered in her mind.

All the Kearsleys were cursed, and invariably died or would die a tragic death, but they also fell head over toes in love and had that love returned. Such had been the case with her father and mother, her grandparents, and her grandparents-parents, and so on.

Not Anwen.

Phineas' great bellow of laughter from some distant hall brought Anwen's eyes flying open. That raucous swell—bright and light and all things joyous—didn't allow misery to share in its company. His laugh had always been that way for her.

Anwen gave her head a hard, clearing shake. "Stop it," she muttered into the quiet.

She might be a bookworm and bookish. She might be a wallflower who spent more time buried in books than on dance floors. But one thing she was decidedly *not* was a self-pitying creature.

A sliver of energy penetrated the soles of her slippers and tingled her toes like when she tread upon this same carpeted floor in her bare stockinged feet gilded frame. She glanced up at the place where she'd stopped—the rendering of her smiling father stared benevolently down at Anwen.

Anwen hovered her fingers over his where they rested upon the back of his favorite walnut and leather upholstered armchair. She let her hand linger there but did not bring herself to touch the oil painting lest she damage the last image they had of the late viscount.

"Papa, how did you do it?" she whispered, desperate for a reply, yearning for one. "How were you able to fall in love and have a big family and pack a lifetime into the short time you were given?"

Whereas Anwen? Anwen couldn't even manage *one* of those feats.

Silence and her father's jovial grin, frozen in time, remained her only company. Touching her fingers to her lips, Anwen blew a kiss at her father's painting and resumed her stroll through the halls.

Mayhap, it's because you've not attempted to take control of your own fate. Mayhap, all along you've been so afraid of dying that you've let yourself linger in the shadows and kept yourself invisible to even Phineas.

As she walked, she considered that possibility. Perhaps that's just what she'd done. What if she'd not been so afraid and attempted to win his affection years earlier? Even dying as she soon would, they would have had almost ten years to be a family. To build a family.

Anwen turned the corner and stopped.

At some point, Phineas had shed his jacket. It now lay in a haphazard heap upon the floor. Her feet were already carrying her over to that well-tailored article. The moment she reached it, she sank to her haunches, scooped the garment up, and drew it close. The material still bore the heat of his body.

Anwen smoothed a hand tenderly over the wrinkled wool. The scent of him lingered on the fabric, and she brought the material nearer her nose so that she could inhale deeply of that masculine trace of sandalwood. She'd never breathe of that scent and not think of him, or that one kiss they'd shared—which he'd vowed would never happen again.

Anwen came to her feet and gave Phineas' jacket several snaps to free it of wrinkles—when her gaze snagged upon a whisper of white in his inside pocket.

She stilled.

It isn't your business. You've no place reading another person's correspondence.

And yet—

Anwen stole a peek around the hallway.

Empty.

She stood there, trapped in a vicious battle with herself: the part that said she'd no right looking through Phineas' things, and the other part, that…well, that wanted to.

Curiosity won out.

Fumbling hastily with the jacket, Anwen tugged free the page, when the cloying scent of rosewater immediately flooded her nostrils. A lover's note.

Her courage flagged, and a black and unreasoning jealousy formed a vise around her heart. Did she dare?

Ultimately, curiosity triumphed.

She scoured the sheet which was decidedly not a note, but rather…

Names. Written, not in his hand, but a cleaner, more delicate, more feminine hand. More specifically, the names of five young debutantes.

Names of potential wives.

None of which were hers.

Granted, Anwen wasn't young. Respectable, virtuous like the other ladies on the page, yes. Girlish, certainly not.

Lady Louise Marshfield
Lady Margaret Sallow
Lady Olive Fernsby
Lady Harriet Hatt
Lady Eliza Stankworth

What other reason did a gentleman go about putting names of proper ladies to paper…?

Except, she knew the answer: No other reason. With fortunes to their names, and not so much as a scandal in their family's history, any one of the five women would make an ideal bride for any gentleman in the market for a wife.

Phineas' intentions toward an innocent lady would only ever be honorable. He intended to court and wed one of those women. Why, there wasn't even a mere Miss within that group.

Anwen's fingers tightened involuntarily around the corners of the page.

Had she fallen on the wrong end of a war hammer like one of her distant, cursed relatives, it couldn't hurt more than this.

What did you expect? How many other women had he courted over the years, with the intention of wedding them? Through the years, there'd been any number of ladies, Anwen had been forced to sit on the sidelines and watch him waltz around ballroom floors or sit next to in theatre boxes. Or read in the gossip pages about the morning visits he'd paid to respectable households and the ladies who resided there.

It hadn't been Anwen then, either.

This time, however? This time was different. Before she'd only pined for Phineas from afar. Now, that she'd tricked him into the courtship she'd dreamed of from him before she died, she'd a taste of what it would be like if he truly cared for and wanted her.

Which was, of course, ludicrous. He never had, and never would. She, on the other hand, now knew the magic feeling that came from him wrapping his arms around her, or from being the subject of his singular focus.

And his embrace. God help her, she now knew the wonderment of his kiss: the feel of his firm, confident lips on hers, and the glide of his tongue against hers in a dance more erotic and headier than any waltz.

Only, some other woman was destined to be the rightful owner of those gifts. They'd know not only his kiss but all of it—what it was to make love with him. More specifically, one of the ladies on the page Anwen still held between her fingers would be the recipient of all that Anwen longed for.

She stared sorrowfully at the names of the prospective ladies he'd chosen as his future marchioness. His future with some other woman had always been a certainty. Even if Phineas had fallen in love with Anwen—which he decidedly hadn't and wouldn't—she was destined to die, and a man like the marquess would never be alone, even after her inevitable passing.

"Stop it," she whispered, her voice quavering slightly. She was making a cake of herself, and this, when she'd always prided herself on not being pathetic by pining after Phineas and longing for what would never be.

She made herself relax the death-like grip she had upon the list and in a bid to flatten the tell-tale mark she'd left, smoothed a hand over the slightly crumpled corner.

As Delia forever sprouting Shakespeare frequently said: *...what though care killed a cat, thou hast mettle enough in thee to kill care.*

"You escaped rather neatly—"

Anwen whipped her head up so quickly, all the muscles in her neck screamed out in painful protest.

Phineas stood there, still sans jacket, in his bare shirtsleeves, trousers, and boots. Of course, he was sans jacket. Said jacket currently rested at Anwen's slippered feet while she had a white-knuckled grip upon the page she'd availed herself to inside that garment.

Phineas' gaze went from Anwen's face to the damning page in her fingers.

"This fell out," she said stupidly, and then unable to meet his eyes, she dropped to a knee and belatedly stuffed the note back inside the pocket she'd pilfered it from.

She stood and shoved the garment towards him. "Here you are."

Wordlessly, he took the black wool jacket from her fingers. Anwen proved unable to remove her eyes from the sight of him. There was something so very intimate seeing him dress before her.

Granted, she'd witnessed when he'd been bare-chested in her family's lake, but that had been different. Clayton had been around, as had any number of the many Kearsley siblings.

Now, it was only her and Phineas.

It became apparent, as he finished buttoning up his wool jacket, he'd not speak about the list she'd discovered, and she must certainly be a glutton for pain and suffering for it proved too much for Anwen.

"Tell me, Lord Landon, do you make it a habit of keeping on your person lists of respectable young ladies?" she asked, unable to keep the archness from her voice.

"Only if you tell me, Miss Kearsley," he dropped a shoulder lazily against the wall in a devastatingly negligent pose that sent butterflies dancing in her breast, "do *you* make it a habit of snooping through another person's belongings?"

Must he be so blasted charismatic? "Yes."

He just stared at her.

"I have half a dozen siblings," she said, taking delight in having unsettled him with that bit of truthfulness. "And when you *have* a half a dozen siblings, snooping is a requisite survival skill."

"Given all that experience, one would expect you'd be better skilled at it so as to not get caught." Phineas gave her an annoying brotherly-like tap on her nose.

She swatted at his hand. He'd certainly not behave brotherly-like to any of those five women; one whom he intended to seriously court.

"Furthermore, it fell out of your pocket," she lied.

The glimmer in his eyes, however, indicated he'd easily spotted that fib.

Say something. Just tell me your reason for having those names so it was confirmed. That way as soon as he took leave of his obligatory visit, she could go on to wallow in her own self-misery.

With the long stretch of passing silence, it became apparent he'd no intention of helping the discussion along. That, if she wished to hear him say it, she'd have to be the one to point-blank ask the question.

Unable to meet his amused and still-knowing gaze, Anwen dropped her gaze briefly to the floor and then made herself look at Phineas.

"Given you don't bother with innocent young women, I trust they aren't...*conquests*."

"They are conquests of a different sort."

She stared blankly at him.

"Potential future wives," he murmured, confirming that which she'd already known. Still, hearing him speak it freed a river of pain within. Literally everything hurt: her muscles tensed at his revelation. Her heart, her lungs, her very soul.

"Oh."

Of course, that was what they were. Why else would he have them listed?

"Why don't you say what it is you want to say, Anwen?" he said, his voice colder than she ever recalled.

Why can it not be me?

Only, she was more cowardly than she'd previously credited, for she couldn't bring herself to utter that desperate query.

"Hmm?" he demanded and took an angry step toward her, and Anwen reflexively moved away from him.

The wall met her back, blocking escape, and also steadying her.

"I don't have any choice."

"Because of the choices you made prior," she said. "If you hadn't gambled and taken mistress after mistress—"

"That was always destined to be my way. I'm a profligate rake and gambler and wastrel just as my father before me and his father before him. I am my father's son."

"You're not, Phin—" she insisted. "I knew your father. I know the manner of man he was. You are not that—"

"Do not give me that shite. You're only seeing what you want to see."

"I'm not!" she said earnestly.

Anwen gripped him by the lapels of his jacket and willed him with all that she was to see the same man she'd always seen. "Your father was a mean, miserable bastard who didn't pay you any notice. He wouldn't have managed to tell a jest or turn a smile if his family's estates depended upon it."

"The fact that I'm some glib, vapid fellow means I'm *better* than my father?" He let out a laugh teeming with cynicism. "That is some paltry praise, Anwen."

"That isn't what I mean," she said, desperate to make him see that he was far more than the man who'd sired him.

He sharpened his gaze on her face. "Then why don't you say exactly what it is you *do* mean."

"When I was eight, I fell from my pony, and it was you who carried me in your arms to my parents. All the while you did, you told me outrageous jests until I forgot the fright I'd just had."

He made to look away, but Anwen gripped his chin and guided

his gaze back to hers. "And when my father died, and my sisters were desolate, you gave them each a day doing something they each loved."

Again, Phineas made to pull away. She wouldn't let him.

"Knowing Brenna lives on the pages written by Enlightened thinkers, you coordinated for Archibald Alison to leave Edinburgh and give a talk on his Essay on the Nature and Principles of Taste, and then personally escorted her to the essayist's previously unplanned visit to London." Without so much as pausing to take a breath, she continued. "Knowing Cora's love for science you took her to visit Miss Etheldred Benett who shared her fossil collection with my sister."

His eyebrows shot up.

"Yes, I know you did all that." One who'd admired and watched him from afar as long as she had, she'd have never failed to see all those great kindnesses he'd shown her hurting siblings.

Anwen joined her hands with his and looked briefly down at her knuckles looped through Phineas'.

She lifted her gaze to his. Phineas' eyes went opaque and then he effortlessly disentangled their twined fingers.

"Yes," he said on a low, husky drawl she'd wager her soul he saved for his lovers. Then, with an infinite slowness, he skimmed two fingers along the lace bodice of her gown.

Her heart did a leap at that distracted but deliberate caress, and the hard glint in his eyes bespoke a man who knew the effect his touch was having on her. He stopped his stroking and trapped between his thumb and index, teased the white lace bow at the center of her neckline. He played with it. Tested the fragile fabric with his fingers. Fondled it.

Unbidden, her eyes slid shut, and she harkened back to that day he'd taken her in his arms and massaged her buttocks. Anwen's breath quickened. A dull ache settled between her legs. Her chest rose and fell with an unmistakable sign of her hungering.

The right corner of Phineas' lips lifted in a tempting smile Satan would have envied the marquess for.

Over the years, Anwen had pitied the women who'd failed to know Phineas-the-man and had only known him in a carnal sense.

Now, God help her, with his lust-filled gaze searing her straight to her soul, she at last discovered why those other women had been content.

"You were saying?" he purred.

His was a jeering taunt. One that demanded she acknowledge the seductive game he played with her in the middle of her family's halls and the possibility of anyone stumbling upon them. He did that as a lesson in his wickedness. He did that to prove he wasn't the man she knew him to be.

He slipped the pad of his thumb over the top swell of her breast.

Anwen took a slow, steadying breath. "And Delia, you took to Shakespeare's performance of The Comedy of Errors," she said, her words hoarsened by desire.

"Ah," He gave her bow another suggestive little tug. "But then, I'm well-known for my appreciation for the *theatre*."

As in *actresses*. He sought to remind her of all the famous singers and ballet dancers he'd been linked to. He was filled with so much self-loathing. He was so certain he was bad, he'd remind her of the darker parts of his reputation and deny any good he'd done.

"Wastrels who care only about drink and wagers certainly don't go about spending funds to bring *ministers of religion essayists* to London to make a sad girl smile, Phineas," she reminded him softly.

A muscle twitched in his jaw. His eyes darkened; tumult glinted in their depths.

Having knocked him off-balance, she, along with her voice, grew more and more steady.

Anwen continued. "You escorted Daria to the Serpentine and joined her in a water burial she held, sending off one of my papa's kerchiefs. Eris you bought a new rattle for. And for Mama, you sent primrose. Even though they weren't in Season and had to have them procured from a special hothouse, you did it, because you *knew* they were her favorite."

His lips curled in an icy smile. "You speak as if I did something for all of you after the viscount's passing, but tell me, hmm? If that is the case, what did I do for you, *Anwen*?"

A memory whispered forward: of her alone that night, seated on the stone bench in her family's gardens in the midst of a rainstorm.

Her knees drawn tight to her chest and her cheeks damp from rain and tears. When suddenly, the storm stopped, a scrap of white fluttered just over her shoulder.

Anwen blinked and looked up. Through the film of misery covering her eyes, Anwen stared at the blurred letters embroidered on that kerchief until they came into clear focus.

PCL, MofL

Anwen whipped her gaze up to the umbrella Phineas now held over her. He shrugged out of his jacket, and then, holding the umbrella in one hand, he, with an effortless grace, draped the wool article around her shoulders.

Wordlessly, he slid onto the bench beside her. She immediately leaned her head against his broad, shoulder. He rested his cheek on her head. And they sat together that way, in complete silence.

Anwen blinked slowly and came back to the present. Phineas watched her through heavy, hooded lashes.

"You just sat with me," she said softly. "Because you knew I didn't need anything or want anything other than y—"

His piercing eyes locked on her face, and she stumbled.

"Your," *You,* "company," she finished weakly.

For if he knew she'd longed for him then and now, he'd walk out of her family's household, and she knew he wouldn't return—likely, *ever*—his lifelong friendship to her brother be damned.

CHAPTER 9

PHINEAS HAD BEEN MANY THINGS in his life: a wastrel, a rake, a charmer, a gambler. But he'd prided himself on never being a coward.

That was, until now.

Standing here in this Kearsley corridor, while Anwen challenged him, while she *insisted* he was in any way different from his father, Phineas wanted to flee.

She was determined to see good in him. Stubborn as she'd always been, she'd fight him tooth and nail. Mayhap doing so proved easier for her. Mayhap it helped for her to think the man she kept close company with now, and had known since she'd been a small girl, was, in fact, a depraved, debauched rake, without a farthing to his name.

"Do you want to know the truth?" he asked.

She hesitated a moment, that slight pause indicating she'd rather not hear.

"The day your father died, Anwen, your brother sent word and asked that I come help him with looking after all of you so that he could focus on the funeral preparations."

Anwen drew back. Something flickered in her eyes. A flash of hurt, and then…disbelief.

"I don't believe that."

Clever girl. She'd always been smarter than any woman he'd ever known.

"You'd call me a liar?" He laughed. "I'm more than certain

that questioning of my honor rather refutes your argument quite handily, love."

"When caught between admitting your own good and telling a lie?" she countered. "Then, yes, I believe you would prevaricate, Phineas."

He gnashed his teeth. Damn her for knowing him well enough to spot a fib on his part.

"You're making more of it than there is," he gritted out.

Why couldn't she…just be like everyone else who saw him, Phineas Lesar, charming rake, without a jot of substance, and a massive debt to his disgraced name?

"I felt *obligated* to do those things, Anwen."

"I don't believe that. Perhaps you can *try* and argue as much if you'd only shown that consideration to my brother. You didn't. You extended your support to five young ladies."

He had. Because he…loved the Kearsleys. When he'd been a boy, then a young man, they'd always been the family he'd wished for.

She pounced on his silence. "And even if it were true, Phineas," she smoothed her palms over the front of his jacket and the muscles in his chest jumped under that soft, innocent caress. "Even if it were true," she repeated, "and you looked after my mother, my sisters, and me out of some sense of loyalty to my father or brother or anyone else, then that in and of itself sets you worlds apart from your father who only put his own pleasures and comforts f—"

He thumped a fist against the wall beside her head. "*Enough!*"

Anwen gasped and recoiled away from him.

Phineas stared back at her. "You're afraid of me." Why did that realization not bring him any sort of glee? Why did it leave him feeling hollow and empty inside?

She shook her head. "You won't hurt me."

"You're trying to convince yourself, love."

"No," Anwen said softly. "I know that to be true. You would never hurt me."

A cold sweat popped up on his brow, and moisture slicked his palms. Why? Why did she have so much faith in him when it was undeserved? How could she see anything redeeming in Phineas when none of the world did? That devotion didn't warm him the way he expected it ought. It scared the everlasting hell out of him.

"Do you know what I find the height of irony, Anwen?" he asked coolly, determined to disabuse her of that devotion.

She shook her head.

"You insist on standing here stating all the reasons, I'm different from my sire," he hissed. "All the while, you're the *same* woman who believes her entire future is pre-determined because of your family history."

A flummoxed Anwen drew back.

She found her voice. "It is different."

"Is it?"

She gave a jerky nod.

"Enlighten me as to how, Miss Kearsley?" he whispered.

With her mouth near his, he felt the sough of each, ragged breath she drew. Hers wasn't the uneven inhalation and exhalation of a fearful lady. A lifetime of debauchery had taught him the evidence of a woman's desire.

"Hmm. No explanation, Miss Kearsley?" he taunted. "Well, then let me answer the question *for* you. Our circumstances? Yours and mine? They aren't in any way different," he whispered. "And you know it. Be it through blood or legacy, we all carry the curse of our family before us."

And then, God help the last shred of soul he had worth saving, Anwen darted the pink tip of her tongue out, bringing all his focus to the lushest lips he'd ever seen. Hers was a mouth that beckoned, tempted. It begged a good man to sin and invited a bad man to explore, and never had he more celebrated his status as the worst of men.

Growling, Phineas took Anwen's mouth under his in an angry kiss, just as he'd longed to since the one they'd shared days earlier.

She instantly went pliant in his arms; she sagged and he caught her right hip in one hand and drove her back against the wall. Through the fabric of her muslin skirts, Phineas squeezed that supple flesh, in a grip both punishing and possessive. He ran the fingers of his other hand along her delicate jaw.

"Open for me," he demanded. And with a trust and surrender

he didn't deserve, she let him in to that place he wanted to be. *Needed* to be.

Incapable of anything more than a growl of appreciation, he swept inside and tasted of her—again.

Phineas lashed that flesh against hers in a primitive battle, and she may as well have been the formidable Joan of Arc, legend for opting the offensive.

She whimpered.

"Do you want more, love?" he rasped between kisses.

Anwen gave a frantic nod.

He tightened his hold upon her hip, his grip punishing. This time, it would be enough. He'd sear the memory of the taste and feel of her in his mind so that it could purge whatever mad fascination he'd developed for Anwen Kearsley.

Not breaking contact with her mouth, Phineas grabbed the nearest door handle and squired them inside. The moment he had her within the darkened library, he pushed the door closed and turned the lock.

Lust fired through him, and he continued his assault on her mouth. And with that inherent boldness she'd always possessed, Anwen nipped the tip of his tongue.

Incapable of anything more than an animalistic growl to show his approval, he reached between them and palmed her breasts.

That starched muslin fabric crunched noisily under his hands, in that wicked sound that only made him harder. Lowering the bodice of her gown, he released her, freeing that creamy white flesh for his worship.

"Phineas," she moaned into his mouth, then cried out softly when he ended the kiss.

He filled his hands with her bared breasts, and Anwen instantly stilled.

"Do you like that?" He knew she did.

When she remained silent, but for the shallow, ragged respirations of her breath, he flicked the pad of each thumb against each proud, pebbled peak of her breast.

"Hmm?" he urged.

"Y-yes," she whimpered.

"How much do you like it, Anwen?"

"Very much?"

He hovered his mouth over her chest. "Is that a question?"

Anwen moaned. "N-No. I love it."

"And what of this?" He darted his tongue out and teasingly tasted one of her pale pink nipples.

She whimpered. "A-Also love."

"And this?" He closed his mouth around that swollen peak and drew it deep.

"L-*Looove*," she rasped.

"I'll show you something you love even more, sweet." Phineas shoved up her muslin skirts. The scent of her desire flooded his nostrils, and a groan of hunger got trapped somewhere in his throat.

He sank to his knees, and then slowly began pushing her hemline further up.

"Wh-what are you doing?" she whispered.

He stopped with her skirts just mid-way up her bare legs and peered at her through hooded lashes. "Do you want me to stop?"

Because he would. If she breathed so much as a hint of hesitation, he'd end this. Even unscrupulous, contemptible bastard that he was, he could bring himself to stop. As much as it would nearly kill him, he'd never taken more than a woman was willing to give, and he'd sooner cut off his own hands than steal a thing from *this* woman.

With desire teeming in her chocolaty irises, she shook her head.

"Say it," he demanded, gripping her bare thighs.

"Please, don't stop," she implored.

It was all he needed. With another growl, Phineas shoved her gown up the remainder of the way.

Then, he caught her right ankle and guided her leg around his shoulder.

"Wh-what are you d—?" Her question ended on a noisy hiss as he parted her moist curls with his tongue.

She rocked her hips slowly, knocking the wall softly with every undulation of her hips.

Phineas paused and placed a kiss against her inner thigh. "Shh, love," he breathed. "Or you'll bring the household down on us. Or mayhap you'd like that?" he teased. "To have one of the big, strapping footmen discover you in this way, with me on my knees, feasting on you."

"N-No!" that denial exploded from her. *Too* quickly.

"You're sure?" he flicked his tongue over the swollen nub at her center. "I think you might like putting on a show, Anwen."

Another hungry little whimper escaped her lips.

"But I don't think I like the idea of sharing you," he whispered against her, startled motionless by the truth of that admission.

As on the heels of that came an image of Anwen and some other man—Benedict, the Earl of Wakefield, feasting on her the same way Phineas now did. Only, that man, a far better one than Phineas had ever been or would ever be, would have a claim to Anwen. One that was respectable, and one that marked her as belonging to him.

With a deep, bestial growl, he shoved back the gross and hateful image. In this moment, Anwen belonged to him and only him, and he'd have her in this way.

He slipped his tongue in her channel.

She promptly collapsed against the wall, against him, in his mouth, and he devoured her. He laved her. Drank her. Learned, and memorized the faint, earthy smell of her.

Anwen tangled her fingers in his hair and anchored him where she wanted him, and he all-too happily obliged her.

Then, drawing her nub between his lips, he sucked.

Anwen released a quiet, scandalous curse, and bucked. Only, he took her hips firmly, to prevent that unrestrained movement.

She moaned and thrashed against him.

She was close. So very close. He could tell by the jerkiness of her undulations and the rasps of her breath.

"I want you to come, love," he urged between each glide of his tongue. "I want you to flood my mouth with the taste of you. You'd like that, too, wouldn't you?"

She released an incoherent sound part-growl and part-sob.

Phineas gave another flick of his tongue. "Is that a 'yes'?" he teased. "Tell me you want to come."

He stopped, and she cried out softly.

Anwen pushed her hips against his mouth in a tell-tale quest to find relief. "Yes!" she rasped. "I want to come. Please."

"Good girl." With that, he rewarded her with what she yearned for.

Phineas plunged his tongue inside her and simultaneously teased her with his finger. Anwen stiffened, and then she was coming inside his mouth as he'd longed for her to do. She bucked and thrust against him, and this time he let her to those wild undulations, even as she thumped loudly against the wall.

And then, she collapsed, sated.

Phineas placed a lingering kiss upon the silken softness of her inner thigh. This was enough.

It had to be.

CHAPTER 10

The following morning, Phineas sat in his office and stared sightlessly over the top of a pen he'd balanced between his left and right index finger.

He'd been wrong yesterday.

Since he'd cleaned her with his kerchief, righted her skirts, and taken his leave of that library, he'd thought of Anwen and only Anwen: the mewling sounds she made when he'd sucked her. The downy softness of those dark curls between her legs. The unbridled passion she'd let herself feel…and show. Should he have expected anything different from the spirited minx?

And it was surely a mark upon his already black soul, that he'd not given a thought or a damn about his friendship to the lady's brother, then or now. With a groan, he tossed aside his pen. Ink splattered, as it sailed forgotten over the opposite side of the desk.

He'd thought one taste of her would be sufficient to get this hungering for Anwen Kearsley out of his blood.

Only, it hadn't.

"Yes…I want to come, Phineas. Please."

He'd had a taste of something so gloriously sweet and perfect that he'd now be left to forever starve like a hungry man set adrift in a desert.

When had he ever been selfless in matters of lovemaking? He'd brought all his partners to climax, but he'd also expected to have his lust slaked. That hadn't been the case with her. With Anwen, he'd not thought first of his own gratification. He'd cared only about bringing her surcease.

Granted, he'd left aching and been hard for her ever since—a need which, in the past, he'd have gone and assuaged himself with some wanton beauty. Now? Hell and damnation, he couldn't even think about bedding another.

In short, Anwen Kearsley had ruined him for all women.

Phineas dropped his head onto the desk and proceeded to knock his forehead slowly in a rhythmic beat against the smooth mahogany surface.

What had he done?

Suddenly, footsteps sounded in the hall. Two sets: one softer yet determined and accompanied by the tell-tale click of a cane. The other, the heavier ones of a butler struggling to keep up.

Phineas clenched his teeth. Splendid. Absolutely splendid. The final flourish to this godforsaken moment.

He stood, just as his aunt came bursting into the room. She gave him one swift, disapproving up-and-down look. "You look like hell," she said, by way of greeting.

From over her shoulder, his butler mouthed an apology, one that Phineas waved off.

The other man, who'd served the Lesar household since Phineas had been a boy, had proven far more loyal than any Lesar had ever deserved.

Smith drew the door closed, leaving Phineas alone with his godmother.

"Nothing to say to your aunt?" she asked, sweeping over with a grace and ease that belied her need for that serpent-headed cane.

"So good to see you, Aunt."

The duchess snorted and helped herself to a seat. She eyed Phineas as he stood there.

"Well, don't you intend to join me?"

"Do I have a choice?"

"No, which is why I suggest you sit."

The moment he'd reclaimed his chair, she continued to assess him. "You're rumpled, boy. Your eyes are bloodshot. Another late night, I gather."

He toasted her with the bottle of brandy that had sat forgotten at his side. "Another late night, indeed."

She grunted.

Good, let her think it was drink. That was better than confessing the truth—he'd been ensnared by an innocent lady whom he'd called friend through the years. *Stupid bastard.* Hadn't he always known ladies and gentlemen couldn't be friends? It couldn't work. It never did.

"I trust you're wondering why I'm here."

"No, I expect you're here to lecture me." And he'd deserve it. Along with a beating and a bullet through the chest from St. John.

"If I thought it would help, I would," she said. "Alas, I think it will take a good deal more to save you than any lecture I can give."

At least, he'd be spared that. "Instead of beating about the bush, why don't you tell me what it is you've come to say?" So that he could get back to pining in the misery of his own company.

"You've been playing with that Kearsley girl."

He froze.

"You don't deny it. Good. At least, there is something honest about you."

"I'm not *playing* with her," he said between tightly clenched teeth.

She scoffed. "You think I'm unaware of the games you're up to? Do you expect I believe you are actually courting St. John's white-haired sister?"

He frowned, and a healthy dose of annoyance snaked through him. "And tell me, just what is the problem with Miss Kearsley?"

"Not one that I can see. But if you'd been of that opinion, you'd have courted the gel any of the almost ten years she's been on the shelf, and not conveniently at a time when I'd laid out very specific terms about your bachelor state."

"It has nothing to do with you," he gritted out.

She latched onto that. "There is *something* at play then, because you certainly aren't marrying her."

No, he wasn't. "You don't know that."

The duchess released another snort. "I do." His far-too-astute godmother leaned forward. "Because if you *did* intend to marry her, you'd have done so during any one of the girl's eight seasons."

She sat back. "Though, it's generous for me to call her 'girl' given she's long in the tooth."

Fury turned his vision briefly black. "The lady is not old."

His aunt frowned. "Isn't she?"

"She's a good number of years younger than me."

"Ah," she held a finger up, "but women are held to different standards."

"Well, they shouldn't be, because she isn't old. She's perfectly young and vital and spirited and—"

His aunt gave him a funny look.

Phineas stopped talking.

"I know what you're up to with her," she said quietly.

Unsettled for a second time, Phineas went absolutely motionless. God help him, he didn't even know how to sort out what his relationship with Anwen Kearsley had become, and yet his aunt somehow had?

"And you needn't deny it," his godmother continued.

His pulse pounded. "What exactly am I denying?" *Only, you know.* His skin went hot, then cold, then hot again. *You know and have been fighting it tooth and nail. You know that somewhere along the way—*

"You started up a pretend courtship to put me off." His aunt's blunt pronouncement brought a swift death to those panicky musings.

She was close. Just not in the way she thought.

A sardonic grin twisted at his lips.

She thinned her eyes on him. "Do you find this amusing? Do you think I don't know what is going on between you and the eldest Miss Kearsley?"

When had everything gone all topsy-turvy for him where Anwen was concerned?

"And what is it you believe is going on?" he asked out of a genuine, desperate need to know.

She leaned forward again, in her seat. "You're thinking you can pretend to court the lady as you did those other women."

"I didn't pretend to court those women," he said tightly. Ironically,

Anwen had been the only one he'd only pretended to, and also the only one he truly wanted in his life. "I *did* court them."

"Only this one," she continued as if Phineas hadn't spoken, "will then go on to marry that far more reliable Wakefield boy who *is* seriously courting her. At which point, you'll come back to me once more, with your hands outstretched, and try and convince me you *really* intended to wed, this time."

So that was the conclusion she'd reached. *And why shouldn't she?* a voice in his head jeered.

Granted, he'd agreed to help Anwen snag a suitor, but that certainly hadn't been for Phineas' benefit, but no one would suspect that, because hell, when had he ever done something for anyone else?

Furthermore, when had Phineas Lesar, the Marquess of Landon, *ever* had his world turned upside down by a virtuous lady? Never, the answer was, never.

Until now, that was.

His aunt's assessment of his character shouldn't rankle, and yet it did.

The duchess crossed her arms. "Hmph."

"Hmph, *what?*"

"So, I'm right."

"Usually you are," he said. This, however, wasn't one of those instances. "But, it isn't like that."

"Where you're concerned, Phineas, it *is* always like that."

"I'm not shirking my duties."

"This time?"

"I didn't shirk them before, either," he gritted out.

His godmother scoffed again. "Don't tell me you truly attempted to find a bride before."

"I did. No one wants to marry me," he exclaimed. "And why should they? I'm a wastrel, a rake. I drink too much. I wager."

"You're also a charmer."

"A charmer? Charm only goes so far in courtships, dear aunt," he said bitterly. The many deficits in his character hadn't mattered before—until now.

Until Anwen.

He briefly closed his eyes.

His godmother looked him up and down. "Wallowing in self-pity doesn't suit you, my boy. Particularly when you have only yourself to blame for your current circumstances."

Her eyes were his mother's eyes and seeing the disgust in her gaze hurt as much as if it had been the late marchioness lecturing him.

"No," he said. Tiredly, Phineas slumped slightly in his chair. "You are right on that score."

And what was the real kick in the teeth? It hadn't mattered… until it had. Anwen had been standing there right beside him, all along. He could have worked to make himself a better man. He could have defied his father by not becoming him. Instead, he'd become *this*—a shallow, detestable fellow unworthy of so much as licking the soles of Anwen Kearsley's slippers.

And…in that instant, he stopped balking at the discovery he'd been so fighting.

I love her.

He always had.

And he always would. Even when she did precisely as his aunt predicted and went on to wed another, more worthy man. Phineas would be left wanting her from afar and hating with every fiber of his rotted being that another man had a right to touch her and love her and—

Suddenly, it became a chore to breathe around the vise that had a tight grip on his lungs and heart.

He felt the duchess's eyes on him and looked over to find her contemplating him in that unnerving, piercing way of hers.

"It is time to end whatever game it is you're playing with Miss Kearsley," she said quietly.

More bitterness crept in. "You have such a low opinion of me you think I'd dally with my best friend's sister?"

"You have earned such a reputation that I honestly cannot say what you're up to with her. What I do know is this: it is time for you to settle down." She shoved back her chair. "Find a bride, Phineas. Find a bride, get her to the altar, and marriage documents signed, and the funds are yours again." With that, she swept to her feet and left.

Phineas stared at the panel long after she'd quietly shut it behind her.

Find a bride.

How many times had he attempted that very feat? He'd gone about the task for the chore he'd seen it as. Having witnessed his parents' marriage, he'd not held onto any grand illusions of a loving union. Only to now want that very thing with Anwen… and be wholly unworthy and unable to take it.

And as he sat there in the quiet of his office, Phineas wished he'd been a better man before Anwen and not because of her.

Then, reaching for a sheet of paper and pen, he began to write.

CHAPTER 11

Anwen,
I'd request a private audience at dawn, in the North
Side of Hyde Park. The copse you used to sneak off to
and feed the swans.
P

THICK CLOUDS ADDED A LAYER to the London sky that the morning sun, when it came time to rise, would struggle to penetrate.

Seated on her family's carriage, with her maid quietly snoring on the opposite bench, Anwen smoothed her fingertips over the note she'd received last evening from Phineas, then dropped her chin in her hand.

He wanted to see her. So much so that he'd penned a letter and had one of his footmen pass it along to her lady's maid.

Butterflies danced in her belly. After yesterday's intimacies, honorable as Phineas was, he likely felt obligated to offer for her.

Anwen gently pressed the handle and let herself out.

Her driver immediately made to climb down, but she waved him off before he could quit his spot on that box. "I'm merely off to feed the swans," she said softly. Anwen displayed the small basket of bread she'd had the sense to pilfer from the kitchens to aid along in her ruse.

And then, with bated breath, she made her way through Hyde Park.

As she walked, a dense fog swirled around the empty walkways and riding paths usually bustling with lords and ladies; a thick white mist that leant an ominous air to the unnaturally quiet grounds.

Gooseflesh popped up on Anwen's arms, and she snuggled deeper into her cloak, in a bid to escape the chill which lingered from the night's recent hold. The grass still bore the hint of the early rain she'd listened to ping the windows in the wee hours while she'd been unable to sleep from thoughts of Phineas, and the memory of his touch.

She'd replayed every wickedly scandalous, magnificent kiss and caress until her body had grown flush, and an ache had formed between her legs, so much so, she'd been desperate enough to touch herself as he'd done—until she'd found some relief.

It hadn't succeeded in quieting those memories.

For the first time in all the time she'd known Phineas, she felt shy at the prospect of being with him. What did one say to a man who'd explored one's body in that most intimate of ways?

As Anwen crested the rise, she stopped and studied the wooded sanctuary in the near distance.

What do you think he intends to say to you? Do you truly believe he will profess his love?

Her heart kicked up a beat at the thought. And yet—she grimaced—Anwen was no starry-eyed debutante. She was a grown woman, with years enough of maturity to know a man such as Phineas didn't simply fall in love overnight, because of a stolen interlude behind a locked door.

Nay, more likely, he'd summoned her here out of more of that guilt.

Her stomach lurched. What if he…sought to propose to her out of a sense of pity and moral obligation?

Oh, God.

Moisture slicked her palms and for the first time since she'd snuck out to meet him, she felt a frisson of uncertainty. She cast a glance over her shoulder and contemplated the path she'd traveled—a path, long since devoured by the morning mist.

Stop this. You are not a coward, Anwen. You are a Kearsley.

With a strengthened resolve, she brought her shoulders back

and headed the remainder of the way to her meeting place with Phineas.

She made her way past a row of looming English oaks interspersed with London planes. Those trees stood like insentient guards over a sacred woodland. And the moment she stepped into the barren forest, she found him, with his back to her, and considering the smooth surface of the Serpentine.

How funny. All these years, she'd believed the memories of her time here with Phineas were ones that only she recalled. Only to receive a note from him just last night and in two sentences he'd revealed his own remembrances of times they'd spent together. She touched a hand to the letter in her pocket.

"You're here," he called, without looking over.

"Did you believe I wouldn't come?" Anwen set the basket she'd used as a decoy down on a small stump and ventured closer. Breathless, she stopped just beyond his shoulder. "Have you invited me to duel at dawn, my lord," she said teasingly.

And here, she'd worried she would not know how to be around him after the intimate things he'd done.

At last, he turned, and she waited for his like-bantering reply, when her gaze locked on the grim set to his features.

Unease traipsed along her spine. "What is it, Phineas?"

An ominous rumble filled the sky, and she brought her hands up and rubbed her arms through her cloak in a bid to erase the chill that had suddenly taken hold.

"I cannot see you anymore."

It was a moment before she registered, he'd truly spoken those words aloud.

Anwen rubbed her suddenly aching chest. "If this is because of yesterday—"

"It isn't," he said brusquely.

"Because if it is, you needn't worry," she finished anyway.

"It has nothing to do with what took place. I'm simply no longer able to help you."

It became apparent, he didn't intend to say anything more.

Anger reared its head. "That's it, Phineas? Just: I'm simply no longer able to help you?" She took an incensed step towards him. "There is nothing *simple* about that, my lord. You promised—"

"I know what I promised," he gritted out.

Anwen fumed. He was frustrated. He was?

"We had an agreement. You cannot just rescind your offer to help me."

"I have…obligations I must see to, Anwen."

"Which are more important than mine?"

"Yes. No." He dragged a hand through his tousled blond locks, and then let his arm fall to his side. "Anwen, this was a terrible idea."

"Trying to quit before the time you'd agreed to help me. I agree. Now," she held her fingers towards him. "Let's leave and forget—"

"Anwen, I'm in debt, on the edge of debtor's prison, and I've a responsibility to set my circumstances to right." He spoke with the finality of a man who knew the solution to his financial woes.

And she knew. Her heart thudded at a sickening beat.

"How does a gentleman go about setting his 'circumstances to right'?" she quietly asked.

How is my voice steady?

Phineas gave her a pitying look. "Come, Anwen. You know."

Yes, *he* knew that *she* knew. He knew because he knew so much about her, and she him. Anwen knew and didn't want to. She wanted to fasten her hands over her ears and block out the inevitable admission coming.

In the end, it became easier saying it herself than hearing him disclose his future.

"You're going to marry," she said softly.

There she'd said it. How had she said it? And more, how was she still standing after having done so?

"Yes." Phineas slid his gaze over the top of her head. "I'm going to wed."

A lone raindrop hit her nose.

Even the sky cried.

Phineas continued. "My aunt…she has been the gracious funder of my dissolute lifestyle. She's since tired of my rakish ways and decided to cut me off. She requires me to find a suitable bride by the end of the Season. Failure to do so will certainly land me in debtor's prison."

The wind tugged free several curls, and to give her trembling fingers a purpose, Anwen tucked them behind her ear.

"And…has she selected a bride for you?" Her question emerged thick to her own ears.

"Of a sort," he said wryly. "I'm permitted some freedom of choice."

Anwen waited. Foolishly, desperately, and pitiably wished, hoped, and prayed he'd say he'd already found that woman, and that woman was, in fact, Anwen.

Only, he didn't. Because of course, it wasn't. He possessed a list. She'd seen it with her own eyes and held it in her own hands.

She bit the inside of her cheek so hard a metallic hint of blood filled her mouth.

"And have *you* selected a bride yet, Phineas?"

His mouth twisted in a grimace. "I've not had the opportunity." His gaze caught and held hers.

It took a moment, and then, Phineas' meaning became glaringly clear. She fluttered her hands at her breast.

"Because of me," she whispered. "The time you've spent with me prevented you from seeing to your duties."

He gave a slight nod.

She braced, waiting once more. This time, for him to offer some kind of assurance that he'd enjoyed the time they'd shared.

Assurances, that never came.

Everything hurt. Absolutely every muscle in her body physically ached.

Anwen hugged herself in a desolate embrace. "I see."

Phineas stretched a hand out, to brush back those errant strands which had escaped once more. "And what exactly is it you see?" Phineas murmured.

"You are taking the easy way out."

The harsh plains of his face turned glacial, and he dropped his arm stiffly to his side. "I'm taking the *only* way out."

"Because of past decisions—"

"Yes, it is because of past decisions," he hissed. "Do you think I do not know? Do you think I don't realize I've made an absolute mess of my miserable life, and that I've no one to blame for my current circumstances but me?" His voice climbed to a shout, and a pair of birds, previously quiet and unseen until now, took flight from their perch in the oaks overhead.

She took a frantic step towards him. "But it doesn't have to be this way. You...you said yourself, Lord Wakefield's father left him in similar circumstances, and look what he did. He—"

"I am not Wakefield," he snarled.

"I know that," she said soothingly. "I'm not saying you are."

"He inherited and immediately set to work righting his circumstances. I continued wagering. I continued adding to that debt." Phineas slammed a fist against his chest. "*Me.*"

God, she was making a mess of this. But when she'd come here, of all the things she'd thought he might say, his ending their time together and marrying some other woman had not been it.

Anwen stretched up a shaking palm. "You don't have to enter into a loveless marriage."

"Actually, I do."

She stared at him. Another rumble from that distant storm filled the copse.

"Don't do this, Phineas."

"What *do* you advise I do?"

"Not this," she said, her voice growing frantic. "You can find a woman who...cares about you and not your situation."

A harsh laugh tore from his lips. "And tell me, where do I find such a paragon of a woman?"

"Here. Me," she said softly.

Phineas just stared at her.

Somehow, courage continued to grow inside of her, and she took another step closer. "You could marry me."

Anwen's heart pounded. Her mouth went suddenly dry. Where had that come from? More, where had she found the courage to say it?

He stared dumbly at her.

"You could wed me," she repeated.

"Are you asking me to marry you, Anwen?"

"I…" She drew back. "I believe I am." Then, it hit her. The wheels of her mind turned quickly, as did the words that fell from her lips. "You are in need of funds, and you will have them. And I? I'm on the shelf, Phineas, a spinster who is destined to die young."

"You're offering me an arranged marriage, then?"

She nodded. She loved him enough to have him any way she could.

His eyes darkened. "What of Wakefield?"

"I don't want the earl. I never did. You know that." She held a hand out toward him. "You could marry me," she said again. "We could marry each other."

Phineas flashed a sad, empty smile. "I could, but I wouldn't."

Hurt lashed at her already bruised heart, and she let her arm drop falteringly to her side.

"I see," she said, with as much steadiness and pride as she could manage.

"Do you?"

"I'm not the manner of woman a man like you would marry. You needn't have me spell out all my inadequacies, Phineas," she said, her voice catching, and she cursed herself for being so very weak for him in this moment.

His gloriously golden eyebrows went shooting up. "You think this is somehow about failings on your part?"

She paused. "It isn't?" she whispered.

"My God, Anwen, you do need me to spell it out. I'm a rotter. A rake. I inherited next to nothing, and squandered what I did have, away." He took a step closer and stretched a hand close to her cheek, but then, before he gifted her that touch she so craved, he let his arm fall back to his side. "You are in love with another, and yet you'd offer yourself to me in marriage."

And finally, she made herself—let herself—tell him the truth.

"It is you, Phineas," she said, and that tranquil admission…lifted a weight she'd long carried and left her free. "It was always you."

He stared blankly at her and then shook his head.

Anwen nodded.

The blood gradually drained from his cheeks.

She nodded once more. "It was always you, Phineas."

The sound of her voice seemed to snap him from his mute state.

With a gasp, Phineas stumbled and staggered back; in his haste to get away from her, he tripped and then righted himself. "No. You are just saying that." His eyes, crazed as she'd never seen them, darted about the forest.

"I've loved you forever," she murmured, approaching him the way she had the injured doe she and Cora had discovered years earlier.

Phineas dragged an unsteady hand through those loose golden curls. "You are St. John's sister."

With all those reasons he'd given, she could only think of the one he'd not: 'I don't care for you'. That, he'd not said. So perhaps... Like a flicker of fire, hope, sputtered to life in her breast.

"You are my brother's best friend, Phineas," she said quietly.

Color splotched his cheeks. "Precisely."

"And you somehow think a man my brother finds worthy enough to be his best friend to also be unworthy of his sister?"

"Absolutely I believe that," he said without hesitation. "The men we keep company with, aren't the men we want to see our sisters marry."

"You don't have a sister."

"If I did, I can say definitively I wouldn't want her to marry me."

"I should hope," she said in a bid for levity. "She would, after all, be your sister."

The Phineas she'd grown up with and loved would have burst out laughing. She didn't recognize the distant stranger before her, and that proved even scarier than laying herself bare as she now did.

"Phineas, I lo—"

"Don't," he rasped sharply. "Do *not*," he repeated and held a staying hand up.

"Me not saying it doesn't make it untrue," she moved closer to him.

He backed away.

Anwen stopped, allowing him to have the space he needed. Still, he continued retreating, and she'd wager he'd have walked himself all the way back into the Serpentine if his rearward path weren't cut short by a noble oak behind him.

"You don't know what you're saying."

"Phineas," she said tenderly. "Of course, I do. I asked you to spend these past days with me, I let you believe there was another, but it was you—"

He clamped his hands over his ears.

Anwen caught his palms in hers and forced them back to his side. "I wanted to spend time with you and dance with you. I—"

"You're merely confusing lovemaking for something more."

"*I love you*," she finally managed to get all the words out through his objections. "I've loved you nearly all of my life."

The branches overhead swayed and set the leaves to dancing.

She waited.

And continued waiting. For words that did not come. But for that faintest rustle, there came not a hint of sound, and from that abrupt and profound silence, Anwen's declaration lingered, awkwardly and unreturned.

Determined to have some response from him, she approached him. "I have loved you since—"

"No!" he exclaimed.

She finished anyway. "I was sixteen. You joined me in that game of hide and seek I was determined to win and climbed the tree to help me up. We both went tumbling. I landed on you."

A panicky glint lit his eyes. "I don't even remember that day."

"Yes, you do," she said with absolute confidence.

He blanched, and then his features smoothed into that hard, unforgiving mask he'd arrived with. "You think you know, do you? You presume much, Miss Kearsley."

"I know you call me 'Miss Kearsley' when you're cross or scared—"

"I'm not scared," he hissed.

"And that you *behave* cross when you *are* scared."

Phineas went tight-lipped.

"You think you're somehow unworthy."

"You think that's what this is about?" he demanded. "You believe I'm rejecting your feelings because I'm some upstanding, principled man? My, that is presumptuous of you, *Anwen.*" He burst out laughing in an empty expression of cold, condescending mirth, and her previous confidence wilted.

"Why are you behaving this way?"

"And what way is that, Anwen?" he asked, almost jeeringly. "Do tell me."

That unexpected frostiness somehow steadied her.

"Like you're a stranger," she said flatly. "You're behaving like *we* are strangers. I don't like you this way, Phineas."

"What way?"

"Mocking and harsh. It doesn't suit you."

"*This*," Phineas dragged both hands up and down before him, "is who I am."

"No, it's not. Your father poisoned you into thinking you were the same as he, but you aren't. You are good and decent and kind and—"

His harsh laugh cut across her list of praise. "Ah, right, of course." He stuck a foot out. "Because I'm an honorable fellow." Phineas gave her a hot look. "Tell me, would an honorable man eat your muff in your family's library?"

Anwen winced. How was it possible for him to turn something magical into something so crude? Only...

She inhaled slowly through her nose. "I know what you are doing." And it wouldn't work.

He took an angry step towards her. "What exactly is that, Miss Kearsley?"

"You're trying to turn me away. To make me hate you." Anwen stretched a beseeching hand out. "I know you're afraid, Phineas. You think we cannot be together *because* I'm Clayton's sister. But I know you care about me."

His harsh, ugly laugh cut her off. "You make more of my attentions than there is. I've had any number of women. Do you think making love with you was somehow different?"

Had he knifed her open at her chest, it couldn't have hurt more.

"Why are you doing this, Phineas? What we've shared, isn't something that can be faked."

"Couldn't it?" That frosty question brought her up short.

Anwen stared at him.

"The only reason I agreed to help you is because your brother asked it of me."

The wind gusted in a forlorn little cry; it sent leaves and brush kicking up about her skirts. She hugged her arms tight around her waist. "I don't believe you."

He looked down his hard, aquiline nose at Anwen, and never had she felt so small.

"You needn't have wasted your time visiting my rooms at the Albany that night, Anwen. St. John met with me before he departed for London and requested that I look after you in his absence. I'd already taken on the responsibility of watching after you."

Watching after her. As if she were a child. And perhaps with her naivete and innocence and trust, she'd been no different than.

"Though, I expect, me shoving your skirts about your waist wasn't *quite* what he had in mind." Phineas lifted one broad shoulder in an unapologetic shrug. "But then, what can one expect of a rake?"

Anwen flinched. "You *are* trying to make me hate you," she whispered.

He gave her a pitying look, and this? This proved somehow worse than his mocking condescension.

"See, that is what you haven't ever understood, Anwen. I've never tried to make you feel one way or another about me. I've only ever been myself—including now."

It began to rain. Alas, numbness wrought by hurt proved a barrier against even the cold.

Phineas grunted and started back over. "Come," he said. "I'd see you home."

"You'll see me home?" she echoed. A half-mad laugh bubbled past her lips. He'd rebuffed her. Rejected her love, scoffed at the idea of a future with her, and would *now* offer to escort her home?

"Why, because I'm Clayton's sister?" she asked, embittered.

"Yes, because you are Clayton's sister."

That's all she'd ever been to him. And the tiny, splintered pieces of her heart tinkled about like shattered glass; that battered organ falling from her chest to her toes, until an empty hole existed in the place it once occupied.

Tears pricked her lashes, and she blinked furiously. If even one fell, she'd dissolve into a puddle upon this beaten path.

"You are worthy, and good and honorable," Anwen said thickly, "and someday, *someday* you will find a woman, and she will help you see the good in you, and you will love her." He would love her as he'd never loved or been capable of loving Anwen. "And I want that for you." No matter how much he'd hurt her.

Through her blurred vision, she thought she saw his features spasm. "Now, please," she said when she trusted herself to again speak. "Leave."

Phineas bowed his head. "Of course."

He hesitated.

Please, she silently implored. Tell me you didn't mean it. Tell me you're only seeking to drive me away because you're scared of feeling. Hope flared to life in her breast.

Only, he didn't. Without so much as a goodbye, he walked from the copse, until she stood there alone.

And at last, she lost the fight to hold herself together. She let her shoulders sag, and then clamping her hands over her face, she wept. She wept for what she'd always wanted, and what she'd never have. She wept for the circumstances Phineas had gotten himself into. And she wept until her chest ached and her body hurt at the realization she'd never be enough for him.

It hurt. It hurt so very much. She would never, ever be the same.

There came a flash of lightning, a violent rumble of thunder, and then the telltale crack of a tree that had been struck.

Anwen looked up, and all the broken pieces of her heart dropped. *Oh, hell.*

She opened her mouth to scream, the same moment the severed tree branch slammed into her forehead.

Pain exploded in her skull, and as blackness filled her vision and the weight of the blow knocked her face-forward on the muddy, earthen floor, Anwen remembered no more.

CHAPTER 12

PHINEAS FLED.

And he kept on running, not breaking stride. His horse. He needed his horse. Only every step he placed between himself, and Anwen didn't erase her quiet profession.

I love you…

Phineas quickened his pace. He'd made himself finally come to terms with his feelings for her. This, however? *Her* loving *him*? That was different. Women didn't love him. At least, aside from his late mother, who, God rest her soul, hadn't seen the rotter Phineas had become; and his aunt, who'd proven more tolerant than he deserved.

But ladies? Respectable ones or scandalous ones? They didn't truly care about Phineas. They loved the pleasure he brought them, or the good time they had in his company. But one couldn't love a shell of a man, and that was what he was, and had always been to the world.

Only, Anwen was different. She'd known him all his life. She'd known the man he'd briefly been, and the one he'd ultimately become.

And she loves you, anyway.

Nay. She didn't. She couldn't.

And yet…his steps slowed, as the memory of how he'd left her standing there took hold and refused to let go.

Phineas stopped.

He'd fallen in love. He thought, mayhap, he'd always loved her.

His throat worked painfully, and he squeezed his eyes shut. He'd absolutely nothing to offer her. He was a bounder and a rake, and St. John's best friend. But he wanted her anyway. It was a mark of his selfishness. He—

A shrill cry pierced through the tempest raging around him, and Phineas jolted to a stop so quickly the slick earth slipped out from under his feet.

Heart hammering, he righted himself and turned toward the place from where that cry had come.

A surge of relief attempted to calm the panicked beat of that organ in his chest. It hadn't been Anwen's cry. He knew Anwen's cry. He'd heard it any number of times over the years: when St. John had pushed her off a swing and into the lake at their family estate. And the mournful wail she'd emitted when her father died.

It isn't her. It isn't her.

But that also meant another woman required help.

Cursing, Phineas sprang into movement. He set off at an all-out run.

A moment later, a young woman came crashing through the woods from which Phineas had just left. Waving her arms wildly, the girl screamed and sobbed.

Oh, God. His stomach dropped. Anwen's maid.

Phineas lengthened his strides.

"M-My lord," the girl rasped, the moment he intercepted her. "L-lightning…" She gesticulated wildly as she attempted to speak through her sobbing.

Lightning? Terror burned the back of his throat and threatened to choke him.

A buzzing filled his ears.

"*…She told me my end was near. There will be a great storm, and a tree and lightning…And I'm not certain how, but during a great tempest, I'll be struck down…*"

"A tree…" the girl sobbed.

He didn't hear the rest of that. He didn't want to hear the rest of that.

"Anwen!" he thundered. As he charged into the copse, his gaze automatically went to that spot he'd left her moments ago. Then, she'd been standing, and looking back at him with the most stricken eyes, and—

And then, he found her. Exactly where she'd last been standing. Only, now, she lay sprawled, face-down in the mud, unmoving.

His breath came harsh and hard; each intake and exhale an agonizing chore for his lungs.

Phineas staggered to a halt beside her prone form. A three-inch-thick branch lay, a barrier over her. He yanked that deadened piece off, tossed it aside, and sank to his knees beside her.

"Anwen," he rasped and turned her over.

She was still. So still. She'd never been still. She'd only ever been vibrant and animated.

He slipped a hand under her back, and her head fell limply.
Dead. She is dead.

The curse.

'I'm on the shelf, Phineas, a spinster who is destined to die young...'
All her past revelations rolled together. *'There will be a great storm, and a tree and lightning...'*

"Nooo," he groaned. She couldn't be dead. Because if she was, then his own heart would surely have ceased to function, too. For she was the only reason that organ beat in his body.

Her. It is for her.

"Please, don't be," he rasped, as he brought shaking hands up, and searched for a pulse.

And then he felt it: faint and slow, but still the smallest of thumps indicating she still lived.

For now...

Forcibly thrusting back the Devil whispering in his ear, Phineas scooped her up. He adjusted her head against his shoulder to keep it from falling forward at that awkward angle, and then, this time, with Anwen in his arms, he took off running.

I shouldn't have left you...I shouldn't have lied to you...I should have told you precisely how I feel. How much I love you. How much it will kill me to lose you...

A strangled sob exploded from Phineas; that sound of his misery swallowed by another clap of thunder.

The moment he broke through the clearing, he kept on flying

toward the place he'd left his mount. Lucky pawed nervously at the ground.

"Shh, boy," he said.

Phineas lay Anwen gently over the front of his horse, and then hurriedly climbed up behind her. The moment he'd properly seated himself, Phineas drew Anwen into his arms, collected the reins, and set Lucky off into an all-out gallop.

The skies opened up in a deluge that blurred his vision, blinded him. Those drops fell faster and harder. And then, he realized: *Me. It is me weeping.* It was his tears that left the world blurred before him.

The last time he'd cried had been when the marquess had sent Phineas's mother away. That day, he'd wept until his soul hurt, and he vowed then, he'd never cry again. He'd never open himself up to being hurt by caring about anyone or anything beyond his own pleasures. Whoring and wagering didn't wound a man's soul. Not as loss and love did.

Now, to realize, he'd not kept himself insulated inside and safe the way he thought he had. Because he loved Anwen. He may have loved her forever. He'd just not let himself see her in that light because to do so would have meant opening himself to more of that agonizing pain.

On and on his thoughts clattered as fast as Lucky's pounding hooves. Until at long last, they arrived at her family's residence. A dutiful footman came rushing through the front doors and down to meet him.

"Hurry! She's hurt!" Phineas handed Anwen into the other man's arms, then jumped down.

As soon as Phineas' feet hit the earth, he snatched Anwen back, and, holding her close, he raced up the steps. He stormed the foyer, leaving a trail of water in his wake.

"Dunster?" The dowager viscount's voice sounded overhead. "What is the commot—" Her query ended on a sharp gasp, as her gaze locked with Phineas'.

"There was an accident," he rasped. "Lightening. A tree…it shattered, and—"

The always graceful lady now staggered on the steps, but she caught a hand on the railing, managing to keep herself upright.

She emitted a plaintive wail and then yanked at her hair. "She's dead?"

He spoke at the same time as the dowager viscountess. "She lives." *For now,* the devil jeered Phineas once more for his faith.

His words seemed to moor Anwen's mother. The color returned to the dowager viscountess's cheeks, and her movements measured, and her voice no-nonsense. "Fetch Dr. Carlson!"

Somewhere behind Phineas, a servant emerged from the shadows and took off running out the front door.

"Follow me," she ordered, and something in her firm, steady voice managed to calm him. The dowager marchioness led him through the doors of a bedroom. *Anwen's room.* Had he ever taken a moment to think about where she rested her head each night, the vision he drew up would have been…this; adorned in the colors of seawaters and summer skies.

A George III lady's mahogany writing desk nearly filled at every corner with unevenly stacked books and a lone leather journal. A painting of the late viscount's favorite foxhounds, Romeo and Juliet, so named by Dalia, hung in a frame near her bed.

A memory whispered forward, of him and Anwen, the first to arise one summer sat alone at the breakfast table.

Anwen handed a piece of bacon each to Romeo and Juliet. "Will you have dogs one day, Phineas?"

"I've never been much of the dog sort."

"You must. They're loyal friends, and you deserve a loyal friend."

"What of you, Wynbug? Can I not consider you a loyal friend?"

"Here." He glanced up dumbly, at where the dowager viscountess stood alongside the bed.

She gestured his way, and Phineas came jolting to the present. He lay her gently down upon the corner of the mattress indicated by the dowager viscountess. The moment he set Anwen down, he was rushed from the room by a bevy of servants who swarmed Anwen and her mother.

He staggered out, into the hall, and then, there was only silence. Silence and the muted exchange taking place on the other side of that panel.

All the life went out of him. Phineas sank to his haunches and brought his hands together, clasping his fingertips at his face.

She would live.

She had to.

A lady didn't go from being vibrant and lively and spirited, to… His mind balked; for he couldn't finish the thought. Because there was no world worth living in with Anwen Kearsley not in it.

And yet, she'd given him her love, and how had he responded? With disdain. He'd rebuffed her profession, and instead let her believe she'd been a chore he'd taken on because of an agreement he'd made with her brother.

His jeering words and icy tone possibly the last ones she ever heard.

A piteous moan spilled from his lips, and restless, he yanked his fingers through his soaking hair. The rain remnants pinged the pretty blue carpet under his feet.

Plink. Plink.

Anwen's room was so…quiet. Not even the muted conversation of those on the inside could be heard. He squeezed his eyes shut. Surely that proved promising. If she…if…the worst had happened, there'd be wails and screams. The silence, however, left a blank place for his mind to replay every ugly, hateful, hurtful word he'd hurled at Anwen.

"You make more of my attentions than there is. I've had any number of women. Do you think making love with you was somehow different?"

He clamped his hands over his ears to blot out the echo of their voices and the memory of her anguished expression. But they penetrated through that flimsy barrier, and he deserved to have his soul sluiced open with each revolting lie that had left his lips in that copse.

"Tell me, would an honorable man eat your muff in your family's library?"

"You needn't have wasted your time visiting my rooms at the Albany that night. St. John met with me before he departed for London and asked that I look after you in his absence. I'd already taken on the responsibility of watching after you."

"Though, I expect, me shoving your skirts about your waist wasn't quite what he had in mind. But then, what can one expect of a rake?"

"It was the thunder, wasn't it?"

That muffled question brought Phineas' eyes flying open. He blinked slowly, and then let his arms fall to his side.

"Eris," he greeted dumbly.

In her oversized white nightshift, she shifted on her still bare feet. Her usually sunny smile had been slayed by the storm that now darkened this household. Her enormous eyes filled with so much grief, too much grief for a small girl, that it ripped apart his already broken heart.

"She's dead."

"No!" That denial ripped from Phineas, and he forced himself to take a calming breath. When he spoke, he did so with a collectedness from he knew not where. "No. She is not dead."

She will not die. She will not die. She will not.

Hope lit her small, delicate features. He patted the spot beside him, and Eris instantly joined him on the floor. She rested her little head against his shoulder. "But she will die," she whispered, her voice trembling.

"She won't," he stated emphatically, willing it into existence.

"Madam Pomfret *said* she would."

Phineas stared down at her brown curls, quizzically. "Madam Pomfret?" He didn't know the lady but hated her for having given life to the thought of Anwen's end.

"Mama's fortune-teller. She said thunder would take Anwen. I shouldn't have let her go outside, but I never saw the curse kill someone. Papa died when I was a babe, and so I didn't believe it, and—"

"And *don't* believe it."

"But Madam Pomfret said thunder."

"Madam Pomfret can go straight to hell," he said harshly, *too* harshly.

Phineas dragged an uneven hand through his still-damp curls. "My apologies."

Eris smiled the first smile he'd seen of her since the world had gone dark. "That's all right. I like that you cursed about Madam Pomfret."

There came the thundering of footfalls, and they both looked up. The butler, along with an entirely too young doctor, came tearing down the hall.

Phineas leapt to his feet. *This* is who they'd called for? The man couldn't be many more years older than Phineas.

"You seem too young to be a doctor," Phineas snarled, ready to order the Kearsley butler to find the oldest, most experienced fellow in the whole of London.

As unperturbed as if they were two men speaking over brandies, the bespectacled fellow inclined his head. "Would you prefer they send for an older one who would only bleed the patient without actually treating her, and in so doing, leave her weaker?" The doctor didn't bother waiting for an answer. He rapped once.

"Enter," Anwen's mother called.

The doctor opened the panel, and let himself in.

Phineas managed to catch a glimpse of Anwen and her chambers. Her wet garments lay strewn about the room; that same dress and chemise and slippers she'd worn when she'd professed her love, now set in the same tatters as his aching heart.

In the center of her bed, Anwen, with a coverlet drawn up to her chin, now lay still and silent and so very pale. His throat worked painfully. *She's so lifeless.* In all the years he'd known her, she'd been vibrant and thrumming with vitality. She'd been—

One of the maids pushed the panel closed, cutting Phineas off from the scene playing out within those bedchambers. A light tug on his trousers brought Phineas' blank gaze downward.

"Is she–?"

"No," he cut Eris off from speaking that question aloud.

They sat with the silence for a moment. All the while, Phineas strained to pick up anything from the muted exchange taking place on the other side of that door.

"I shouldn't have let her go," Eris said softly.

He glanced down at the little girl's tousled brown curls. They were Anwen's strands.

"Anwen," Eris clarified, mistaking the reason for his silent study of her. "She said it would be a storm, and I should have believed the curse and never let her go anywhere when it rained."

And I shouldn't have left her. The young girl's blame was misplaced. Phineas was the only one at fault for Anwen's circumstances. His chest ached. Nay, every part and piece of his soul ached.

"Given we reside in rainy old England, you would have had to keep her indoors forever," he said solemnly.

Eris edged back a fraction and passed her gaze over his face. Her lips twitched up at the corners. "You're making a jest."

"I'm telling the truth. I'm not sure if you're aware but one can count on one hand the sunny days in this kingdom we call home."

Her smile widened. "You're trying to make me feel better."

"Yes," he allowed. Phineas tweaked her nose. "But I'm also telling the truth."

She giggled.

"There you are."

They looked up. Brenna, the second eldest Kearsley sister, smiled gently at Eris. That smile, however, looked forced and strained.

"I've been looking for you," Brenna said. She'd stepped in to fill a role Anwen had always assumed, and Anwen's absence here hit him so keenly, that he wanted to toss his head back and wail.

"I've been here, with Phineas."

Brenna briefly shifted her focus to Phineas, then she turned it back to the younger girl. "I see that. But Cora, Daria, Delia, and I have been searching for you."

Eris set her chin at a defiant little angle. "I'm not leaving."

Brenna gave a small shrug. "That is unfortunate. We were drawing pictures for when Anwen wakes up."

Eris hesitated. "What are you drawing?"

"Cora had the idea we paint and sketch images of Mama's newly planted carnations. There's such an array of colors, she thought it would be a—"

"A terrible idea!" Eris exclaimed. "A terrible idea is what it is."

Brenna frowned. "Well, do you have a better i—"

"Roses. We must make drawings of *roses. Everyone* knows roses are Anwen's favorite."

Phineas hadn't. But he wanted to discover those unknown pieces that collectively joined to make Anwen, *Anwen.*

Brenna stretched out a hand, where the little girl immediately placed her smaller palm.

"I must go, Phineas," Eris said. "There's pictures to be drawn." She paused. "Unless you'd rather I stay and keep you company? Or you can join us?"

He shook his head. "I'd spare her that. Any drawings I made for Anwen would surely make the lady weep when she awakes."

If she awakes, the devil taunted him once more.

Eris giggled and allowed her older sister to usher her off.

Over the top of Eris's head, Brenna mouthed a silent, 'thank you'.

He waved off her thanks—that *undeserved* thanks. Were the Kearsleys to know he was the reason Anwen now lay in that bed, they'd certainly feel a good deal less magnanimity for him.

After the girls had slipped off, Phineas rested the back of his head against the wall. He couldn't have her. He didn't deserve her. Mayhap that was why he'd never let himself truly see her. Mayhap because, somewhere deep inside, he'd known she was untouchable. His own failings and his connection to her brother put her forever outside of his reach.

Time stretched eternal.

Suddenly, the door opened, and hope brought Phineas flying to his feet.

Anwen's mother looked at him with sad eyes, and she shook her head. "She is still…asleep."

"Asleep," he repeated dumbly.

The dowager viscountess nodded.

Except, this state Anwen now dwelled in, was no *slumber.* For sleep implied a natural state one went into and then came out of.

She pressed a fist against her mouth. "I…the doctor cannot say if or when she will awake. The branch that hit her left a sizeable lump, and he explained head injuries vary so greatly, and there is no saying for sure, and the only thing to be done…"

What? he silently screamed. *Tell me and I'll do it this instant.* He'd *stand on his head, sell his soul, snatch a star from the sky. Anything, if it meant she lived.*

"Yes?" he begged.

Lady St. John took in a shaky breath. "The only thing to do, is wait."

"Wait."

She nodded. Wait for Anwen to either wake up, or stop breathing, or…never wake up.

A pained groan swelled in his chest and climbed his throat; grief that demanded to be set free.

"None of that, Phineas," the dowager viscountess chided.

Phineas dragged his hands over his face, and then let his arms fall to his side. "Tell me what to do," he implored. *Give me some purpose or I will go mad.*

"I know Clayton's babe is just born, but, if…" The dowager viscountess stopped talking, but she needn't have finished. Her meaning was clear. If Anwen died, and Clayton hadn't been brought to her side, he'd never forgive himself or any of them.

"Will you get her brother?"

"Of course." St. John needed to be here. He needed to be told what had happened to Anwen, and that information should come, not from a servant, but from a best friend—a best friend now responsible for the state Anwen found herself.

Shoving aside thoughts of guilt, Phineas bowed his head. "I'll leave immediately."

With that, he went racing a second time that day.

This time to fetch Anwen's brother.

CHAPTER 13

ANWEN WAS DYING.

There was no other accounting for the jagged pain hammering away at the back of her skull; a throbbing so miserable, she'd have moaned if doing so wouldn't have caused her further misery.

There'd only been one time where she'd felt anything close to this degree of suffering. Some years earlier, she, Brenna, and Cora had been determined to enjoy the same pleasures as their brother and other gentlemen who visited their respectable clubs. They'd snuck into Clayton's office, pilfered a bottle of whiskey and a decanter of brandy from his liquor cabinet, then headed to the billiards room, where they'd sat around the table smoking cheroots and drinking liquor, and playing cards.

The following morning, they'd paid the price for their sins, and they'd paid *tenfold*. It'd been enough for Anwen and her sisters to declare men mad for drinking as they did, and forever swear off spirits.

Only, this time, Anwen hadn't been overindulging in brandy. Her lashes, like that long-ago day, felt the same heaviness. It was as if they'd been weighted down. Still, she forced them open a fraction. An inky darkness enveloped the room, and she blinked slowly to orient herself to her surroundings. The slight crack in the curtains revealed a hint of the night sky and her room.

She struggled to push back the cobwebs in her brain which continued to pulse.

Anwen touched a hand to the spot which seemed the source of the pounding; her fingers collided with an enormous lump.

What in blazes? What had happened…?

And then, it came rushing back to her.

Hyde Park.

The storm.

The lightning strike.

Phineas…and his rejection.

"You make more of my attentions than there is. I've had any number of women. Do you think making love with you was somehow different…?"

This time a new wave of hurt came up to meet her; this one fierce and wrenching. And she didn't want to remember. She wanted to close her eyes and fade back into the oblivion of before, but now that the pain had found purchase inside, it held her in its vise and would not let go.

Perhaps death would have been a preferable fate. In death, a person surely didn't feel the agony of a broken heart and bruised head.

A light snore penetrated her self-misery, and she forced her eyes open once more. With an agonizing effort, she angled her head. A tall, broad, figure sat slumped in the chair next to her.

Anwen's heart jumped, and then promptly fell as she registered the identity of that noisily slumbering figure.

"Clayton," she whispered. Her brother.

Who did you expect would be here next to you? Did you truly think after everything Phineas said, and every hateful, hurtful truths he'd hurled your way, that he would have taken up a place beside you?

Of course, it made sense that he wouldn't be here, but that didn't stop her foolish heart from wishing it was him. Tears pricked her lashes, and she pulled the edge of the woven linen sheet up and wiped the moisture from her cheeks.

When she lowered the sheet back to her chin, her gaze collided with Clayton's. His eyes, now open, were bleary and bloodshot as if he'd been the one crying.

"Anwen," he whispered. "You're awake!"

"Should I not be?" Even as the effort proved an excruciating chore for the muscles of her face, Anwen made herself force a smile for her brother's benefit.

His big Adam's apple moved wildly. "No," he said, his voice thick with emotion. "You very much should be."

Anwen looked at her brother. A beard covered his usually clean-shaven cheeks. At some point, he'd discarded his jacket and yanked his now heavily wrinkled shirtsleeves from the waist of his dusty trousers.

Clayton scrambled so quickly from his chair the upholstered piece went flying backward; it toppled noisily upon the floor. He fell to his knees next to her bed and joined their hands.

"Anwen," he whispered, his voice breaking.

"You...look like hell," she said, her own voice weak and hoarse to her ears. "I...hope I look better than you."

Then, Clayton began to laugh. "You look perfect, Anwen. So very perfect," he said, between great gasping breaths and, lowering his forehead on the mattress next to her, Clayton wept.

Panicky desperation built within her. Never, not when Papa or Clayton's dear friend, the Earl of Norfolk died, had she seen her brother shed a tear. At least, never in front of her. Even then, during those most awful of times, he'd managed to be in control of his emotions.

Not now. In this instant, he, the big brother who when Anwen had been a girl, had always dusted the tears from her cheeks and chased away her sadness with a smile, now wept while she searched for ways to comfort him.

"Shh," she urged, the throbbing at the base of her skull and back of her head an afterthought.

Still, her big brother only sobbed all the harder. "I-I th-thought... I-I th-thought..."

"Please, don't cry," she pleaded, in vain.

"I thought you were going to die," he finished between great, gasping breaths. "The curse."

"But I didn't die." That managed to penetrate her brother's well of emotion.

"No," Clayton said hoarsely. "You are alive."

Funny that. She lived, even with her heart having been broken into a thousand million shards that could never be pieced back together.

"I'm alive," she made herself say for her brother's benefit.

Only, Madam Pomfret hadn't been altogether wrong. While that storm raged, just as the fortune-teller predicted, Anwen had died a death, just one different than the physical one people thought of, and quite different than the one Anwen had previously fretted over.

The anguish of Phineas' rejection hit her as hard as it had the moment he'd lashed out at her in Hyde Park. Her body hurt all the way to her very soul. Tears filled her eyes, and she blinked to keep them from dropping. But, not unlike her efforts to make Phineas fall in love with her, her attempts at stopping those crystalline beads from falling, proved futile.

"Anwen," Clayton rasped. "I'll get the doctor." Dragging a hand through his unkempt blondish hair, Anwen's brother flew to his feet and took off towards the door.

"No," she called, her weak voice managed to reach him.

Clayton faltered, then staggered to a stop. He whipped around, facing Anwen once more. "No?"

"I'm…I-I don't want to see the doctor. Not yet."

"Anwen," he gently protested. "You're in pain. You're crying. Let me fetch Dr. Carlson. I had him put up in the rooms next door. I'll be just a moment." He made a move toward the door.

"No! I'm fine," she assured Clayton. It was the biggest lie she'd ever uttered. Which, considering she'd shamelessly and furtively snuck a courtship out of Phineas, was saying a good deal, indeed.

Clayton hesitated. His gaze vacillated between Anwen and the door, then surprisingly, but welcomingly, he heeded her request. Instead of leaving, however, and granting her a much-longed-for moment to be alone with herself in her sadness, Clayton returned. He righted the upended chair and then reclaimed his previous seat beside her. Joining his fingers together, Clayton considered her over the tops of them.

Unnerved by that penetrative gaze he kept on her, Anwen fiddled with her blankets.

"How long have I been asleep?" she asked.

"Eight days."

Shock brought Anwen's eyebrows shooting up. That quick muscle movement taxed her still aching head, and she promptly winced.

"Eight days?" she echoed dumbly.

He nodded. "The doctor warned us that if you'd not awakened after seven, that it was…that you…" Clayton took a long, slow breath. "It was unlikely you'd awaken."

"And today is day eight," she murmured.

He nodded. "You defied the odds." Her brother placed his hand over hers. "But then, we Kearsleys are defiant like that, aren't we?"

Anwen looked around at the dark room. "You've been here this whole time." He'd a family of his own. A new babe. Guilt instantly took root where pain and heartache had previously dwelled. "You had to leave Sylvia and the ba—"

"Wyndham and Sylvia are doing splendid."

Wyndham. Wryness brought her lips tipping up at the corners. "It appears my new nephew and I share the whole stormy connection."

"Indeed." Clayton grinned. "Granted, I'm now worrying Sylvia and I may have portended a future for the little fellow. But for now, he's resting and tiny, and so I'll save those worries for another morrow."

Her brother sat back in his chair. "I've not been the only one here the whole time. Me, Mother, Cora, and Brenna have all taken turns sitting next to you." He paused. "And Landon has been stationed outside your rooms."

Landon. "How… Why?"

Misunderstanding that incomplete, and incoherent musing, her brother elucidated. "It is my understanding, after you were injured, your maid found Landon in the park, and the marquess carried you back home. Afterward, at Mother's behest, he raced to inform me of your injury and continued on with me to London, where he's remained. He's here, even now."

"*Here?*"

Clayton clarified. "Yes. Just on the other side of the door, to be exact."

Her heart thumped wildly. She struggled up onto her elbows. "Phineas is here?" she whispered.

Clayton sharpened his eyes on her face. "I referred to him as Landon, but, yes, one and the same."

Of its own volition, Anwen's gaze slipped back toward the door. *He's here even now.* He'd been stationed outside of her rooms for *eight days?*

Why? Why, if he didn't care, even in some...The minute the desperate thought grew, it withered on the vine of reality. Exhausted from the exertion of propping herself up, Anwen collapsed back into her mattress.

Guilt.

He'd been clear that his loyalty lay with Clayton. That is and was all Anwen had ever been to Phineas: Clayton's younger sister. He'd promised Clayton he'd watch over and after Anwen in his absence.

All the while, she'd snuck into his private suites at the Albany and put her own request to him, Phineas had agreed, not because of his relationship with her, but instead because of the meeting he'd had before with her *brother.*

Anwen cringed. *What a fool. What an absolute wretched, pathetic fool, I am.*

"Anwen?" Clayton's questioning voice slashed into her melancholy.

She glanced over to find her brother scrutinizing her through narrowed eyes. "Aside from your accident and injury, is there anything *else* that I as your big brother, should be concerned about?" he asked, his meaning clear.

And Anwen did the only thing she could do—she lied. "I don't know what you're asking."

Her brother's mouth tightened. "I'll speak more plainly. Should I be concerned at the sad, longing look you keep pointing in *Phineas'* direction?"

At her delayed response, a dawning horror crept over Clayton's face. He leaned closer to her mattress. *"Anwen?"*

"I don't—" Want to do this. She didn't want to have this discussion with Clayton, now *or* ever.

"You don't 'what'? Know exactly what I'm asking, *still?* Or you don't want to talk about whether I've reason to be concerned that something transpired between you and Landon?"

He wavered. "*Did it?*" he asked, desperation and dread all co-mingling in his faltering question.

And suddenly, it was too much. The secret she'd kept from him, from her mother, from Phineas, from all the Kearsleys.

"I love him," she said raggedly. "Is that what you would have me say?" she asked, pushing herself back up onto her elbows. "Would you have me say he proved staunchly steadfast as your friend and was properly gentlemanly and horrified when I expressed my feelings for him?"

Her brother's features wavered. "Anwen, we don't have to talk about this now."

She ignored his attempted interruption. He didn't want to hear anymore. Well, to hell with him.

"Would you like me to tell you that I've loved him since I was just a girl, but he never, *ever* saw me as a woman, because he only ever did and only ever *will* see me as *your sister*. So no, you don't have anything to worry about, Clayton." Anwen couldn't keep the bitterness from creeping into her voice. Nor did she try. "Phineas... Lord Landon, passed the friendship test with flying colors. He's been loyal to you and indifferent to me."

The fight drained from her exhausted body. Anwen fell back against the bed and turned her head to look at the opposite wall, and away from her brother.

Clayton's chair groaned, and the floorboards joined that creaky chorus, indicating Anwen's brother had stood and moved nearer to her.

Just go. Why will you not just go? she silently pleaded.

"Oh, Anwen." Her name emerged from Clayton with an aching regret, sorrow, and worse—pity. "That does not make me happy."

She snorted but still did not attempt to face him.

"Anwen, I have known Landon nearly all my life. I love him like a brother. He is a good man, but..." Clayton paused, like one searching for the right words, "he is a *flawed* man," he finally said.

"And *other* men are somehow perfect?"

"No. That isn't what I'm saying."

"Then, what are you saying, Clayton?"

"He is incapable of loving any woman in the way you want or, more importantly, *deserves* to be loved."

"Incapable of loving any woman?" she echoed. "Is that what *Phineas* thinks? Or everyone around him?" What other outcome would there have been but for Phineas to believe himself incapable and unworthy of loving?

"Anwen," her brother began in pained tones.

She'd, however, had enough.

Without a care for the further strain it caused, Anwen angled her head and leveled a look on her brother. "If you, Phineas' *best* friend, trust he's incapable of loving, then how do *you*, a man who by your own admission sees the marquess as a brother, expect Phineas would trust himself deserving of that emotion?"

Taken aback, Clayton's mouth moved several times before he managed words. "Anwen," he tried again, "all I'm trying to say is I want you to fall hopelessly in love with—"

"A man who can love me in return?"

He gave a small nod. "Precisely."

And Phineas, wasn't that man. The remainder of that thought couldn't have been clearer than had her brother spoken it aloud.

"Unfortunately," she said achingly, "the heart isn't the most cooperative of organs. One cannot simply direct it to love where it does not love."

She slid a glance back his way. "Given you fell in love with your late best friend's former wife, I thought you should know that," she said without recrimination.

Her brother took her hand in his. "Tell me what to do," he implored. "Tell me how to make this right."

Except, Clayton couldn't. For he couldn't give Anwen the only thing she longed for in this life—Phineas' love. In the end, she took the coward's way out.

"I am tired, Clayton," she said on a broken whisper.

Her brother was already climbing to his feet. "I'll fetch Dr. Carlson."

"No! Please, I just...would like some quiet."

Turmoil raged in his eyes. "Anwen, I don't want you to sleep. I'm afraid—" He stopped himself.

"You're afraid I'll not wake up again?"

He paused and then gave a slight nod.

Anwen forced a grin. "As you said, we are the Kearsleys too stubborn to give in to the curse."

They shared a smile, and she closed her eyes. How much easier it would be to sink back into one of those blessedly still rests where the memory of Phineas' rejection couldn't touch her.

Alas, there was no rejecting that reality...or the misery it wrought.

CHAPTER 14

WHOM THE GODS LOVE DIES young.

That fact and fate had been inked into Herodotus tablets because the all-knowing man had known. Just as Phineas knew.

It was why Phineas' mother had perished years and years ahead of her time. And it was why Phineas lived even now. The Lord had no use for a soul as sullied as his.

Seated on the floor, with his back against the opposite wall facing Anwen's still-closed door and his head buried in his lap, Phineas at last made himself acknowledge the truth.

Anwen is going to die. Phineas knew that.

He'd known that the minute he'd heard her maid scream and had raced back to find Anwen buried under that branch, still and silent. He'd known when he scooped her lifeless body up in his arms and rode like the devil through the torrents of rain, and with the pounding of his horse's hooves as he'd set out to inform St. John the tragedy which had befallen the Kearsleys.

Except, even knowing the fate certainly awaiting Anwen, even trusting that her death was the only outcome, Phineas had still allowed himself to hold out for a different one. For buried deep inside, there'd been a part of Phineas' cynical, cold being where a glimmer of light had dwelled, and hope inhabited.

And then the week…it had come and it had gone, ushering in a new day, the eighth day.

A faint, but deep murmur brought Phineas' head up, and he stared with bleary eyes at the two doves etched in ivory upon

Anwen's door. St. John spoke to his silent sister. *Again.* Just as the other man had done countless times now.

The first time Phineas detected his friend's muffled voice on the other side of that panel, Phineas had thought the viscount talked *with* Anwen. Only to realize, the exchange was a one-sided one between St. John and Anwen's lifeless form.

Yes, Anwen was destined to die, and Phineas' world would cease to exist without her in it. There'd only be darkness with her dying, and the last smile he would have smiled was the one that had spread across his lips after he'd made love to her in the Kearsley library.

His chest ached. A vise compressed his lungs, and breath became an impossibility.

Please. Just let her live, he silently entreated a Lord whom he'd only put an appeal to once before—and then, it had been a plea that He give him back his mother. Now, he prayed that there was a God and that He'd spare Anwen.

I'll beg her forgiveness, and then, I'll leave her alone forever. I'll let a better, worthy man have her, and let her live her life happily. Just please, please, do not take—

Click.

Phineas looked up and stared dumbly at the enervated figure at the entrance of Anwen's room: St. John, haggard as Phineas had never before seen him, and his eyes bloodshot in ways befitting a man either drinking or crying.

Oh, God. Bile burned the back of his throat. A low, animalistic moan reverberated in his chest.

The viscount opened his mouth to speak.

"She's dead," Phineas said, flatly, then withered and himself died inside at having spoken her fate aloud.

St. John shook his head. "She lives," he said quietly and drew the door closed behind him. He looked briefly the way of the footman who'd been stationed nearby. "Fetch Dr. Carlson at once. Miss Kearsley is awake."

The young servant took off running.

"She is awake?" Phineas echoed.

She is awake. She is awake!

Had there ever been more beautiful words uttered than those?

Phineas dropped the back of his head against the wall. "Thank God," he whispered, and it was the first time in his life he'd confirmation of the Lord's very real presence.

Euphoria twined with exhaustion, and Phineas shoved himself unsteadily to his feet.

St. John spoke, "I—"

Whatever words he'd been set to utter were cut off by Dr. Carlson's approach. Phineas stepped aside, as his friend exchanged quiet words with the doctor. With a nod, Dr. Carlson let himself inside; Phineas caught a glimpse of Anwen.

Since the moment he'd laid her upon the mattress, he had hungered for each and every small glimpse he could catch of her. For, even if she were in a deep sleep in that bed, it meant she still drew breath.

Now, his heart hurt all over again at the sight of her sprawled on her side; her brown curls hung in a tangle about her shoulders and face.

"No one could be bothered to plait her hair?" Phineas snapped the moment Dr. Carlson pushed the panel closed. "It'll be hopelessly knotted, and—" He felt St. John's gaze and looked over.

The other man stared sharply back. "Yes?"

Oh, hell. He'd said too much. *Revealed* too much. Phineas shook his head. "Nothing. It is nothing."

St. John continued to study him a moment, then, "I wanted to speak with you," he began quietly.

And not for the first time, Phineas proved unable to meet the other man's eyes. This time it was the clamor of approaching footsteps that saved Phineas from the deserved interrogation his friend was certainly about to deliver.

Because a sea of Kearsleys converged upon them, with the dowager viscountess leading the charge. The gaggle of ladies, ages eight to fifty-eight, spoke excitedly, over one another, their words all rolling together.

"What…say…?"

"How…she…?"

"When did Anwen…?"

Blasted with a peppering of questions, St. John held his arms up. "Ladies," he called. "Ladies!" he repeated, more loudly.

A shrill whistle pierced the cacophony, and the din instantly died.

Lady St. John removed her fingers from her lips, and let her arms fall to her side.

"Now," she said into the quiet she'd managed to bring over the hall. "Your sister is going to be tired and sore, and the last thing she needs is our raised voices. We will be quiet. We will be proper. We will be composed. Failure to do so will see your immediate expulsion from Anwen's side. Is that understood?" she directed her attention to each daughter.

"Yes," they murmured, with an uncharacteristic Kearsley acquiescence.

With that, Lady St. John led the way, and, in what Phineas would have staked his life was a losing feat, each girl and woman followed in a neat, silent, line one after the other.

The dowager viscountess brought the panel closed behind them, leaving Phineas and St. John...alone. Neither man said anything for a long, awkward moment.

St. John was the first to speak.

"Quiet, proper, and composed," he said, bemusedly. "And here I thought that was an impossible feat."

"Yes, but the Kearsleys love deeply," Phineas murmured. "And would do anything to spare one another from pain. As such, they could manage even those endeavors we'd have taken as impossible if it meant sparing Anwen further suffering."

St. John continued to contemplate Phineas in that unnervingly discerning way.

His neck went hot. "What?"

"It is nothing...Just..."

"If there is a 'just' then it is certainly not 'nothing'," Phineas said in a futile attempt at humor, and self-preservation. He didn't want to know exactly what insight his friend had suddenly attained.

"It appears a day for firsts, as I can't recall you ever speaking about that emotion." He paused. "In fact, I didn't even know you...believed in love."

That conversation he'd had with Anwen some weeks ago whispered forward.

"Do you ever wonder if you're afraid to love because you're afraid to be hurt...?"

Phineas balled his hands. How bloody sapient. Absolutely anything would be better than discussing his late-in-life discovery—that he was in fact, capable of love, and he knew it because he loved Anwen with every fiber of his worthless being.

Fortunately, St. John proceeded to let the matter rest. "I wished to thank you for standing in wait with my family and myself," St. John said and held out a hand to Phineas. "And also thank you for everything you've done..."

A deserved shame threatened to swallow Phineas whole.

"In my absence, you watched after Anwen..."

With every word his friend spoke, St. John notched another nail of guilt into Phineas' chest.

"The only reason I agreed to help you is because your brother asked it of me."

"My mother informed me you visited almost daily to visit with Anwen and my other sisters."

St. John's unending homage twisted and twined with every last lie Phineas had fed to Anwen.

"You needn't have wasted your time visiting my rooms at the Albany that night..."

"Mother even ventured you attended more respectable affairs this Season than every previous Season before...." St. John droned on and on.

"...St. John met with me before he departed for London and asked that I look after you in his absence...I'd already taken on the responsibility of watching after you."

Phineas' reasons for spending day after day with Anwen hadn't been because of St. John and any damned favor.

If Anwen or St. John truly knew Phineas, they would have also known the truth all along—his purely selfish yearning to be with her, and see her smile, and *make* her smile had been stronger than any aphrodisiac he'd ever partaken in.

St. John rested a palm on Phineas' shoulder; that touch jolted him out of his own thoughts.

"Not many men can say they have a friend who will take on the responsibilities of looking after a young lady who is not their sister, as you did with Anwen."

"Though, I expect, me shoving your skirts about your waist wasn't quite what he had in mind…But then, what can one expect of a rake…?"

It was too much. Phineas shrugged off his friend's hand. "I neither want nor need, and certainly do not deserve your gratitude!" Phineas exploded. "I didn't do any—" *Of this because of you.*

At the penetrative look the other man leveled on him, Phineas stopped his word flow.

"Yes?" St. John prodded.

My God, man, get control of yourself?

"I didn't do anything that any other friend wouldn't do," he finished lamely, and with a lie.

Something flickered in the viscount's eyes; a brief glimmer that looked very much like disappointment. It was gone so quickly; Phineas may as well have imagined it.

"I see," St. John said.

Except, he couldn't. For if he did, he would have known Phineas was a damned liar. Then and now, his only reason for being here was because of Anwen. He just hadn't realized it at the time.

"I should return home."

"Yes, again, I thank you for being a friend and staying with me here through this hell."

Phineas bowed his head, and at last quit his vigil outside Anwen's rooms.

CHAPTER 15

IN THE COMING DAYS, PHINEAS didn't leave his residence. Not for his clubs—the wicked nor respectable ones. Not to bed a whore or a widow—Anwen had thoroughly ruined him for all women.

Instead, he spent the better part of a fortnight first conducting interviews for new stewards and a man-of-affairs. Each man came recommended by his friends, Scarsdale, St. John, Waters, and Rothesby.

Then, for hours, Phineas remained locked away in appointments with the men new to his staff. The first order of business had been to sell the little that was left of value so that he could pay salaries and buy additional time from his debtors.

From sunup, until the early evening hours, he discussed the state of his long-neglected estates and strategized a path forward for improving those lots and lands. No stone went unturned. No new business venture not considered.

And long after his new employs left, Phineas stayed in his offices, working into the wee hours of morning, whereby he'd bathe, steal several hours of sleep, and then do it all again. Through it all, no matter the effort, hours, questions, or considerations that went into his work, there remained one constant—the numbers in the ledgers didn't change.

With a curse, Phineas tossed his pen down and glared at his books. Though, it wasn't the books to blame. Nay, the fault lay solely with their owner. Giving a black expletive, he slammed closed the ledger he'd been staring at, and shoved it across the surface of his now tidy desk.

It was futile. And yet, there had to be a way.

Only, he knew the truth. Men like him weren't granted second chances, for the sole reason they didn't deserve them. Eventually, the devil came due.

The door opened with a quiet click. Tiredly, he looked up.

His aunt stood framed in the doorway, a folio in one hand, and a cane in the other. "I told your butler I could show myself in."

"Splendid." He infused all the drollness to convey how he truly felt.

The last thing he required was a lecture.

Deserve one? Yes.

Require one? No.

The duchess stopped at the foot of his desk. She used the tip of her cane to nudge the pile of old ledgers stacked there. She turned an assessing stare from those books back to Phineas. Her gaze went to his bearded cheeks.

"I'm not in the mood for another lecture," he gritted out the moment she'd seated herself.

"Perfect, as I've come to discuss the terms, I laid out for you," she said, getting right to business.

He'd spare the both of them a lengthy back and forth. "I'm not marrying," he said quietly. "At least not any of the women on that list you gave me." He paused. "Not any woman."

She sat back. "I see."

No, she didn't. She never did.

"Does this have anything to do with the Kearsley girl."

So mayhap she did.

It had *everything* to do with the Kearsley girl. More specifically the Kearsley girl who'd stolen his heart.

His aunt proved unrelenting. "More specifically, does it have to do with the reports of your riding like a madman through London in the middle of a rainstorm with the lady in your arms, fetching her brother, and then riding all the way back to take up a spot with the family."

Phineas said nothing, just silently cursed whichever gossip lived in the Kearsley household that had violated that worthy family's trust.

"Or," his aunt leaned forward, "does it have to do with you locking yourself away in your office and righting your books?"

Apparently, he had gossips in his own midst.

Phineas massaged the taut muscles under the base of his skull.

The duchess leaned back in her seat and rested her palms on the arm of her chair. "You love her."

Phineas didn't pretend to misunderstand. He didn't bother denying it. He'd spent his whole life in a state of denial. "I have nothing to offer her," he said, shame burning his tongue. "But you were right. Self-pitying doesn't undo my past transgressions."

"No," she agreed. "But hard work goes a good way towards the building of a new future. And my sources also indicate you've been hard at work here." Tapping that leather folio against her leg, she cast an approving glance around his tidy office. "My sources appear to be good ones."

He managed his first smile in weeks. "Only you, dear aunt, a duchess, would laud hard work."

She snorted. "Come, I'm not snobbish when it comes to the topics of money." Quite the opposite, given she even mentioned them. "Either way, Phineas, you *do* have something to offer Miss Kearsley." Wordlessly, she slid her folio across the desk.

He looked at it. "What is this?"

"Go on. Look at it."

At her urging, he flipped the leather case open and stopped. He whipped his head up. "What is this?"

"Funds both I and your mother have kept safe for you."

His mind raced. "Why…would you give it to me?"

"Your mother, she would not touch the funds our father, your grandfather, insisted be set exclusively in her name. Even as she could have used it when your miserable cur of a father ran through everything and had her in rags. She said she was saving it for you. She asked I hold onto it until the love of a good woman saved you." Her eyes grew misty. "And I believe you found that woman in your Miss Kearsley."

Phineas' mind raced as he attempted to make sense through his shock.

"Before now, you were only worried about what those funds offered you," she explained. "Finally, you see and ask how you could use them for another.

"I never had a child of my own, but you have been like the son I never had and I'm proud that you've begun changing your life around."

"And you've been like another mother," he said gruffly.

"A sterner one than my sister."

He smiled. "A deservedly sterner one." His grin died, and he slowly brought the leather folio shut. "I cannot marry her."

"Bah?" She gave a wave of her hand. "Out of some misbegotten sense of honor? You've been selfish for most of your adult life, Phineas. Do not choose this moment, the one when you've finally fallen in love with a woman, to be the one when you become too noble."

In the span of a twenty-minute visit with his aunt, all at the same time, everything and nothing had changed. He now possessed a small fortune, but money did not erase past transgressions. It did not bolster a wicked reputation.

There came a knock at the door. Who in hell was it now?

"I'm busy," he shouted.

His butler opened the door anyway. "The Viscount St. John," Georges announced.

St. John. *Splendid.*

"I informed His Lordship you were in a meeting," Georges said worriedly.

"But I insisted you'd want to see me."

The viscount was wrong. He didn't want him here. Seeing him reminded him of Anwen, and—

As if he'd been invited, and with a newspaper in hand, St. John strolled over to the other chair which had since been supplied from the dining room, for meetings with his servants.

St. John greeted Phineas' aunt warmly. "Your Grace."

"So good to see you, my boy," she returned. "And how is your family?"

"Prodigiously well."

"And how is the eldest Miss Kearsley?"

Anwen. Unconsciously, Phineas arched forward in his seat, before catching himself. He needn't have worried. His godmother and best friend required no input from him.

"Vastly improved."

"And is there truth to the rumors in the papers, St. John?"

At his aunt's question, Phineas puzzled his brow. *The rumors?*

The viscount chuckled. "As they say, there is some truth to all rumors."

What rumors?

The pair shared another laugh.

"*What* rumors?"

The duchess and St. John both looked over, like they'd only just remembered his presence.

"Why, the wonderful news about the eldest Miss Kearsley."

"What—?"

St. John dropped the newspaper on his desk. Phineas glanced down and found her name in an instant.

His hands contracted.

Anwen's name…twined with another.

He read quickly the article.

Given the Earl of W's daily vigilance,

following Miss AK's collapse at Hyde Park,

it is expected banns will be posted…

A low rumbling sound started in his throat. It was too much.

"You are letting Anwen marry *Wakefield*?" he thundered.

St. John bristled. "Here, now. I'm not the manner of brother who'd ever dare presume to tell my sister who she should and should not love."

Love?

"Do you truly *believe* she loves him?" Phineas spat.

She didn't. She couldn't. She loved Phineas. Or she had before he'd gone and scorned her love.

He gnashed his teeth.

"Who do *you* think she loves?" St. John asked with a weighty solemnness that gave Phineas pause. Then, the pair of them seated themselves, folded their arms, and stared pointedly at him.

He resisted the urge to squirm. *Oh, hell.* "I walked into a trap, didn't I?"

St. John and the duchess nodded.

"She loves *you*, Landon," St. John said.

Phineas' shoulders sagged. "It's not enough."

His friend's eyes narrowed into dangerous slits. "Do you love her?"

"Of course, I love her! What would you have me say?" he exploded. "That I hate, absolutely despise, that I spent my life being a man who'd never be deserving of her? That I wish I could be better for her? That I love her?" That profession echoed in the room.

The fight went out of Phineas, and he collapsed in his chair. "Yes."

It was a moment before he registered St. John had spoken. Confused, Phineas picked his head up.

"That is precisely what I would have you tell me."

Phineas shook his head. "I..."

His aunt looked at St. John. "Will you be so good as to tell your friend he *is* good enough for your sister?"

The viscount shook his head. "I don't need to tell him that." He looked at Phineas. "I trust he already knows. But in the event you don't, old friend? You've been the brother I never had. I've welcomed you into my family. How could you believe I'd believe you unworthy of my sister? I know if you love her, you will be faithful and good to her." Clayton paused. His eyes formed hard, threatening slits. "Also, I'd kill you if *you weren't.*"

"I *would* be true. I *will*..." He dragged a hand through his hair.

His aunt's face lit up and she clasped her hands at her breast. "What are you saying?"

"I'm saying—"

There came a commotion in the hall. "Where are they?" the dowager viscountess's battle cry rent the corridor. A moment later, Lady St. John stormed his office. She looked around the room. "Why is he still *here*?" she demanded of her son.

St. John shrugged. "I'm afraid you will have to ask the gentleman himself."

Her eyes pure fire, Lady St. John swept over in a whir of mauve skirts. Situating herself between her son and the duchess, Lady St. John lay her palms on Phineas' desk. "Listen now and listen good, Phineas. I did not go through all the trouble of arranging for you and my daughter to be together for her to only go on and marry a man she does not love."

Phineas stared dumbly at the unlikely trio before him. "You..."

"*We* all knew what it took you long enough to realize?" St. John supplied for him. "Yes."

Phineas slowly shook his head. "The request for me to attend the same affairs as your mother and sister..."

"*My* idea," Lady St. John crowed.

St. John frowned. "I'd argue credit belongs to the both of us."

Phineas looked at his aunt. "And the horr—" He stopped himself.

"The less than kindly things I said about Miss Kearsley?" she asked. His aunt smiled. "All meant to nudge you along, dear boy."

Nudge him along.

"Though, I must admit," his aunt went on, "I was exceedingly disappointed my ultimatum that you cease seeing Miss Kearsely went awry." She looked to Lady St. John. "What gentleman does not chafe at being told what to do by a domineering aunt and do the exact opposite?"

"I daresay, I can't think of a single one," Anwen's mother commiserated.

St. John cleared his throat, putting an end to that fast-spiraling conversation between the pair. "Yes, well, I suggest we answer any further questions you may have later," St. John consulted his watch, "because as we speak, Lord Wakefield is paying a visit, and I have it on authority he—"

Cursing, Phineas took off running.

"I took the liberty of having your mount readied," St. John called laughingly behind him.

Laughing? His bloody best friend was *laughing*?

Phineas took off on Lucky at a dead-run.

Wakefield was going to propose. Dread licked at his insides. Only one thought went through his head, the whole interminable way to the Kearsley residence.

Do not marry him. Do not accept his offer. Do not...do not...

I love her. He'd always loved her. And he hadn't been a good man before now, and he'd always be deeply flawed, but he'd consecrate his life to Anwen's happiness.

A lifetime later, Phineas wheeled his mount to a stop outside the Kearsley townhouse. The place where she, even now, met with Wakefield. The bloody perfect paragon.

Phineas stormed the steps, and the old butler Mr. Georges, held the door open, as if he had anticipated Phineas' arrival. Just as his aunt, best friend, and Lady St. John had known his heart before Phineas himself had.

His breath ragged from the mad pace he'd set, and terror clutching at his heart, Phineas looked frantically about the foyer.

"She is in the White Room, my lord," Georges supplied. "I suggest you—"

Phineas tore down the hall. "Anwen!" he cried.

"Hurry," Georges finished in the distance.

Do not say yes. Do not. Please, do not. Choose me, instead.

His heart knocked painfully against his ribcage, and gasping for air, he caught himself against the door panel. Then, grabbing the brass knob, he tossed the door wide.

"Don't!" he rasped.

A wide-eyed Anwen sat perched on a white sofa with an apple poised at her lips.

Frantic, Phineas looked about...before registering... "You're alone." A giddy lightness suffused his chest.

"Yes. I'm alone."

God, the sight of her. And with too many days spent apart, Phineas devoured the image she made before him.

A healthy ivory color had returned to her wan cheeks, as if she'd spent the days in the gardens, with her face tilted up towards the sun. Her lustrous dark brown hair, with that enthralling strip of white. Her cupid's bow mouth.

Phineas came forward hesitantly, and when she didn't issue a protest, he continued over. The moment he reached her, she stood. Her satin skirts fell around her ankles.

Then it hit him. In his frantic rush to get here and interrupt Wakefield's proposal, he'd not thought about how his being here likely taxed her.

"How are you feeling?"

Carefully, she set her apple down on a nearby side table. "Well?"

"Is that a question?"

"No," she said softly. "I'm…well."

I'm well. What did that mean? Did she speak to her physical health? Or…was she saying she'd found happiness without him in her life?

She smoothed he palms over the front of her dress. "Phineas, what are you doing here?"

And then, he registered something else.

She was…different. Changed. Distant. Hesitant. And he mourned that change that had come between them. A change, *he* had wrought with his cruelty and lies…and fear. He now knew that fear had compelled him.

"I thought…I believed…"

Anwen angled her head. "Yes?"

Relief brought his words out in a rush. "I thought Wakefield was here."

"He was," she said, deflating Phineas' all too brief elation. "He left just before you arrived."

Oh, God. A kick between the legs would have been preferable to that utterance.

"He was," he repeated hollowly. There. He'd managed words.

Anwen nodded.

"And…the papers, they said, it's been suggested that he…that you and Wakefield…" It was too much. Phineas couldn't make himself finish it.

Anwen took a step closer. "Yes?"

"That you are to wed."

He'd said it. *Now, I'm going to be ill.* "I…"

Anwen just stared patiently.

"I'm a liar," he said.

She tipped her head.

"I remember. You were dangling from a tree," he said hoarsely. "You were about to tumble, and then we both tumbled, and you didn't want to lose, and I was determined you wouldn't."

Her lips went soft.

And the words, they all came tumbling free. "And we ran, Anwen. We sprinted through the forest because Daria and Delia and Brenna were close on our heels. I pulled you down, and you tumbled a second time that day, onto me."

"You do remember," she whispered.

"I remember it all." He lowered his brow to hers. "And that day, I'd been about to kiss you but caught myself. I asked if you'd something—"

"In m-my eye." Her mouth trembled. A tear trickled down her cheek.

Phineas caught that drop with the pad of his thumb. "I asked if you had something in your eye, because I saw the look there, and God, I wanted to kiss you, and how I hated myself for it."

Twining his fingers with hers, he brought them up, so that they pointed at the stone bench across the way. "And that day, the day your father passed, Anwen, you sat right over there, so forlornly, and I didn't buy you books or take you to museums because I knew that all you wanted was for me to be there with you, as I wanted to be with you."

A sob tore from her lips.

Phineas raised her knuckles to his mouth and kissed them, one at a time. "I love you, Anwen. I've been a cad and a bastard." She made a sound of protest, but he stopped her. "But I have been working to improve my circumstances, and I've learned I have an inheritance that will allow me to care for you in the way you deserve."

"Phineas, I never cared about all that," she said, her voice aching.

"You should have," he said. "You deserve so much better than me. Please, don't marry Wakefield."

"I told him 'no'."

He went motionless. She'd told him no.

Anwen smiled tenderly up at him. "I told him I could not marry when my heart belongs so wholly to you, Phineas. I love you."

"Marry me. Please, Anwen?" he implored. "Marry me, and I will devote my entire life to your every smile. I want to build a new future with you. I want to have a dozen girl babes with you, all spirited, hilarious, clever girls like their mother." He paused. "If you want that, that is. Because if you say you do not want babes, you will be enough."

Anwen lifted luminous eyes up to his. "On one condition."

"Anything," he said before she'd fully formed that sentence.

"*I* want a dozen boy babes who are witty and loving and loyal like their father."

And a sheen glazed his eyes. "Yes. I want all of that with you." He lowered his mouth to take her lips, but Anwen edged back. Phineas stared at her, a question in his eyes.

"It is just, well, given we've committed to twenty-four babes," she said, "I'd venture ours should be a quick engagement."

"Agreed, my love." And then with a half-laugh, half-sob he caught her in his arms. "Agreed."

Anwen twined hers about him and held him in return. While he spun her in a dizzying circle, their laughter joined like their souls and hearts had forever been, as they looked eagerly and joyfully towards the future awaiting them—together.

EPILOGUE

℮NSCONCED IN THE PRIVATE SUITES of Forbidden Pleasure and seated on the blue floral silk, Canapé à Oreilles, between her friends, Marcia and Faith, Anwen listened absently to their happy chatter.

Her focus remained on the game of faro taking place between Viscount Waters, Lord Rutherford, and Anwen's husband.

Well, that was the game between Lord Waters and Lord Rutherford. Phineas, positioned between the two men, served in the role of dealer to the two other gentlemen's gameplay.

My husband, she moved her lips, silently sounding out those two words.

Married for nearly a fortnight now, and she still became giddy at the mere word of what Phineas now was to her.

As if she felt his gaze, Phineas glanced up from the gaming table, and caught Anwen's eye.

"I love you," he mouthed.

She went all soft inside. Anwen touched a fist to her breast and returned that avowal.

"A little focus, if you will, chap," Lord Waters chastised. "I've a winning hand here."

Lord Rutherford's mouth formed a droll grin. "I've heard *that* many times before."

The viscount bristled. "Beg pardon, ole' chap, but I've—"

Phineas turned a card, and Lord Waters' words, dissolved to a long groan.

Even as Anwen and Marcia both fought back a smile, Lord Rutherford erupted into laughter.

"Behave," Faith called over.

Lord Rutherford pushed back on the legs of his chair. "It's just a friendly game over pennies, my love," he assured.

Since his marriage to Marcia, that was the extent of Lord Waters' wagering; the viscount had forsaken high-stakes gambling.

As had, Anwen's.

The marquess looked to Anwen's husband. "What of you, Landon? How's about joining in at least one hand this evening?"

Phineas sipped his brandy. "I must decline."

"Now, *that*, I've *never* heard from you before," Faith's husband said wryly. "You're sure I cannot entice you to a hand of faro?"

"Alas, my gambling days are over," Phineas insisted. He slid his gaze Anwen's way, once more, and just like that, everything and everyone melted away so that only two existed in the moment.

Anwen's heart filled with so much love.

Among the vows he'd pledged Anwen, in addition to loving, honoring, and caring for her in sickness and health, until death did part them, had also been a promise to give up gambling, and dedicate himself to his estates and those reliant upon him.

Marcia sighed. "Did you ever believe you'd see the day, Anwen?"

Anwen reluctantly pulled her attention away from Phineas. "No," she said softly. "I only ever dreamed of marrying him."

The viscountess draped an arm around Anwen's shoulders. "I referred to the day our rapscallion husbands made friends with Lord Rutherford," the viscountess said gently.

Faith bristled. "My husband is not as scary as all *that*."

Both women looked at her.

"He's perfectly funny and warm...to those he calls friends," Faith finally allowed.

Though, Lord Rutherford had been kind and gracious and good to Faith's friends, neither was he the manner of man who'd only ever be considered funny or warm. But then, that was love. It allowed one to see the parts of a person other people couldn't necessarily see *or* appreciate.

"What do you think they're talking about?" Marcia whispered.

Their trio of friends turned their collective focus on the men across the room at the gaming table.

A somberness had replaced that group's early levity, and Lord Rutherford led whatever discussion now took place.

Suddenly, Phineas tossed his hands up, and gave his head a hard shake.

Anwen frowned. "I…don't know."

What had occurred between the two marquess's? They'd been getting on so well. The conversation, however, had turned heated between Phineas and Lord Rutherford.

Lord Waters appeared a forgotten, hanger-on.

The nervous viscount looked back and forth between Anwen and Faith's husbands, pushed back his chair, and jumped up.

Crossing over quickly, Lord Waters took his wife by the hand. "I suggest we leave them to a bit of privacy."

As the husband and wife bustled from the room, Marcia flashed a grin back Anwen's way. "I'll see you soon." Her eyes twinkled.

Smiling? Her friend was really *smiling*? At least, one of them found amusement in the breakdown between Anwen's husband and Lord Rutherford.

The moment they closed the door with a click behind them, Anwen returned her attention to Phineas and Faith's husband.

The fight appeared to have died down.

Phineas, however, had been left with flushed cheeks and red eyes, and was a moment away from crying.

Fury filled her. Phineas had insisted a relationship between himself and the man who held most of his vowels was an impossibility. He'd insisted Rutherford had seen the worst of Phineas over the years, and that was all the other man could possibly see.

Anwen too, had been adamant. She'd promised him Faith's husband was a good man and could be a friend to Phineas as he'd become a friend to Anwen.

Only to be proven wrong.

Faith touched a hand to her shoulder. "It is fine," her friend said, with a soft, knowing smile.

"It isn't," Anwen said tightly, unable to take her gaze from the triumphant grin now worn by Lord Rutherford.

It was *too* much.

Anwen jumped up and planting her hands on her hips, stormed across the room. "How dare you?"

Phineas looked up, startled. "Anwen."

She ignored him. "My husband is a good man."

"Anwen," said husband made the mistake of trying to interrupt her. He offered Faith's husband a sheepish smile. "She's more devoted than I deserve."

"I see that," Lord Rutherford drawled.

The wry set to the gentleman's hard features sent Anwen's annoyance ratcheting up a notch.

"You don't see anything, Lord Rutherford," she countered, deliberately using that title which he hated and usually substituted in favor his surname alone.

"Anwen, *please*," Phineas said, more insistently. He gathered her hand in his.

"I'm *speaking*, Phineas." Anwen pulled free and kept her ire where it belonged—on Lord Rutherford. "My husband *feared* you would judge him. He *feared* you'd only ever see him as the wastrel patron he'd once been. But he is *so* much more. He is good and kind and deserving of a second chance."

"I know," Lord Rutherford said.

"He is a loving husband and a devoted friend and—" She stopped abruptly and scrunched her brow up. "You know?"

Faith's husband nodded. "I know."

"Then…" Befuddled, much the way Lord Waters had been, Anwen glanced between the two men. "What were you fighting about?"

Faith, who'd hovered just beyond the fray, moved to her husband's side, and took his hand in hers. "They weren't fighting."

"You…weren't?" Anwen asked.

Phineas shook his head. "We weren't."

At sea, Anwen attempted to make sense of any of it. "But…but you looked about ready to cry, Phineas."

Color splotched her proud husband's cheeks, and he wrestled with his snowy white cravat. "I wouldn't say I was ready to *cry*," he mumbled.

Lord Rutherford's grin widened.

Faith, at last, helped Anwen through her confusion. "Rex was giving Lord Phineas a wedding gift."

"One I insisted I absolutely couldn't take," Phineas said on a rush.

"And one I was adamant he must accept," Lord Rutherford spoke in the same gravelly tones he adopted for both moments of happiness and anger.

"He forgave my debt, Anwen," Phineas finally explained.

Reeling, Anwen rocked back on her heels.

"I told him I couldn't accept that generosity, as it is a fortune," The crimson color on Phineas' cheeks went a shade deeper, and he coughed into a fist.

"We arrived at a compromise," Lord Rutherford came to his rescue.

"Money would be set aside as gifts to our future children," Phineas explained. "and I'd donate a significant portion to charities and hospitals throughout London."

Staggered by that generosity, Anwen pressed a palm against her mouth, and looked at Lord and Lady Rutherford.

Hand in hand, the loving couple, smiled back at Anwen.

Tears filled her eyes, and their visages blurred. "I...I am s-so sorry," she said thickly. "I c-can't believe. I d-don't believe...just thank you," she sobbed. "Thank you s-so much."

Faith surged forward, and wrapped her arms about Anwen. "We are sisters, not by blood, but in every other way, and Phineas is now family, too. Isn't that right, Rex?"

Lord Rutherford inclined his head. "That is correct," he said solemnly. "My wife taught me that found family is family, and that friends help one another."

Alternately laughing and weeping, Anwen hugged her friend back tightly.

Over the top of the smaller woman's head, Anwen caught Phineas' gaze.

"I love you," he mouthed.

More tears pricked her lashes. "I love you, too."

A voice called out from the other side of the thick oak paneled door. "Can we return now?" Marcia's asked, her words slightly muffled.

"Yes, but you didn't have to leave in the first place," Faith shouted.

And as the rest of Anwen's friends came streaming into the room, Anwen slid over to her husband.

Phineas immediately looped his arms over her, and she leaned back against him.

She'd the heart of the man she'd always loved, laughter, and the dearest friends and beloved family.

This was paradise.

THE END

COMING NOVEMBER 2023

Enjoyed Once a Rake, Suddenly a Suitor? Be sure and check out the next installment coming in the Scandalous Seasons series!

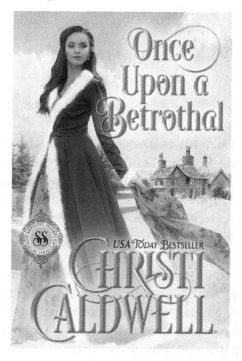

Once Upon a Betrothal, brings readers a winter-set romance between former lovers, Mr. Broden Burgess and Miss Harmony Beresford.

OTHER BOOKS IN THE HEART OF A DUKE SERIES

BY CHRISTI CALDWELL

TO HOLD A LADY'S SECRET
Book 16 in the "Heart of a Duke" Series

Lady Gillian Farendale is in trouble. Her titled father has dragged her through one London Season after another, until the sheer monotony of the marriage mart and the last vestige of Gillian's once-independent spirit conspire to lead her into a single night of folly. When her adventure goes so very wrong, she has only one old friend to whom she can turn for help.

Colin Lockhart's youthful friendship with Lady Gillian cost him everything, and a duke's by-blow had little enough to start with. He's survived years on London's roughest streets to become a highly successful Bow Street Runner, and his dream of his own inquiry agency is almost within his grasp.

Then Gillian begs him to once again risk angering her powerful father. The ruthless logic of the street tells Colin that he dare not help Gillian, while his tender heart tempts him to once again risk everything for the only woman he'll ever love.

To Tempt a Scoundrel
Book 15 in the "Heart of a Duke" Series

Never trust a gentleman…

Once before, Lady Alice Winterbourne trusted her heart to an honorable, respectable man… only to be jilted in the scandal of the Season. Longing for an escape from all the whispers and humiliation, Alice eagerly accepts an invitation to her friend's house party. In the country, she hopes to find some peace from the embarrassment left in London… Unfortunately, she finds her former betrothed and his new bride in attendance.

Never love a lady…

Lord Rhys Brookfield has no interest in marriage. Ever. He's worked quite hard at building both his fortune and his reputation as a rogue—and intends to enjoy all that they can offer him. That is if his match-making mother will stop pairing him with prospective brides. When Rhys and Alice meet, sparks flare. But with every new encounter, their first impressions of one another are challenged and an unlikely friendship is forged.

Desperate, Rhys proposes a pretend courtship, one meant to spite Alice's former betrothed and prevent any matchmaking attempts toward Rhys. What neither expects is that a pretense can become so much more. Or that a burning passion can heal… and hurt.

BEGUILED BY A BARON
Book 14 in the "Heart of a Duke" Series

A Lady with a Secret… Partially deaf, with a birthmark marring her face, Bridget Hamilton is content with her life, even if she's been cast out of her family. But her peaceful existence—expanding her mind with her study of rare books—is threatened with an ultimatum from her evil brother—steal a valuable book or give up her son. Bridget has no choice; her son is her world.

A Lord with a Purpose… Vail Basingstoke, Baron Chilton is known throughout London as the Bastard Baron. After battling at Waterloo, he establishes himself as the foremost dealer in rare books and builds a fortune, determined to never be like the self-serving duke who sired him. He devotes his life to growing his fortune to care for his illegitimate siblings, also fathered by the duke. The chance to sell a highly coveted book for a financial windfall is his only thought.

Two Paths Collide… When Bridget masquerades as the baron's newest housekeeper, he's hopelessly intrigued by her quick wit and her skill with antique tomes. Wary from having his heart broken in the past, it should be easy enough to keep Bridget at arm's length, yet desire for her dogs his steps. As they spend time in each other's company, understanding for life grows as does love, but when Bridget's integrity is called into question, Vail's world is shattered—as is his heart again. Now Bridget and Vail will have to overcome the horrendous secrets and lies between them to grasp a love—and life—together.

To Enchant a Wicked Duke
Book 13 in the "Heart of a Duke" Series

A Devil in Disguise

Years ago, when Nick Tallings, the recent Duke of Huntly, watched his family destroyed at the hands of a merciless nobleman, he vowed revenge. But his efforts had been futile, as his enemy, Lord Rutland is without weakness.

Until now…

With his rival finally happily married, Nick is able to set his ruthless scheme into motion. His plot hinges upon Lord Rutland's innocent, empty-headed sister-in-law, Justina Barrett. Nick will ruin her, marry her, and then leave her brokenhearted.

A Lady Dreaming of Love

From the moment Justina Barrett makes her Come Out, she is labeled a Diamond. Even with her ruthless father determined to sell her off to the highest bidder, Justina never gives up on her hope for a good, honorable gentleman who values her wit more than her looks.

A Not-So-Chance Meeting

Nick's ploy to ensnare Justina falls neatly into place in the streets of London. With each carefully orchestrated encounter, he slips further and further inside the lady's heart, never anticipating that Justina, with her quick wit and strength, will break down his own defenses. As Nick's plans begins to unravel, he's left to determine which is more important—Justina's love or his vow for vengeance. But can Justina ever forgive the duke who deceived her?

One Winter with a Baron
Book 12 in the "Heart of a Duke" Series

A clever spinster:

Content with her spinster lifestyle, Miss Sybil Cunning wants to prove that a future as an unmarried woman is the only life for her. As a bluestocking who values hard, empirical data, Sybil needs help with her research. Nolan Pratt, Baron Webb, one of society's most scandalous rakes, is the perfect gentleman to help her. After all, he inspires fear in proper mothers and desire within their daughters.

A notorious rake:

Society may be aware of Nolan Pratt, Baron's Webb's wicked ways, but what he has carefully hidden is his miserable handling of his family's finances. When Sybil presents him the opportunity to earn much-needed funds, he can't refuse.

A winter to remember:

However, what begins as a business arrangement becomes something more and with every meeting, Sybil slips inside his heart. Can this clever woman look beneath the veneer of a coldhearted rake to see the man Nolan truly is?

To Redeem a Rake
Book 11 in the "Heart of a Duke" Series

He's spent years scandalizing society.

Now, this rake must change his ways.

Society's most infamous scoundrel, Daniel Winterbourne, the Earl of Montfort, has been promised a small fortune if he can relinquish his wayward, carousing lifestyle. And behaving means he must also help find a respectable companion for his youngest sister—someone who will guide her and whom she can emulate. However, Daniel knows no such woman. But when he encounters a childhood friend, Daniel believes she may just be the answer to all of his problems.

Having been secretly humiliated by an unscrupulous blackguard years earlier, Miss Daphne Smith dreams of finding work at Ladies of Hope, an institution that provides an education for disabled women. With her sordid past and a disfigured leg, few opportunities arise for a woman such as she. Knowing Daniel's history, she wishes to avoid him, but working for his sister is exactly the stepping stone she needs.

Their attraction intensifies as Daniel and Daphne grow closer, preparing his sister for the London Season. But Daniel must resist his desire for a woman tarnished by scandal while Daphne is reminded of the boy she once knew. Can society's most notorious rake redeem his reputation and become the man Daphne deserves?

To Woo a Widow
Book 10 in the "Heart of a Duke" Series

They see a brokenhearted widow.

She's far from shattered.

Lady Philippa Winston is never marrying again. After her late husband's cruelty that she kept so well hidden, she has no desire to search for love.

Years ago, Miles Brookfield, the Marquess of Guilford, made a frivolous vow he never thought would come to fruition—he promised to marry his mother's goddaughter if he was unwed by the age of thirty. Now, to his dismay, he's faced with honoring that pledge. But when he encounters the beautiful and intriguing Lady Philippa, Miles knows his true path in life. It's up to him to break down every belief Philippa carries about gentlemen, proving that not only is love real, but that he is the man deserving of her sheltered heart.

Will Philippa let down her guard and allow Miles to woo a widow in desperate need of his love?

The Lure of a Rake
Book 9 in the "Heart of a Duke" Series

A Lady Dreaming of Love

Lady Genevieve Farendale has a scandalous past. Jilted at the altar years earlier and exiled by her family, she's now returned to London to prove she can be a proper lady. Even though she's not given up on the hope of marrying for love, she's wary of trusting again. Then she meets Cedric Falcot, the Marquess of St. Albans whose seductive ways set her heart aflutter. But with her sordid history, Genevieve knows a rake can also easily destroy her.

An Unlikely Pairing

What begins as a chance encounter between Cedric and Genevieve becomes something more. As they continue to meet, passions stir. But with Genevieve's hope for true love, she fears Cedric will be unable to give up his wayward lifestyle. After all, Cedric has spent years protecting his heart, and keeping everyone out. Slowly, she chips away at all the walls he's built, but when he falters, Genevieve can't offer him redemption. Now, it's up to Cedric to prove to Genevieve that the love of a man is far more powerful than the lure of a rake.

To Trust a Rogue
Book 8 in the "Heart of a Duke" Series

A rogue

Marcus, the Viscount Wessex has carefully crafted the image of rogue and charmer for Polite Society. Under that façade, however, dwells a man whose dreams were shattered almost eight years earlier by a young lady who captured his heart, pledged her love, and then left him, with nothing more than a curt note.

A widow

Eight years earlier, faced with no other choice, Mrs. Eleanor Collins, fled London and the only man she ever loved, Marcus, Viscount Wessex. She has now returned to serve as a companion for her elderly aunt with a daughter in tow. Even though they're next door neighbors, there is little reason for her to move in the same circles as Marcus, just in case, she vows to avoid him, for he reminds her of all she lost when she left.

Reunited

As their paths continue to cross, Marcus finds his desire for Eleanor just as strong, but he learned long ago she's not to be trusted. He will offer her a place in his bed, but not anything more. Only, Eleanor has no interest in this new, roguish man. The more time they spend together, the protective wall they've constructed to keep the other out, begin to break. With all the betrayals and secrets between them, Marcus has to open his heart again. And Eleanor must decide if it's ever safe to trust a rogue.

To Wed His Christmas Lady
Book 7 in the "Heart of a Duke" Series

She's longing to be loved:

Lady Cara Falcot has only served one purpose to her loathsome father—to increase his power through a marriage to the future Duke of Billingsley. As such, she's built protective walls about her heart, and presents an icy facade to the world around her. Journeying home from her finishing school for the Christmas holidays, Cara's carriage is stranded during a winter storm. She's forced to tarry at a ramshackle inn, where she immediately antagonizes another patron—William.

He's avoiding his duty in favor of one last adventure:

William Hargrove, the Marquess of Grafton has wanted only one thing in life—to avoid the future match his parents would have him make to a cold, duke's daughter. He's returning home from a blissful eight years of traveling the world to see to his responsibilities. But when a winter storm interrupts his trip and lands him at a falling-down inn, he's forced to share company with a commanding Lady Cara who initially reminds him exactly of the woman he so desperately wants to avoid.

A Christmas snowstorm ushers in the spirit of the season:

At the holiday time, these two people who despise each other due to first perceptions are offered renewed beginnings and fresh starts. As this gruff stranger breaks down the walls she's built about herself, Cara has to determine whether she can truly open her heart to trusting that any man is capable of good and that she herself is capable of love. And William has to set aside all previous thoughts he's carried of the polished ladies like Cara, to be the man to show her that love.

THE HEART OF A SCOUNDREL
Book 6 in the "Heart of a Duke" Series

Ruthless, wicked, and dark, the Marquess of Rutland rouses terror in the breast of ladies and nobleman alike. All Edmund wants in life is power. After he was publically humiliated by his one love Lady Margaret, he vowed vengeance, using Margaret's niece, as his pawn. Except, he's thwarted by another, more enticing target—Miss Phoebe Barrett.

Miss Phoebe Barrett knows precisely the shame she's been born to. Because her father is a shocking letch she's learned to form her own opinions on a person's worth. After a chance meeting with the Marquess of Rutland, she is captivated by the mysterious man. He, too, is a victim of society's scorn, but the more encounters she has with Edmund, the more she knows there is powerful depth and emotion to the jaded marquess.

The lady wreaks havoc on Edmund's plans for revenge and he finds he wants Phoebe, at all costs. As she's drawn into the darkness of his world, Phoebe risks being destroyed by Edmund's ruthlessness. And Phoebe who desires love at all costs, has to determine if she can ever truly trust the heart of a scoundrel.

To Love a Lord
Book 5 in the "Heart of a Duke" Series

All she wants is security:

The last place finishing school instructor Mrs. Jane Munroe belongs, is in polite Society. Vowing to never wed, she's been scuttled around from post to post. Now she finds herself in the Marquess of Waverly's household. She's never met a nobleman she liked, and when she meets the pompous, arrogant marquess, she remembers why. But soon, she discovers Gabriel is unlike any gentleman she's ever known.

All he wants is a companion for his sister:

What Gabriel finds himself with instead, is a fiery spirited, bespectacled woman who entices him at every corner and challenges his age-old vow to never trust his heart to a woman. But…there is something suspicious about his sister's companion. And he is determined to find out just what it is.

All they need is each other:

As Gabriel and Jane confront the truth of their feelings, the lies and secrets between them begin to unravel. And Jane is left to decide whether or not it is ever truly safe to love a lord.

LOVED BY A DUKE
Book 4 in the "Heart of a Duke" Series

For ten years, Lady Daisy Meadows has been in love with Auric, the Duke of Crawford. Ever since his gallant rescue years earlier, Daisy knew she was destined to be his Duchess. Unfortunately, Auric sees her as his best friend's sister and nothing more. But perhaps, if she can manage to find the fabled heart of a duke pendant, she will win over the heart of her duke.

Auric, the Duke of Crawford enjoys Daisy's company. The last thing he is interested in however, is pursuing a romance with a woman he's known since she was in leading strings. This season, Daisy is turning up in the oddest places and he cannot help but notice that she is no longer a girl. But Auric wouldn't do something as foolhardy as to fall in love with Daisy. He couldn't. Not with the guilt he carries over his past sins… Not when he has no right to her heart…But perhaps, just perhaps, she can forgive the past and trust that he'd forever cherish her heart—but will she let him?

The Love of a Rogue
Book 3 in the "Heart of a Duke" Series

Lady Imogen Moore hasn't had an easy time of it since she made her Come Out. With her betrothed, a powerful duke breaking it off to wed her sister, she's become the *tons* favorite piece of gossip. Never again wanting to experience the pain of a broken heart, she's resolved to make a match with a polite, respectable gentleman. The last thing she wants is another reckless rogue.

Lord Alex Edgerton has a problem. His brother, tired of Alex's carousing has charged him with chaperoning their remaining, unwed sister about *ton* events. Shopping? No, thank you. Attending the theatre? He'd rather be at Forbidden Pleasures with a scantily clad beauty upon his lap. The task of *chaperone* becomes even more of a bother when his sister drags along her dearest friend, Lady Imogen to social functions. The last thing he wants in his life is a young, innocent English miss.

Except, as Alex and Imogen are thrown together, passions flare and Alex comes to find he not only wants Imogen in his bed, but also in his heart. Yet now he must convince Imogen to risk all, on the heart of a rogue.

MORE THAN A DUKE
Book 2 in the "Heart of a Duke" Series

Polite Society doesn't take Lady Anne Adamson seriously. However, Anne isn't just another pretty young miss. When she discovers her father betrayed her mother's love and her family descended into poverty, Anne comes up with a plan to marry a respectable, powerful, and honorable gentleman—a man nothing like her philandering father.

Armed with the heart of a duke pendant, fabled to land the wearer a duke's heart, she decides to enlist the aid of the notorious Harry, 6th Earl of Stanhope. A scoundrel with a scandalous past, he is the last gentleman she'd ever wed…however, his reputation marks him the perfect man to school her in the art of seduction so she might ensnare the illustrious Duke of Crawford.

Harry, the Earl of Stanhope is a jaded, cynical rogue who lives for his own pleasures. Having been thrown over by the only woman he ever loved so she could wed a duke, he's not at all surprised when Lady Anne approaches him with her scheme to capture another duke's affection. He's come to appreciate that all women are in fact greedy, title-grasping, self-indulgent creatures. And with Anne's history of grating on his every last nerve, she is the last woman he'd ever agree to school in the art of seduction. Only his friendship with the lady's sister compels him to help.

What begins as a pretend courtship, born of lessons on seduction, becomes something more leaving Anne to decide if she can give her heart to a reckless rogue, and Harry must decide if he's willing to again trust in a lady's love.

FOR LOVE OF THE DUKE
Book 1 in the "Heart of a Duke" Series

After the tragic death of his wife, Jasper, the 8th Duke of Bainbridge buried himself away in the dark cold walls of his home, Castle Blackwood. When he's coaxed out of his self-imposed exile to attend the amusements of the Frost Fair, his life is irrevocably changed by his fateful meeting with Lady Katherine Adamson.

With her tight brown ringlets and silly white-ruffled gowns, Lady Katherine Adamson has found her dance card empty for two Seasons. After her father's passing, Katherine learned the unreliability of men, and is determined to depend on no one, except herself. Until she meets Jasper...

In a desperate bid to avoid a match arranged by her family, Katherine makes the Duke of Bainbridge a shocking proposition—one that he accepts.

Only, as Katherine begins to love Jasper, she finds the arrangement agreed upon is not enough. And Jasper is left to decide if protecting his heart is more important than fighting for Katherine's love.

In Need of a Duke
A Prequel Novella to "The Heart of a Duke" Series

In Need of a Duke: (Author's Note: This is a prequel novella to "The Heart of a Duke" series by Christi Caldwell. It was originally available in "The Heart of a Duke" Collection and is now being published as an individual novella.

It features a new prologue and epilogue.

Years earlier, a gypsy woman passed to Lady Aldora Adamson and her friends a heart pendant that promised them each the heart of a duke.

Now, a young lady, with her family facing ruin and scandal, Lady Aldora doesn't have time for mythical stories about cheap baubles. She needs to save her sisters and brother by marrying a titled gentleman with wealth and power to his name. She sets her bespectacled sights upon the Marquess of St. James.

Turned out by his father after a tragic scandal, Lord Michael Knightly has grown into a powerful, but self-made man. With the whispers and stares that still follow him, he would rather be anywhere but London…

Until he meets Lady Aldora, a young woman who mistakes him for his brother, the Marquess of St. James. The connection between Aldora and Michael is immediate and as they come to know one another, Aldora's feelings for Michael war with her sisterly responsibilities. With her family's dire situation, a man of Michael's scandalous past will never do.

Ultimately, Aldora must choose between her responsibilities as a sister and her love for Michael.

BIOGRAPHY

Christi Caldwell is the *USA Today* best-selling author of the Sinful Brides series and the Heart of a Duke series. She blames novelist Judith McNaught for luring her into the world of historical romance. When Christi was at the University of Connecticut, she began writing her own tales of love—ones where even the most perfect heroes and heroines had imperfections. She learned to enjoy torturing her couples before they earned their well-deserved happily ever after. Christi lives in Charlotte, North Carolina where she spends her time writing, baking, and being a mommy to the most inspiring little boy and empathetic, spirited girls who, with their mischievous twin antics, offer an endless source of story ideas!

Visit www.christicaldwellauthor.com to learn more about what Christi is working on, or join her on Facebook at Christi Caldwell Author, and Twitter @ChristiCaldwell!

Printed in the USA
CPSIA information can be obtained
at www.ICGtesting.com
LVHW020950091023
760566LV00008B/146